Krystal Pederson

Life & Breather

FINDING THE FIVE

ISBN 978-1-961644-00-7 (paperback)

ISBN 978-1-961644-01-4 (hardcover)

ISBN 978-1-961644-02-1 (ebook)

To my husband Dave and our five children. My treasures.
…and to the moon.

The Meadow

"Have you ever found an old worn out dandelion, plucked it out of the ground then blew the wishes off?"

On the day of Leena's birth, daisies bloomed in late October, covering the meadow. Odd behavior for daisies. Odd and miraculous.

Mum knew Leena was not like other children.

Mum knew Leena had the gift.

Mum knew Leena was a Life Breather.

Three-year-old Leena reached out and took the wish flower Mum held in her outstretched hand. Leena held it carefully so as to not disrupt the wishes too soon, standing perfectly still just as Mum taught, waiting for instructions.

"You, Leena, have a gift," Mum said gently. "It is a gift that has been passed down from your great great-great-grandmother." Leena gazed at Mum's hazel eyes that sparkled with hints of green and gold in the sunlight. "My baby girl, you were given the gift of breath. With practice, hard work, and time, you can learn to control your breath, and with that, control the world around you. But only if you truly connect with your spirit and if your intentions are pure. You are a Life Breather — one of only a few left in this world. A time will come when your gift will be needed and you will need to find the others. Be ready, my darling."

Leena nodded. Mum had recited this same lesson to her since the day she took her first breath. Warmth spread through Leena's insides as she heard these familiar words and absorbed the power in them.

"If you learn to control your breath, you will be able to give life to nature when nature is out of breath. Do you understand, my little sunbeam?"

"Yes, Mum. I understand," Leena said in a steady voice, even though she didn't fully. She looked intently at the puffy dandelion and closed her eyes. Inhaling a deep breath, the air moved gracefully through her nostrils and filled her lungs. As she exhaled through her nose, she focused her breath on one single wisp. Visualizing the flower she held in her hand, she could see it in her mind's eye. Her breath flowed back out through her nostrils and lifted the seed from the stem, blowing it out into the meadow. She repeated this practice over and over, one wisp at a time until the wish flower stood bald in her hand. Leena opened her eyes, tossed the bare stem, and laughed with delight as she watched the wisps float in the afternoon breeze.

This was Leena's first memory, blowing wish flowers. She learned to use her breath steady and strong by blowing wishes all over the meadow. Mum taught her how to focus her mind on the wisp and focus her breath to be firm and controlled. Eventually, with time and practice she learned to control where each seed landed.

Two years passed. In the middle of the meadow, Leena laid her head in Mum's lap, though there was not much room since the baby inside Mum's tummy took up most of her lap space. Leena gave the baby inside Mum a tap.

"You are getting too big. When are you coming out?" Leena said loudly, talking straight to the belly. Looking up at Mum, Leena smiled and combed her fingers through Mum's long, straight, nut-brown hair that fell towards Leena's face and said, "I hope it comes out soon. I want a friend."

"You have Prickle," Mum suggested as Leena's goat sauntered up beside them. Prickle stood stiffly, his beady goat eyes staring straight ahead, unblinking. They both laughed. Crawling out from Mum's lap, Leena hugged Prickle. The goat grunted disapprovingly, his beard twitching into a frown.

"I love you, Prickle. I don't care if you are grumpy, you old grump." Leena patted his head. More grunting. Last week Prickle escaped the garden fence again and ate all the best buds on the new rose bushes. Mum had still not forgiven him.

"I don't know what we're going to do with that goat." Mum sighed and rubbed her stomach. "Let's finish up your breathing lesson for the day with a final quiz." Mum, a light that never got dull, made everything a game and every game magical.

Five-year-old Leena sat up straight with wide eyes, listening for the final questions of the day.

"The three keys," Mum said. "Question one. What is the key that unlocks the door to life?"

"Breath," Leena answered without hesitation. She sat, slightly leaning forward anticipating the next question.

"Yes. Good. Breath is the first of the three keys. Next question: When is your *mind* in perfect alignment with your *heart*?" Mum asked. Silence. Leena sat pondering. Twisting a piece of grass in her fingers, she reviewed the question in her mind. "Alignment…mind to heart aligned. Head to body," she whispered as she mentally went through her lesson from earlier that day.

"Good Posture!" Leena blurted out as it came to her suddenly. She laughed at herself. Mum laughed, too, which sounded to Leena like a perfect tinkling bell.

"Yes, the second key is good posture. Now for the third key: When is your *heart* aligned with your *soul?*"

"When I quickly forgive myself and others," Leena answered.

"Yes, exactly. Forgiveness is the third key. If you forgive yourself when your mind wanders during your breathing exercises, it will teach you to forgive yourself when you make mistakes, too, and to forgive others quickly when they make mistakes."

"Guess that means you have to forgive Prickle for eating those rose buds" Leena said matter of factly and shrugged.

"I suppose I do." Mum smiled. "So Breath, Good Posture and Forgiveness are the three keys. All done for today — now let's go make some biscuits," Mum said, attempting to stand, holding her stomach with her free hand.

"Yesssss!" Leena said, grabbing Mum's other hand to pull her up.

Leena hummed a funny song and skipped all the way back home, across the big green meadow, over the stream with the brand new bridge that Dad built, past the farm, and through the orchard to their tiny cottage.

Leena ran up the front porch and flung the door open. Dad sat inside, reading on his blue chair.

"Well, hello there." Dad jumped up and twirled Leena around. Then, changing pace quickly, he carefully guided his pregnant wife up the steps with his strong hands — hands that showed he knew how to work the land. "You should sit down and rest. That's too long of a walk for you, darling," Dad said and Mum nodded in agreement.

"Want to play some cards?" Dad asked Leena, looking hopeful.

"We're making biscuits!" Nothing kept Leena laughing and loving life more than being in the kitchen baking biscuits with Mum and Dad, playing with the dough and getting flour all over their faces. Their little family, always making or baking something, and Mum always in her apron. The thrill of baking compared to nothing else for Leena with the exception of the miracle of planting flowers.

Another year went by. Baby Aaron charmed his way into Leena's heart with ease. She loved him from the first moment she saw him. Having a baby brother meant she always had a playmate. Except at naptime. Late morning naptime for Aaron meant quiet time for Leena to practice her breathing.

Even with the knowledge and skills of being a Life Breather, Leena didn't grasp what that meant and what would be required of her. At times it weighed on her mind heavily. Today it didn't. She wore her purple dress today—she wore it as many days in a row as she could before Mum insisted on washing it, and then she wore the yellow one. But today it was a purple dress day.

Light-hearted and care-free, Leena set out early this morning, with thoughts of Mum's bedtime story the night before still galloping through her mind. Stories of Leena's great great great Grandmother Lacey sitting still, breathing in and out, bringing plants to life, flowers into bloom, turning ponds into rushing streams, and changing the seasons just for fun, filled Leena's mind.

Leena found a quiet place by the creek and sat with a tall back and criss-cross legs, resting the back of her hands on her knees to show her palms in a receiving position. Her brown hair matched the dark bark of the black walnut tree beside her. The sun peeked out over the grassy hills miles away. As she meditated, she took three breaths in and out through her nose, slowly. The breathing connected her body to her spirit and focused her mind.

I am a Life Breather. I am a Life Breather. I am a Life Breather.

A small wave rippled through the pond. Leena smiled, feeling proud of herself. It was tricky to move water. Leena wandered down to the deepest part of the stream and jumped in, purple dress and all. The cold water startled her insides, and she struggled to catch her breath. Once she steadied herself, she took a deep breath through her nose and visualized the sun hanging right beside her. Within a minute, the water at her toes gurgled and a bubble of hot air burst under her feet, instantly filling the swimming hole with heat like a warm bath. Leena sighed, and her tense body relaxed in the warmth of the water.

Taking in a big breath, she dunked under the surface. Little by little she had trained herself to hold her breath for unusually long periods of time underwater. Today she easily played beneath the water surface for an hour. The muscles in her lungs got stronger every time she practiced. Holding her breath underwater seemed as natural as eating.

As much as Leena loved the water, her first love was the meadow pasture with the sheep. She climbed out and up onto the bank, shivering a bit from leaving the warmth of the swimming hole and squeezed the excess water out of her purple dress.

And then she ran.

Leena ran as far and as fast as she could until her legs and lungs were so tired that she couldn't take another step. Overcome with the joy of exhaustion, she collapsed onto the soft grass. The feeling of pushing herself to her limit and then going just a bit further thrilled her. She loved the simple life of the meadow. The rolling hills belonged to them—Mum, Dad, Leena, and Aaron. The fields seemed to extend on forever, but in the far distance stood the forest, and beyond that, the village. But everything she needed rested here. She had no need or desire to venture off. Leena belonged in the meadow. The grazing sheep saw Leena and within minutes they made their way over to her.

Leena's small arms wrapped around one of the sheep. It didn't mind the hug like Prickle did. Giggling she buried her face into the warm wool as the sheep munched mindlessly on the grass. This wool would someday be woven into yarn and someday after that, dyed and knitted into a scarf. Her six-year-old mind loved knowing that everything has a purpose here in the meadow. Calm spread through her body. The smell and comfort of the wool soothed her soul. Oh how she loved her little flock. Leena released her grip and flopped back into the grass, spreading her legs out among the dandelions and laying her hands at her sides. Her body breathed in the spring air. A mix of the sweet scent of flowers and the earthy smell of grass that surrounded her filled her nose. Her breath started in her toes and worked its way all the way up to the top of her dark, curly ringlets. Every part of her body breathed. Her shoe-less feet snuggled into the grass. More breathing in through her nose and out through her nose, just as Mum taught her.

Leena practiced on all sorts of flowers that afternoon. Using her gift of breath she opened and closed a rose bud as she breathed in and out. The tight petals clenched and bundled as she breathed in, then as she breathed out a slow steady exhale, the petals relaxed and bloomed wide open, releasing a sweet fragrance from the rose. In the garden she encouraged new carrot seeds to germinate after being in the ground for less than an hour. The carrots would be full grown and ready to eat by tomorrow.

Freckles appeared on her fair skin from staying out in the sun too long and she headed home.

That evening at bedtime, Mum told her a new story. Mum spoke quietly and Leena sensed that she chose her words deliberately and carefully. It made Leena uneasy.

Looking into Leena's brown eyes, Mum told her the legend of the Life Breathers.

"Life Breathers used to co-exist with the Deliverers." Leena's mind opened and she could clearly see the story unfold before her. "The two cultures shared a planet in peace, each providing some-thing for the other. The Life Breathers gave the Deliverers breath, as well as giving all living things breath, and in return the Deliverers provided the raw material to work with, like stone, water, minerals, and metals. But after thousands of years the Deliverers became greedy, dark creatures. Loathsome and lazy. Stealing the breath from everything around them and giving nothing in return." Leena felt sick inside as her Mum spoke. A wave of nausea passed through her. Her young mind had never heard of such injustice.

"Their appearance changed. Instead of tall and upright with

distinct facial features, they became featureless and slightly hunched over. The bones inside them became more prominent until they resembled thin dark skeletons wrapped in black webbing instead of skin. They stopped delivering materials and began harvesting the breath given by the Life Breathers. Stealing it from the Life Breathers and forcing them into a life of suffocated darkness. Little by little, century by century the Life Breathers became nearly extinct." Mum paused, sensing Leena's feelings of despair. "Are you okay, sweetheart?"

Leena answered Mum's question with a question. "Are *you* a Life Breather, Mum?"

"No, I'm not," Mum responded.

"Then how do you know all about it?" Leena asked. "How do you know how to teach me?"

"My great great grandmother was a Life Breather. I've told you about her before. Grandmother Lacey. When I met her she looked about my same age. We could have been twins, she and I. But she was very old and died soon after."

Leena interrupted her Mum with a frown. "But how?"

"Well, Life Breathers live longer than humans. They can live up to 200, sometimes 250 years old—some even older." Leena's eyes grew as Mum spoke. "Grandmother Lacey taught me with the hope that I would pass it on to my children and that eventually a Life Breather would live on incase…" Mum looked down at her hands in her lap.

"Incase what?" Leena was curious and concerned.

Mum spoke quietly—low and reluctantly. "Incase the Deliverers return."

"Return?" Leena squinted her eyes, and her body tensed and leaned slightly back. "*Can* the Deliverers return?" Fear shifted inside her as she thought about the Deliverers hoarding the breath from the earth after stealing it from those who live here. That couldn't happen could it?

"They are no longer called Deliverers. They do not deliver anything now except for fear." Mum paused and swallowed, placing her hand over Leena's hand. "Now they are called Destroyers."

It felt as though ice-cold water poured down Leena's back, causing a shiver through her entire body. The shiver took hold of the nausea and made Leena's skin look like snow. Destroyers. What did this mean for Leena? For her family? What did this mean for the meadow? For the earth? A horror that she had never known before took root inside her, creeping throughout her insides and grabbing onto her heart.

Leena did not sleep well that night. Thoughts of the Destroyer's dark webbed faces and crooked backs haunted her dreams.

The next morning, Dad woke Leena up before dawn.

"It's time to go digging," Dad whispered. Leena knew what this meant. Grateful for the distraction from the fear-filled night, Leena quickly got out of bed. Dad and Leena had spent long hours throughout the year digging for geodes and cracking them open to find the purple crystals inside. And now it was time again. One last time before Dad left for market.

Leena hurried and dressed herself in her purple dress and shoved her feet into her black boots. They left in the dark of the morning. This time they journeyed to a grove of locust trees at the far side of the meadow. When they arrived, Dad handed Leena a small shovel and pick and they began digging around the base of the trees. The sun rose slowly above the hillside, and as soon as the light hit the dirt, the round gray rocks showed themselves. The excitement of finding the rocks, then the anticipation of cracking them open, sent Leena's heart soaring everytime. The fear from the previous night lifted, and her heart raced with excitement.

"There they are!" Leena pointed at the egg-sized rocks.

"Hahaaa! Yes there they are!" Dad looked just as excited as Leena. They piled as many rocks as they could hold into their sacks and headed back to the cottage. The dirt on their hands and the sweat on their faces did not stop the thrill that bubbled inside them.

Dad said these gems called amethyst have special meaning. He'd passed his love of rocks and gems onto Leena along with stories of growing up in the mountains. Dad's stories of caves and magic blue stones deep within the caves filled Leena's mind as they walked back home. It took all morning and into the afternoon, but they cracked open each geode one by one, and when they finished, they had gathered a few dozen more amethyst stones to sell at market. The dig proved to be a success.

Leena had a collection of the purple gemstones that were too small to sell at market. She kept them in a special box under her bed. By the glow of candlelight she admired them each night before she closed her eyes. Dad handed her another one to add to her collection as he tucked her in bed that night.

"Hold onto the amethyst, and feel the calm. It is full of light, and will make your thoughts clear when everything around you feels muddled," Dad said with a wink. "Inner harmony will always be your friend if you can harness the calm of the amethyst. It will be your guiding light." He paused and looked at her with love and admiration. "You are my amethyst, Leena." Dad leaned down and kissed her forehead.

Calm, full of grace, serenity and understanding. Leena was just like an amethyst.

A cold wind blew through the meadow. The trees, plants, and flowers were wrapping up their life cycle, preparing for the change. Market time came with the changing season, from summer to fall. This exciting time of year fluttered in like the fall leaves blowing off the trees with ease.

Twice a year, Dad needed to leave the meadow to sell goods at the marketplace and gather supplies that would last them throughout the coming year. The market, in the village beyond the forest, took five day's travel by carriage. They never knew how long Dad would be gone and what he would bring home when he returned. Sometimes he would be gone for nearly two months, selling Mum's knitted scarves, homemade pies, and the purple amethyst gemstones.

The last day spent with Dad, everyone bustled with excitement. The day began in a simple way—feeding the hens and gathering the eggs. Mum led the way, and Leena followed close behind. Aaron tried to keep up with his big sister, calling to Leena, "Lala wait a me! Wait a me!" Leena tossed the cornmeal to the chickens, and they came running, pecking the ground fiercely. Baby Aaron, silly, slobbering, and without fear, chased the chickens, his toddling legs, chubby and unstable, running and squawking after the hens. As much as he chased, he never caught them, but it entertained him all afternoon.

With Dad leaving for market today, he worked hard to get in the last of the fixing-broken-things list done. All the vegetables were ready to harvest and the wood needed to be split, stacked, and ready by the back porch door because winter would be on its way soon.

Dad, from up on the little cottage roof fixing a leaky spot, called down to Leena and Aaron with his hands cupped around his mouth as if he called to them from far, far away.

"Hellooooo down there!"

Leena waved back giggling hard into her hands. Aaron waved both his hands and blew Dad kisses.

After Leena completed her chores, she stood at the front window and watched Dad pack up the carriage, her nose fogging up the glass. She sighed over and over, her heart sinking deeper and deeper into her stomach with each sigh. The scarves and homemade pies along with the gemstones were loaded up in the carriage, ready to go. Her heart filled with dread for what she knew would be a long winter without Dad. Leena wished she was twelve. Dad said when she turned twelve she could come help him sell at market. Thoughts of all the fine food and clothes filled Leena's mind along with an ache.

The smell of bread baking floated through the kitchen and out into the front room. Dad came in the front door, his nose following the aroma.

"Lunch smells delicious," he said. Leena turned her head slowly from the window. Her nose red from the pressing.

"Please be home in time for my birthday, Dad." Hopping off her chair, she stood in front of him. "I only turn seven once, you know." Leena looked at Dad, her eyes pleading.

"I will do my very best to be home for your special day this year." Dad gently touched her cheek. "But if I am not here, know that my whole heart will be thinking of only you." From inside his jacket he pulled a brown package wrapped in a light purple ribbon and handed it to Leena. Dad smiled lovingly and said, "Just in case, I'll give you my gift early."

Leena's mouth opened. "Oooooh…" She admired the package, surprised at the unexpected gift. Her eyes glanced from the package to Dad's face.

"Can I? Can I open it now?" She could not contain her excitement and did not wait for an answer as she tore off the brown paper. A doll with long, curly brown hair like Leena wearing a purple dress and gray shoes, waited inside the wrapping. Leena pulled the doll free from the paper and held it in front of her, speechless. Hugging the doll that resembled herself, she cried, "It's me! Did you make this?"

"Well, yes." Dad smiled. "Mostly." He looked at Mum and winked. "I had a bit of trouble getting the eyes just right so Mum helped get those beauties sewn on. She is the real gift."

Leena squeezed her gift tighter as she imagined Dad sewing each curly thread of yarn onto her dolls head.

"And look" —Dad held up his fingers— "I have battle scars to prove it." A few tiny needle pricks had left marks in the tips of his fingers.

Leena hugged him. "Thank you, Dad!"

They sat together inside their tiny home, at their wooden table, and ate one final delicious lunch all together—of fresh-baked bread and jam, with cucumbers and carrots on the side.

After the excitement during lunch, the time came to say goodbye. Dad put on his cap, which was a sign that he was ready for an adventure, and kissed them goodbye. He gave Leena and Aaron both a big squeeze and a kiss on each of their noses. Leena did not want him to go. She forced a smile and willed the tears to stay behind her eyes because she did not want Dad to know just how sad she was.

Dad gave Mum an extra long hug.

"I love you my darling meadow girl," he whispered in Mum's ear.

A tear slid down Mum's cheek, and she whispered back, "We will see you when the snow falls." Mum handed Dad a small pouch full of bread and apples, and with that, he got into the carriage and left for the village.

2

Day of Destruction

"Have you ever smelled a memory so vividly you could touch it? Memories are stored inside the scent of a flower."

Mum decorated the fireplace mantle early in the morning with the last of the lavender flowers from the bush out front and knitted a purple scarf to match. The lavender scent filled the cottage. When Leena tiptoed quietly out of her room that morning, she paused at her bedroom door and breathed in the sweet scent of the flowers. Her nose also filled with the delicious smell of her favorite breakfast, apple tartlets with whipping cream. Leena clapped her hands and raced over to the mantle. Gently picking up the purple scarf, she twirled it around her neck, admiring the softness, giggling and squealing with delight. She knew the value the scarf held, the expensive yarn and the time it took Mum to knit. At market it would fetch a high price.

"Happy birthday, big girl!" Mum said, her eyes sparkling with excitement.

"It's the prettiest scarf, Mum! I'm going to wear this all winter! Even when I sleep!"

"I believe you will, Leena girl," Mum said softly.

Breakfast tasted as delicious as it smelled, with the hot apples bubbling out of the tart crust and the whipping cream melting and sliding off the sides. Aaron made a sticky mess all over his hands, face and floor, but thoroughly enjoyed his first experience with apple tartlets. The only thing missing from this perfect birthday morning breakfast was Dad.

Dad had not returned after five weeks. Most mornings Leena sat on the porch swing with wide eyes, watching for Dad's carriage in the distance. Waiting patiently came easily for Leena. Training her body to be still came with her breathing lessons. Being an unusually patient girl came in handy while waiting for Dad to return, but especially today, on Leena's seventh birthday, she wanted him home. He had already missed her birthday breakfast. Her heart sank inside, because deep down, she knew he would not be home today.

Mum wet down a cloth and gave Aaron a good scrubbing before sending him out the door with Leena. Standing on the front porch they could hear the quiet meowing of six kittens. Leena lifted up the loose floorboard and set it aside. They both peeked between the boards under the porch. Betty lay there with her nearly hairless babies, all their eyes tightly, but gently closed.

"Eyes!" Aaron demanded pointing at his own eyes that were wide open. Leena laughed. "They will have eyes soon." Leena said patiently, but her heart longed to play with the kittens, too. Mum said in two weeks they'd be fuzzy and bouncing. But for now, Leena and Aaron watched and waited.

Aaron curled up on the front porch, his arm dangling through the opening reaching down to the kittens and before long fell fast asleep. Mum came out of the house, wiped her wet hands on her apron, and picked up her sleeping boy. She winked at Leena, and Leena winked back. Leena tiptoed in behind her Mum without making a sound and grabbed her doll with the purple dress from her bed.

"What are you up to?" Mum asked Leena as she returned to her dish washing.

"I'm just going out back," Leena said casually.

"Well you and Aaron stayed up late watching all those stars last night, so if you're sleepy you can take a little rest, too, if you like."

"Oh, I'm not sleepy," Leena reassured Mum.

Mum looked at Leena. "I know you're sad that Dad couldn't make it back for your birthday." Mum knelt down in front of her. "Sometimes things don't work out the way we think it should, but in the end, it's always the way it was supposed to be." Mum's eyes brimmed with tears. Leena looked down at her doll. Her insides were torn between the delightful morning, full of fun birthday surprises, and the the ache in her heart when she thought about Dad so far away. Leena thought about the wish she made on a shooting star last night, and a piece of anger darted through her. Her wish had not come true. She squeezed her doll tighter as she held back the tears from her own eyes.

"I'm okay, Mum." Leena gave a half smile. "Don't worry."

Mum lifted Leena's chin. The look in Mum's eyes softened Leena's troubled heart, and the anger and sadness left momentarily.

"Did I ever tell you about the day you were born?" Leena shook her head. "On the day you were born it snowed. Did you know that?" Leena shook her head again. "It was the earliest snowfall we've ever had here in the meadow. It only snowed long enough to cover the ground with a lovely white blanket and then the sun came out, but the snow never melted. But from *under* the snow bloomed a miracle."

"A miracle?" Leena tipped her head slightly to one side.

"Yes, a miracle. A highly improbable or extraordinary event, that cannot be explained by natural or scientific laws and is therefore considered to be the work of a higher law." Leena's mind pricked with curiosity. "We call it the miracle of the daisies. Thousands of daisies bloomed from under the snow the day you were born and completely covered the meadow and over the hills as far as the eye can see." Mum pointed out towards the rolling hills. "So we knew you were different. It was a sign that you were extra special. It was a sign that you are capable of extraordinary and improbable things. You are a miracle."

Leena's heart lightened. "Well, I am a Life Breather."

"Yes you are, Leena. And you must always remember that. And also remember, in the end...everything is always the way it's supposed to be." The look in Mum's eyes and the tone in her voice did not feel familiar to Leena when she said that. Mum sounded far away, like her mind was somewhere else—caught in a storm. She did not have her usual sparkle or optimistic glow. Mum took Leena's face in her hands and stared straight into her eyes. She did not say anything with words but Leena felt words filter into her mind.

A time will come when your gift will be needed, and you will need to find the others. Be ready my darling.

Leena gave Mum a smile and headed out the back door. Leena pushed away her sadness about Dad–pushing it deep down inside her, as well as the thought about her gift. She pushed and pushed until it disappeared.

Leena tucked herself between two hay bales behind the small cottage. The birds darted and swayed in patterns above. Leena watched them as she thought about the miracle of the daisies. She swallowed hard as thoughts about Dad continued to try to come to the surface of her mind. Leena did not welcome the sadness that tried to sneak inside her.

"Go away," she whispered and slightly shook her head. Thinking hard, she replaced her sad thoughts with happy things— daisies, purple scarves, kittens, grass, snow, her family.

Many things in life are happy and good. Leena knew those things. But some things in life are sad. And it is important to know a bit of both. Leena continued to resist the ache inside her. She did not want anything to do with it, especially on her birthday.

As she watched the birds play above, Leena noticed the sky shift. It swayed slightly in the breeze. The sky looked dizzy. It made Leena dizzy. Leena watched carefully, wondering about the strange behavior. Something didn't feel right inside her. The sky began to change. First slowly, almost imperceptibly, it grew darker. Within seconds the change became rapid and parts of the sky faded to charcoal black.

Fear struck Leena to her core. What was happening? Leena, in confusion, could not move.

One large, dark cloud rolled as if tumbling down a hill, gathering speed. Faster and faster. Closer and closer. Leena's heart tightened as she saw the black cloud rolling in furiously and silently.

She clutched her doll.

A thunderous noise erupted like an angry mob of boots stomping on the ground. It filled her ears, quaking and stomping in the distance. Precise and penetrating, hundreds of boots, like drum beats. Hard on the earth. Rhythmic and getting louder. Thump, thump, boom! Thump, thump, boom!

The Destroyers. They were coming.

Leena's insides shook. Shutting her eyes tightly, she stayed tucked in between the hay bales. The stomping got louder as they got closer. A terror like she never could have imagined in her worst nightmares gripped her heart and refused to let go. She wanted to run inside to Mum and be wrapped up in her arms for protection, but, frozen in fear, she sat waiting, her heart clenched and her mind frantic.

The large, black cloud dropped lower to the earth as if it intended to swallow the meadow whole. Thump, thump, boom! Thump, thump, boom! The meadow struggled to breathe. She could feel it, and her heart raced. The meadow was being strangled. Like the meadow, Leena struggled to find her own breath. Gasping for air, she grabbed her throat and drew in a stuttered breath.

When the thunderous beating reached the cottage, Leena's eyes shot open at the thought of Aaron in his crib napping and Mum inside washing dishes. But before she could run inside to warn Mum of the danger, she heard a cry. Aaron's cry. Sharp and terrified, cut short by silence.

Then there was no sound at all. Leena could no longer hear the drumbeat of boots, or a bird, or the bustle of leaves in a tree, or the creek running through the meadow. All lay still. Deathly still. She did not dare cry out. Her heart beat wildly, and her breath quickened, her mind racing ahead trying to figure out what to do. How to help her family. How to save her meadow. Then the beating on the earth began again. Thump, thump, boom! She did not dare look out at the army that lay on her doorstep. But with everything in her, she knew they wanted one thing. Her breath.

One simple thought. *I am a Life Breather.* With all the strength inside her, she focused on this thought.

I am a Life Breather. Leena gently closed her eyes and she saw a wish flower. This time, instead of slowly breathing out to blow the wishes off the stem, she took a smooth, deep breath in through her nose, like she did to prepare to go underwater in the stream, and held onto it tightly. Sitting very still, she held her breath and waited.

Leena became invisible to the Destroyers.

The thunderous charcoal cloud searched the meadow. With one last sweeping motion, the cloud whipped across the meadow and callously rolled on. The sound of boots followed the cloud, heading west, marching on towards the forest. Thumping, beating the earth relentlessly, further and further into the distance until finally completely gone.

Leena let out her breath, her lungs heavy and sore. She sat perfectly still with her eyes closed, terrified of what she would see when she opened them. Silence filled the air. No wind. No thumping. No sweet scent of flowers. Nothing.

Slowly she opened her eyes. Blackness covered everything. Not because of lack of sunlight. It looked as though the world had been burned, but there were no ashes left behind. Everything looked like coal but still in perfect form, not deformed like wood after a cooled fire. Leena's stomach dropped. She did not know what to do next. Her mind and body could no longer function properly. She screamed silently in her mind.

The once brilliantly green meadow, now covered in black grass, stared at her desperately. The trees that only minutes ago had birds nesting in their branches and a rainbow of colored leaves in red, orange, yellow and green, now looked painfully miserable. Black like charcoal. The only remnant of color was Leena, her doll, and her purple scarf. Leena glowed with color against the blackness.

As Leena sat tucked between the hay bales she scooped up a

handful of black dirt and let it drain out of her cupped hand like sand through a sieve. The black dirt fell lifeless to the ground. What happened? What just happened to her perfect world? Everything she loved, gone. Stolen. Destroyed. An aching thought nagged at her mind. *You could have saved them. They are gone because you were not strong enough.*

Leena sat alone, frozen. Nothing breathed. She could feel it. Hollow and cold. Until this moment she had not been fully aware of her own connection with every living thing surrounding her. The breath of the world around her had always pulsed through her, breathing and thriving. Until now. Now she felt nothing but her own beating heart. The Destroyers extinguished everything.

This couldn't be true. It couldn't *all* be gone. Leena closed her eyes and used her mind to reach out, to search for any sign of life, of breath. She reached the edge of the meadow—nothing. But she wouldn't accept it. She reached further, beyond her meadow, into the forest, into the village. Her mind stretched, strained, to the point where it hurt. Still, she could not feel a single breath of life. Leena let out a choked sob as she finally let her mind collapse. Quietly, she came out from her hiding spot between the hay bales and walked carefully up the back stairs that led to the kitchen. Her Mum's final words ringing in her ears. *Remember, in the end...everything is always the way it's supposed to be.*

How can that be! Leena thought angrily, tears flashing in her eyes.

Before allowing a tear to fall, she turned and looked out across her meadow, holding her doll at her side. Looking to the west she could see the forest edge. The cloud had rolled through the forest, and all the trees in the distance stood still in blackness. She knew that the Destroyers had continued on through the forest, to the village, and beyond. With one purpose. To destroy everything that breathes. That meant Dad would have been in the Destroyer's path at market. Leena's heart throbbed thinking of Dad experiencing the same terror. Maybe even right now at this very moment. Heavy and tight, her body collapsed onto the black porch steps, realizing that the Destroyers were sweeping across the entire earth, taking all the breath for their own. Leena lay sobbing on the porch. Her body shaking as the torment became reality.

Entering the cottage Leena saw Mum's dishes she'd been washing, now laying charred in a dry sink. In Aaron's room stood a blackened crib and inside the crib, a black blanket.

Alone. The word echoed in her mind.

I am alone. Repeating relentlessly. *I am alone. I am alone.*

Leena's eyes filled with more tears. She pinched them shut, wishing her life to be back how it had been just a short time ago. Her heart crumbled to the floor. A dark mist enveloped her mind.

Leena sat on the sooty floor of the small cottage and cried, clutching her purple scarf and her doll from Dad. All she wanted was to be in her Mum's arms again and hear her brother laugh. More than anything she wanted to see her Dad's smile again, but in her heart she knew he was gone, too.

Tears flowed as she found her way to her small bedroom with her bed, now looking cold, hard, and uninviting. She fell asleep quietly sobbing on the floor. Her heart breaking into pieces. A dark hole opened inside her. Loneliness filled it.

Today Leena turned seven years old. And today is the beginning of her new life.

For the next five years Leena barely existed. She wandered the meadow without direction or purpose. Questions haunted her. Why had she survived? Where was her family? Were they dead? Were they trapped? Were they in pain? Would she feel sad forever? Would the earth ever live again? These questions tortured Leena's mind, plagued her with the guilt that she had survived.

Her questions and loneliness consumed her, and twelve-year-old Leena no longer remembered her gift of breath. She forgot why she existed. Leena wished she did not exist.

Standing on the bank of the boggy pond, she bent down and scooped a handful of thick mud into her cupped hand and mindlessly held it to her lips, forcing herself to eat. Wiping her mouth with her arm she tossed the remains of mud into the bog.

Leena forgot her wish flowers and she forgot the sound of her Mum's lullabies at night. No more seasons. No more spring crocuses or fall pumpkins. No more summer stars or winter mornings, crisp with new fallen snow covering the meadow. Leena no longer remembered any warmth or cold or color.

Colors that used to fill the meadow in bright yellows, pale pinks, rich greens and fresh blue skies now erased from her mind. She only knew the shadow that covered everything. Leena could not remember what it felt like to smile.

One afternoon Leena sat slumped on the blackened porch swing and mindlessly rocked it back and forth. Her hair was matted and twisted—her face streaked with the dirt she had eaten but not tasted. While she rocked, Leena caught the slightest whisper of a breeze floating beneath the rocking swing. The breeze smoothly drifted up toward her face. Something in the breeze smelled familiar, like a scent that carries a glimpse of a hard-to-describe childhood memory. Leena breathed in the scent again, trying to remember. The memory of the scent swirled in her mind, digging deep into a life that she could not feel anymore.

A scent that would attract the bumble bees. The scent…what was it?

Now her mind curiously longed for the scent. Leena sat up straighter on the swing. What was it that brought the bees? What was it? Now the bees buzzed around in her mind, wanting to be thought about. Why would they come to the cottage?

Leena stopped rocking in the swing and sat very still. She looked out over her meadow. Words that she had not heard for five years found their way into Leena's thoughts.

You will be able to give life to nature when nature is out of breath. Leena blinked and slowly looked around, feeling like she'd woken up from a deep sleep. *With practice, hard work, and time, you can learn to control your breath, and with that, control the world around you. But only if you truly connect with your spirit and if your intentions are pure.*

Gently Leena closed her eyes as she took in a long, steady breath through her nose, filling her body with as much air as her lungs could hold, and then releasing the breath through her nose, slowly. So slowly. With her eyes closed, sitting perfectly still, she repeated the steady deep breaths three times. Pulling in as much of the scent as she could find in her memory, then slowly releasing.

Lavender. She smelled it clearly now. The lavender bush that grew near the front porch. Aaron used to try to pet the bees with their fuzzy jackets as they landed on the dainty purple flowers. For the first time in five years, Leena giggled to herself, shyly as if she had witnessed a cherished experience from someone else's life. She let the tiny breeze soak into her soul as she held the purple scarf, still wrapped around her neck, and remembered the lavender on the mantle for her seventh birthday, smiling at that memory and at the same time aching for it.

Words flowed into Leena's mind and she understood them for the first time.

"You, Leena, have a gift. It is a gift that has been passed down from your great great great grandmother. My baby girl, you were given the gift of breath. With practice, hard work, and time, you can learn to control your breath, and with that, control the world around you. But only if you truly connect with your spirit and if your intentions are pure. You are a Life Breather. There are only a few Life Breathers left in this world. A time will come when your gift will be needed and you will need to find the others. Be ready my darling."

Calm, like a blanket, wrapped around her heart, and after all these years, she let go of the darkness inside her.

This is a story about death and life. About sadness and hope. About destruction and healing. This is Leena's story. About her meadow, her purpose, and how her breath saved her. When the darkness settles in, sometimes there's nothing else to do but keep breathing.

And that is exactly what Leena decided to do.

MEDITATION MOMENT:

Take a breath in through the nose filling your lungs with air. Slowly count to five as you inhale.

Imagine a wish flower. Slowly breathe out through your nose as you blow the wisps off. Slowly count to five as you exhale, scattering the wishes into the air. Exhale completely.

Three deep breaths in and out through the nose.

Breathe in the lavender....Fill your lungs slowly with as much air as you can hold.

Now breathe out through your nose slowly, completely emptying your lungs.

Again. Breathe in....Breathe out.

Breathe in....Breathe out.

3

Amethyst

"Have you ever heard a whisper floating on the edge of a breeze?
Trust the whisper. Trust that it has a message for you."

Leena turned and looked behind her at the door of her cottage. Shifting her body, she faced the door and stared at it, her mind still groggy. She hesitated. Her first impulse was to run inside the cottage and see and touch and feel everything inside her little home that had been invisible to her. But she held herself still. Reaching out her hand she turned the doorknob and carefully walked inside. Eyes wide open so she would not miss a thing.

With new breath inside her, she saw everything with new eyes. Leena walked through the small sitting area and marveled at things she had been blind to all these years. Books on the shelf, a pillow on the soft armchair, her Dad's boots by the front door. Her hands glided over the black table as she passed by. The memory of her Mum and Dad eating a final lunch together the day Dad left, panged her insides sharply, but the memory softened quickly. She didn't know exactly what direction to go, but something urged her down the hall towards her bedroom.

Something caught her eye. A black book on the shelf titled *Riddles of Time, Secrets of Stones* seemed to be gazing at her. She had no memory of this book. Pulling it from the shelf she turned it over in her hands a few times. The worn black leather looked as though it had been read many times, though she did not know by whom. Etched on the cover was the title, but the pages were black, blending in with the words which made it impossible to see the writing. Leena flipped through the pages quickly then slipped the small leather book into the pocket of her dress.

She walked to her bedroom. Reaching under her bed, she found the familiar box of purple amethyst gemstones from her childhood. Lifting the lid a warm, purple light glowed from within the box. Leena's mouth opened in awe. The life of the stones had been protected. The rocks waited patiently for Leena—full of life, full of color.

Her heartbeat quickened as excitement rippled through her body. Leena paused, breathing in and out. She held a glowing stone tenderly in her palm. Closing her fingers around the gemstone, she clutched it to her heart. Gratitude swept through her with such force that she thought she might burst through the roof and fly up into the sky. A deep ache moaned inside her, wanting to be free after it had been shut tightly inside her for all these years. Her eyes filled with tears. The grief and pain fled her body like a cleansing bath as the tears fell freely. She had not cried since the day everything was destroyed.

All at once, memories of Mum, Dad, and Aaron filled her mind, filled her whole body, as though she was experiencing her former life in an instant. Her Mum's fresh baked bread. Arm wrestling with Dad. Aaron shaking his little body, imitating a new chick shaking out of a shell. Mum helping Leena stand when she fell, Dad lifting her into the air and twirling in circles. Aaron begging for kittens. All of it. Fresh in her thoughts. As though it happened yesterday.

Leena laughed through her tears of gratitude, and as she cried, color flowed into her pale cheeks. Streaks of dirt on her face disappeared. Her tangled hair that had lost its curls, came to life again, and smooth silky ringlets took the place of the matted mess. Her favorite purple dress, faded, dirty, and two sizes too small, miraculously altered, transforming into a dress that fit her just right.

As she wept, Leena allowed the goodness of life to seep into her body. Hope replaced the loneliness.

More than anything Leena wanted her family back, but she could not dwell on that painful thought. That was not an option. Right now she needed to focus on giving breath back to the meadow. *Her* meadow. Leena's mind wrestled with these thoughts. She had no idea if she would be able to do all the earth asked of her. What if she failed? What if the evil returned? What would happen if her breath was not enough? Doubt and hope fought for precedence in her mind.

The task standing in front of her overwhelmed her. "I don't know if I'm strong enough," she said out loud.

Nothing made her more afraid than that thought.

She looked at the amethyst still in her hand, and she made a choice.

"Let's get to work. There is much to be done."

Sitting on her front porch with her legs criss-crossed and her hands resting on her knees, she breathed in her steady rhythm. Breathing in for five seconds, then breathing out for five seconds. Smooth, controlled, slow. The largest tree in the meadow grew in the field straight in front of her out in the blackness. Looking abandoned and helpless, the tree waited for Leena.

A picture formed in her mind. Leena could see the tree alive and in full bloom. Every part of her body participated in the visualization. She saw the green leaves and heard them rustling in the wind. The blossoms smelled sweet, and she could taste the tart cherries. In her mind she ran her fingers along the trunk, feeling the bumps and grooves in the bark.

Hours passed. Leena waited patiently, and finally the tree let out an audible, deep sigh that flowed down its trunk and throughout its limbs. Leena opened her eyes. Tiny leaf buds sprouted one at a time with green bursts of light on the tips of each branch. Elation filled her whole body. A feeling bigger than happiness swept through her. Pure joy, extreme and exhilarating, consumed Leena. The leaves spread out and popped open, unraveling their joy that paralleled Leena's. The bark turned a lush, deep auburn brown and spread along each branch and twig, continuing until it reached the base and the very top of the tree.

Leena sprinted out into the meadow. She wrapped her arms around the large trunk, hugging it tightly the same way she hugged Dad when he returned from a long journey. Laughing she yelled out, "I am not alone!" Leena grabbed the lowest branch and twirled under it, dancing with the tree as her partner. She had a friend. A tree. A living, breathing tree.

"Oh my goodness! You are alive! Where has your spirit been?" Leena asked eagerly, running her hands along the bark of the tree. "What have you been doing? Have you been asleep? Are you thirsty? Did you feel me breathing?" Leena told the tree what happened on the day of destruction in detail. As she spoke about her family being taken by the cloud, she wondered if their spirits were close. Could *they* feel her breathing? Could *they*—she stopped mid thought. An ache spread across her chest. No. They were gone. Leena buried the notion.

"Were you waiting for me?" she asked the tree. Of course the tree did not answer back in words, and Leena did not expect it to, but she knew the tree understood—she knew the tree needed her as much as she needed the tree.

Exhaustion took over. Leena did not know the extreme fatigue that followed bringing life back to nature. All she could think about was sleep. She closed her mouth and closed her eyes and fell asleep under the branches of her old friend. Leena slept under the tree for two days.

When she woke up, her insides growled. She remembered a time when Aaron cried and cried while they were out on a walk together with Mum.

"What is he crying about? There's nothing to cry about. Is he hurt?" Leena could not understand why her new baby brother was so sad and in so much pain. Mum answered, "He's hungry."

At the time Leena wondered how it was possible to be so hungry that Aaron would cry angry tears. But now she understood hunger in that way and it made her miss him more.

Gazing up at the tree, she saw hundreds, maybe thousands of cherries dangling above her. Leena could not think of anything more appealing than eating all the cherries on the big tree in one sitting. She pulled on a cherry within her reach, tugging it off its branch and popped it into her mouth. Leena had never eaten anything as sweet and delicious.

Leena filled her stomach and then put a handful of extra cherries inside her pocket to save for later. The leather book was still inside the pocket of her dress. She pulled it out.

"Hmmmm. I wonder."

Opening the book she flipped through the black pages hoping to remember something significant.

"Do you remember my Mum and Dad? And Aaron?" she asked, looking up from the book to the tree. "I miss them...so much." The tree did not answer. Leena looked back down at the book. The tree listened. "On the day of destruction" —Leena paused and clasped her hands tightly around the book— "I think maybe Mum knew something was about to happen. But I can't understand why she didn't tell me if she knew? Why didn't she warn me?" Leena worked hard, digging through her memory. What was the last thing Mum had said to her? Leena remembered Mum holding her face, but what had she actually said. "My Mum told me something just before the Destroyers came. What was it?" Leena stared at the tree waiting. No answer.

She set the book down on the black earth and straightened her back. Resting her hands on her knees, she breathed in. And out. In. And out. The pages of the book fluttered open. Leena opened her eyes and had the distinct feeling that the book wanted to breathe. It was ready and willing. She closed her eyes again and continued to breathe. *There is life all around me. I am not alone.*

The leather softened in color to a rich brown and the pages turned a creamy antique white. The book took a breath, rising off the ground slightly then gently landing back on the earth, looking even older now. Something in the book called to her, something she needed. The feeling of connection could not be denied.

"Riddles of Time, Secrets of Stones," Leena said as she ran her fingers across the title on the cover. Opening the book, she turned to a page that had a folded corner on the upper right side.

On the page it said: *First you see me in the grass, dressed in yellow ray; next I am in cotton white, then I float away. What am I?*

"Well, that one is easy. I am a dandelion," Leena said casually under her breath. She had lots of practice with riddles. Dad quizzed Leena all the time, making her use her mind to figure things out.

She turned the page and read a riddle circled in ink.

At last the child is born, when white stars fall peak of season. Together with summers, belated blooms of bellis perennis. One after six and one before eight, when the lights go out, a decade will harvest. Collect them all. The task is yet to rise again.

What did *that* mean? And why had someone circled it? Was the riddle foretelling about her? Was that a riddle about her birth? And about the Day of Destruction? Leena remembered now on her seventh birthday her Mum had told her the story of the day she was born. The snow falling earlier than usual and the meadow being covered in freshly bloomed daisies at the same time. One after six and one before eight is seven. Her age the day the Destroyers came.

She didn't know how she felt. Astonished. Grateful. Afraid. Curious. Could this book help her know what to do next? *She* certainly didn't know what to do next. Scribbled writing filled the margins on many of the pages throughout the book. Who wrote in it? Who did it belong to?

The task is yet to rise again was underlined. The task of breathing life back into the earth. Leena knew that was the task to which the riddle referred. But did it also refer to something even bigger. It had taken a lot of effort to breathe the tree back, and Leena felt discouraged just thinking about it. The overwhelming, unknown, and possibly dangerous task of giving nature back its breath against the will of the Destroyers. How in the world would she do that? And what if they came back? The fear of their return lurked in the back of Leena's mind like a shadow. How could she face them again? Could she survive another attack?

Leena turned to the inside front cover and saw, in lovely handwriting, the name *Lacey*. Grandmother Lacey. Hope resurfaced. Is it possible that her great great great grandmother, the only other Life Breather she had heard of, could guide her through this with her wisdom from the past?

Leena got in her bed that night but found it hard to sleep. Her mind churned on a riddle.

The soldiers with many arms stand guard, hiding the fungi under their beams. Where am I?

Such a strange riddle. Leena did not know where to begin in solving it. That night she dreamed of soldiers standing guard. But they were not soldiers at all. They were trees.

The next morning Leena sat in quiet reflection while the sun rose. Breathing in and out slow and deep and repeating the phrase in her mind *I am not alone. There is life all around me. There is life in me.* She believed these words. Leena embraced the truth that when phrases were repeated consistently, the words became part of her. Everything her Mum had taught her about her gift of breath made sense now, and a connection formed between Leena and the earth that she had never known before.

Leena spent hours envisioning the rebirth of the meadow by visualizing every single action it would take to accomplish her purpose. Over and over, in her mind, she witnessed all the trees coming back and the pond once again rushing wildly through the meadow. Her mind filled with images of flowers blooming, and she imagined the green fields full of life. Breathing life back into the meadow would take time, maybe even years, but Leena knew she had been born for this purpose.

Making her way to the boggy pond, Leena walked down the hill and crossed over a small bridge that Dad had built so long ago, leading to the bog that used to be the running stream. When she got to the muddy edge she let out a hopeful sigh.

"This will take a bit of time," she said under her breath, "but I know we can bring you back. I need you, and the meadow needs you."

On the bank sitting cross-legged she got into a comfortable position with her back straight and her hands relaxed, palms toward the sky, open, resting on her knees. Inhaling a breath through her nose, then exhaling through her nose. Again, another deep breath in and out. In and out. Focusing on the life that the bustling stream once had. Seeing in her mindseye the water running and jumping over the rocks, playing and laughing as it flowed. Leena peeked one eye open. Nothing yet.

Gently close your eyes. Relax the muscles in your eyelids. Soften your body and allow your jaw to drop. Feel your breath easily flowing in and then out through your nose. Feel your breath move through your body, giving your soul life. Let your thoughts be light and flow freely like water. Visualize the water in the stream. See it clear and free as it hurries along it's path. You are alive. There is life inside you. Feel the joy of the water washing over you. You are alive. There is life all around you. There is life in you. I am a Life Breather.

She continued meditating and focused her mind just as she had learned to control the wish flower seeds as a child. Relaxing and breathing, her spirit became one with the water. She peeked again. The mud gurgled. Leena smiled. More focus, more breath, more seeing the water. More saying the words to give it life. More feeling the life inside the water.

Leena sat on the edge of her stream for over an hour, sitting quietly, patiently waiting and believing that life was coming. And finally she heard it. The sound of dripping water. Like a whisper at first just a few drops, then a bit of chatter, then it broke out into a full conversation with millions of water droplets coming together and rejoicing after not being able to communicate for years! Water! Coming back to life! She opened her eyes. Thrilled to be alive, the crystal clear water inhaled and exhaled, taking its place back in the meadow where it belonged.

Leena stood up and let out a holler, "I knew it! I knew you would come back!" Fully clothed she jumped into the stream, which easily went up to her waist. Taking a huge breath in, she immersed herself under the breathing water. When she popped out of the stream, her long, wet, hair slicked back on her head. Leena filled her cupped hands with water and drank, feeling the coolness from her lips all the way down her throat and into her stomach.

After splashing and playing in the water, Leena relaxed into a back float and stared up at the sky as the current gently pushed her downstream. Gratitude filled her thoughts.

Climbing out of the stream and onto the bank she squeezed out the excess water from her dress and hair. Her mind and body craved rest.

"Thank you, stream," she said reverently and made her way back to her cottage and again slept for days.

Now seventeen-years-old, Leena lived off the land. The past five years she spent bringing life back to her meadow, making friends with every flower along the way. Vegetables grew in the garden and fruit in the orchard. Her daisy patch breathed life again, along with the lavender that grew by the front porch. She even breathed back life into the wood of the cottage and everything in it.

Everything has a soul. Everything breathes.

To Leena's great discouragement she had been unsuccessful breathing life back into the grass across the meadow. She had tried many times, but the miles and miles of dead dirt covering the meadow seemed beyond her strength. Why had the earth not allowed her to bring back the grass and dandelions? Leena tried not to let the frustration overcome her, but the feelings of discouragement won out at times.

After her meditation one morning, Leena called out, asking the earth in exasperation, "What do I need to do to bring back the fields? What more can I do?" She rolled back from her sitting position and laid flat on the earth. Closing her eyes and continuing to breathe steadily she lay waiting. Frustration bubbled inside her.

Rolling over onto her stomach she propped her chin in her hands and stared at the ebony earth.

"What do you need?" she asked again, pointing her finger tapping into the dirt so the earth knew she was serious.

With her fingers she doodled in the dirt, drawing circles to convey her feelings of endlessly going around and around in a path that led her nowhere. Her doodling turned into digging and she dug a small hole in the ground. Still lying on her stomach, she dug until she hit something solid. Her hands worked faster now as she wondered what message the earth wanted to tell her. Working on the solid object, she dug around it until it came loose and finally free.

Leena held the round rock she had dug out in her hands. The rock felt lighter than it should be for its size. It easily filled both of her hands cupped together. She caressed the unusually round stone with its smooth, bumpy texture. Dusting it off, she felt a strange connection to it. The outside of it was gray, not black. Her memory came into focus.

Leena sprang off the ground with the rock in her hands and sprinted to the small shed by her cottage to find her Dad's old caving tools. He used to use a large, heavy mallet to crack open the geodes. Searching through all of Dad's special tools that he knew so well but had been forgotten, she remembered his strong hands making and fixing so many things.

"Leena, pass me that mallet. Let's see what the earth has given us today," Dad said with the excitement of a child. Leena bent down and looked under the shelf and with her little hands grabbed onto the heavy mallet that hung on a hook.

"Dad, what are we going to do with that rock?" asked Leena innocently, lifting the heavy tool using all her strength and handing it to her Dad.

"Today, we are going to find magic inside this rock," he answered as he tapped his fingers on the smooth surface and her eyes lit up.

"Magic? Real magic inside? But how are we going to get the magic out? And how do you know it's a magical rock and not a regular rock?" Leena said with no hesitation to believe whatever answer Dad gave.

"As you know, Princess Leena, I lived my whole life in the mountains, until

I met your Mum at market ten years ago. She's the only one on this earth that could convince me to leave my mountain home and follow her to the meadow." He smiled just thinking about Mum. "And in the mountain there are caves and jewels and gemstones, but not like this one. This one is only found in our meadow. This one is no ordinary rock. It's a geode and you can only see the gems if you break it open."

"We have to smash it?" Dad nodded. "To pieces?" Leena asked in surprise. Her eyes got big thinking about it. She did not want to destroy the rock.

"Not to pieces, little one, but we will need to hit it pretty hard with this mallet," Dad said matter of factly. "So place the geode up on the work table inside that groove so it'll hold still, and then you best step back a bit."

Leena followed the directions and waited with anticipation as Dad lifted the mallet and brought it down hard onto the geode as if chopping wood. And crack! Down the center of the rock split an opening enough to see a purple glow streaming out.

Raising her arms in the air victoriously and jumping up and down, Leena ran over to the work table and gazed at the amethyst gemstones that were beaming magic out of the gray shell casing.

"It is magic, Dad! Let's go show Mum!"

Leena reached for the mallet under the shelf hanging on its hook, still there after all these years. Carefully she placed the rock into the groove on the table. She picked up the mallet and swung it hard, barely denting the rocks shell. Whack! She hit it again and again. On the third time, the rock cracked in half and the beauty of the amethyst spilled out of the geode. Leena wondered if anything could compare to the magic of seeing the amethyst explode with life. The happiness inside her reflected on her face in a broad smile.

Leena scooped up the two halves and held it up into the light of the sun that streamed into the window of the shed. The crystals sparkled as the rays of the sun shone through all the shades of purple that grew out of the inner walls of the rock's shell. Just like when she was a child, the meadow still held the breathing amethyst.

Leena ran back to the work table and placed half of the geode back in the groove. Lifting the mallet only a little, she more gently hit the gemstone, breaking it into smaller pieces. Carrying all her stones to the tree in the meadow, she layed down, placing the gems around her on the dark earth, feeling the quiet protection of the amethyst.

The sun went down in the sky and the stars glittered above. Watching the stars appear, she asked the earth again, "Will you show me? What do I need to do? I will do whatever you ask."

Find the others. Find the five. Together you are the five.

4

Find the Five

*"What do you do when you hear a bird calling your name? You answer politely
and give a whistle back."*

The words repeated in her mind over and over. *Find the others. Find the
five.* "Five? Where are they? Who are they?" she asked the earth out
loud desperately.

That night she dreamed about another Life Breather. And the
forest.

*Leena walked among trees crowded together like soldiers. They looked down
at her, needing her, beckoning her, no, begging her for help. Black moss, pinecones,
and ferns covered the forest floor. As she walked, she climbed over a fallen log.
The pine trees still had needles on their branches, but they looked like charcoal
just like the meadow. She could feel one life among the trees there. She could feel
his breath. His life tugged at her heart, and Leena longed for this stranger—a
stranger she knew nothing about.*

When Leena awoke, the dream sat quietly in her mind, the
images fresh and real. She did not sit up. Instead, she turned her
head to the side, facing the direction of the forest.

Another Life Breather.

A sensation lit up inside her. It swirled in her, a yearning desire for him like she'd never experienced. A sensation so strong that she knew she needed to leave her meadow home and go in search of him. Soon. Now.

The feeling of dread held on to her. She did not feel ready to leave. She knew nothing about the trees in the forest. How would she survive outside her meadow? But she knew no matter how content she was here, life could not go on like this. She had a purpose to fulfill—something more than just her own survival and working her spot of land. More. So much more.

Leena had been called by the earth to give it rebirth. To complete her purpose, she needed to find the other four Life Breathers. Together they would be the five to restore breath to everything.

But before she left, she desperately needed the strength within herself to bring back the grass in the meadow.

She called on every living, breathing soul in her meadow for breath. She sat cross-legged in the middle of her meadow and closed her eyes. In her mind, as she took in her first steady breath through her nose, she called to the trees. All of them.

I need your strength. Air flowed out through her nose slowly, until every bit of air had left her lungs, and she felt as strong as the tree trunk rooted in the ground.

Strong like the trees.

With her next deep inhale through her nose, she called to the water.

I need your power. As she exhaled, she felt the power of the water flow in her veins, rushing through her.

Powerful like the water.

On her third breath in, she called to the gardens.

I need your nourishment. Exhaling, she felt the nutrients of the crops and the flowers united, encircling her, becoming one with her meadow.

As Leena inhaled her next breath, the ground beneath her gracefully lifted and released. Relief flowed like a wave through her insides. The dirt trembled then settled. Her heartbeat echoed the trembling vibration and then also settled. Leena watched as one dirt speck at a time turned from coal black into warm brown. Like a rolling wave over the entire meadow, green blades of grass sprouted one by one.

Leena's meadow breathed life again for the first time in ten long years. Color that had been forgotten on the hills had never been given more life than at this glorious moment. Her meadow glowed with emerald power as the roots to each blade of grass lit up, yellow dandelions dotted the rolling hills like specks of sunshine, hiding and popping out like treasures. The grass grew quickly, and the yellow dandelion's life accelerated and changed to wish flowers before her eyes. Leena's heart leapt in her chest at the sight. The waving green fields flourished just like Leena remembered as a young girl. Just like she had envisioned in her mind for the past five years.

Running through the meadow barefoot became the most important thing. Leena ran to the highest hilltop.

"We did it!" she called out triumphantly. She rolled down the hill, laughing all the way. When Leena reached the bottom, she stood up and looked around at the beauty of the earth. Her heart filled with emotion, like it could burst out of her chest at any moment. Taking a long breath in and out, she raised her hands to the sky and twirled around feeling the wonder of life that surrounded her.

With the grass alive again, her work in the meadow was now complete.

Leena dreamt about the forest for the next three nights. Each night felt more urgent than the last. She knew the answer to the riddle now, even though she didn't fully understand it all. *The soldiers with many arms stand guard, hiding the fungi under their beams. Where am I?* The soldiers were the trees in the forest. Tightly standing together, waiting for Leena. But the fungi under their beams? She did not know what that meant. The forest filled her thoughts. A pressing persistence weighed on her mind, and she prepared quickly to leave.

Just like Dad, she gathered a bag full of necessities, the purple scarf from her Mum, the doll with the purple dress from her Dad, her book of riddles from Grandmother Lacey, her box full of amethyst stones, water from the stream, and as many fruits and vegetables from her garden as she could fit. The food would not last long, but it would be enough to get her through the first two nights and into the next day when she would reach the forest.

Saying goodbye to her daisy patch felt like a piece of Leena's heart might fall to the ground and refuse to leave.

"I'm needed in the forest right now, daisies," she said softly, passing her fingers along the velvety petals. "I'm counting on you to care for the meadow while I'm away. My hope is to return after I've accomplished all the earth has asked of me, but I don't know what my fate will be." She watched them sway in the breeze, drooping their heads showing they understood her. "I need you to be strong. I'm relying on your strength. Look after the lilies," she continued, a lump forming in her throat when she added, "You know how they can be." With a choked laugh and an exaggerated roll of her eyes. "So silly and without a care in the world. I need my daisy girls to take care of the pumpkin patch next summer, too, and the carrots." The pitch of her voice got higher and tears pricked her eyes, blurring her vision, but she did not allow a tear to fall. Pushing back on her emotion she asked, "Can you do that for me? Can you promise me you will?" All the daisies bowed and nodded in respect. Leena's hands floated over the tops of the daisy patch and lightly brushed their petals one last time. She loved them. She trusted them. The daisies, without making a sound, whispered to Leena:

Even through fear of the unknown, the most important thing you can do is keep going, and do what you have been called to do. Keep going. Keep living. Keep breathing.

Without prompting, the last words her Mum spoke finally resurfaced in her mind.

"Remember, in the end...everything is always the way it's supposed to be."

Leena covered her face in her hands. Her Mum knew. All along, she knew and she believed in Leena. Relief came in these words. That is what she needed most, to know that her Mum believed she could do this.

Carefully, she plucked a bundle of the lavender, pressed her nose deeply into the purple flowers, breathed in the sacred scent, and tucked it into her bag. As she made her way through the meadow in the direction of the forest, she picked as many wish flowers as she could hold and blew the wisps through the air as she walked. When she reached the rocky road at the edge of the meadow, she gave one last look at her beloved home and waved goodbye. Her meadow waved back.

5

The Forest

"Are you ever afraid of something much smaller than you, like a mouse or a
spider?
What are you really afraid of?"

Leena headed west toward the forest. Sometimes she skipped, sometimes she sang, sometimes she walked very fast at almost a run. She munched on carrots and apples. A few times she stopped to rest. The scenery around her looked gloomy in its blackness. Her desire to breathe back life around her weighed heavy on her heart, but she could not risk the exhaustion that would come with that task, not to mention the increasing and looming worry in the back of her thoughts that without the protection of the amethyst in the meadow, the Destroyers might find her. A shiver crept down her spine. She forced those thoughts away.

Traveling the same rough, rocky road Dad took twice a year on his way to market proved to be more difficult than Leena had expected. Thoughts of Dad in his carriage pulled by their pony,

Doveton, filled her mind. The carriage full of scarves, pies, and gemstones and Dad whistling all the while. Oh, how Leena missed hearing her Dad whistle. Her heart ached thinking of him, but simultaneously it comforted her. Remembering the times he challenged her to a race or a riddle brought a smile to her face. Her favorite riddle: *I can fill a room, but I take up no space. What am I?* It took her six weeks to figure out that one, but she finally got it. *I am light.*

Leena stumped her Dad good when she challenged him with this riddle: *What kind of room has no doors or windows? A mushroom.* Leena laughed out loud thinking about her six-year-old self believing that was the best riddle ever told. But she had puzzled Dad with that one. Mushrooms did not exist in the meadow. Dad brought loads of mushrooms home from market and cooked them up over the open fire. The really good ones would get crisp on the outside and be light and full of flavor inside when cooked over the fire properly. He called them 'slow roasted 'shrooms'. If you timed it right, the mushroom inflated and burst in the flames like popcorn into a mushroom the size of a fist.

Mushrooms. Dad referred to them as a fungus. A fungus. A peculiar word. But why did this word feel familiar to her? Her mind opened and expanded. The riddle. Of course the fungi under the beams! Were there mushrooms in the forest? Dad had never said where he got the mushrooms. The riddle guided her. Leena knew it, just as she knew her parents guided her along this journey. She was not alone and she needed the mushrooms in the forest.

Leena's stomach grumbled at the thought of a good puffed mushroom. She looked at the darkening sky and the full moon rising in the east. The sky, open and cloudless, looked alive with stars. This was familiar. The meadow sky always overflowed with stars. She bundled her scarf under her head and got comfortable, the air, still warm, clinging to the thought of summer. As Leena lay there she remembered the night before the day of destruction and how she, Mum, and Aaron had stayed up late, stargazing and watching for shooting stars long past bedtime.

Leena thought of something she hadn't before. The sky *had* seemed strange that night. Almost as if it waged a silent battle with itself. One minute clear, and the next minute peculiar and moving. Then clear again. Six year old Leena didn't think anything of it, but seventeen year old Leena could now see the strangeness of that night—the last night with her family. Destruction had already begun around the world. And Mum had known it.

Leena curled up on the side of the rocky black road, the abnormal night sky from her childhood still lingering in her mind. Slowly her consciousness melted into a dream.

Little Leena laid down in the meadow with the sheep grazing around her. Without warning, the sheep bolted, causing a stampede. With so many sheep running, the stomping vibrated the earth loudly. The stampede pulsed into a rhythm. Like a million drums–clamorous, like a storm. The violent, black clouds rolled in closer.

Leena tried to run but she couldn't move her feet, her legs heavy and rooted like a tree trunk deep in the earth. The black cloud overtook the herd of sheep, and they vanished instantly. Leena tried to yell for Dad, but no sound came out —just an airy whisper. Nobody heard her, and nobody came to help. The black cloud came for her. Frantically she tried holding her breath, but she breathed too quickly out of control. Then in one whipping motion, her legs were ripped from the ground, and she flew up into the darkness of the cloud.

All the pounding and stomping crashed loudly around her, forcing her to cover her ears. And then she saw them, down below—thousands of tall, dark, hunched figures moving across the land with long sticks slamming them on the ground in perfect rhythm. Thump thump boom. Thump thump boom. Over and over. Their dark, featureless faces covered in black spiderwebs, gave no emotion. Every time their sticks hit the ground, the whole ground vibrated, and the life in that spot of ground suffocated. The feeling of strangulation gripped Leena's throat. Gathering all the energy in her body she called out:

"I am a Life Breather!"

Leena woke up, cold, sweaty, and shaken on the hard earth by the side of the road. Out of breath like she'd just ran for miles, she gasped for air, face dripping with sweat, despite the chill in the air. Heart racing, Leena's messy mind tried to abandon her nightmare and shut out the thoughts of the Destroyers and dark feelings of the past.

It was only a dream, she reassured herself, but she saw them.

The Destroyers. She saw them. They were hideous creatures, and as much as she tried to calm herself, a dull unease loomed inside her. Somehow she knew they would find her eventually, and she had the strange sensation that the Destroyers watched her every step, lurking in the shadowy places of her journey. The thought created a buzz throughout her body. Leena squeezed her eyes shut.

"I will not let you in," she spoke out loud to the fear.

The land stayed black even as the sun rose quietly in the sky. Her hollow stomach ached for the small amount of remaining food. Sitting up slowly, she drank a bit of fresh water from her jug.

The sun coming up in the east shone brightly over her meadow in the distance. She looked out across the land and could see how far she had traveled the day before. Her heart wanted to walk back to her meadow and forget about the forest. But the forest was only a day away now. She had to keep going. Thoughts of the Life Breather in the forest permeated her mind, and turning back was no longer an option.

Longing for focus, she settled into her crossed-legged position, her hands softly resting on her knees with her palms towards the sky. Inhaling a deep breath through her nose and releasing it through her nose, she instantly felt a connection with her body and mind to the earth. The thoughts of her dream melted away as she focused on the goodness of the sun, grateful that it rises day after day, giving the world hope. Continuing to breathe in and out, using the full capacity of her lungs, Leena felt at home while she meditated. Her mind coming home to her body through her breathing.

I am not alone. There is life all around me. There is life in me.

She repeated in her mind over and over in sync with each breath.

With a straight back, breathing in and out in a steady rhythm, she imagined stepping into the dark forest. The trees did not have leaves like the trees Leena knew in the meadow. The forest trees were much taller and had thick needles. The trunks were enormous. Forest trees were old. Thousands of years old.

She could see every detail in her mind's eye, every branch of the ancient souls of these forest trees. No breath came from the trees; it would take a long time to breathe them all back to life. As Leena pondered in the stillness of her mind, seeing the trees, she vividly pictured them awake and alive, breathing, with the sharp color contrast of rich greens and browns. She saw the pinecones and the moss and the mushrooms. Even though the forest was not yet alive, she could see it clearly in her mind. Opening her eyes she looked out to the edge of the forest. Like a gift, in the distance she saw one small bright green tree standing like a beacon at the edge of the forest amongst the blackness, welcoming her with gratitude to the forest.

Leena took out her lavender flowers and held them close to her face, breathing the sweet scent into her body. She grabbed the last apple out of her pack and her nearly empty water jug and kept walking. With her meadow behind her and the sun at her back she resumed her journey once again.

Leena walked all day, taking few breaks. As the sun sank low in the sky, she reached the living tree at the edge of the forest. This tree looked so much bigger now that it stood in front of her so close. The forest was grander than she had envisioned. Her heart quickened. The mix of emotions filled her body. Exhaustion and exhilaration sharing the same space. Excitement, fear, urgency, and hesitation. All of the feelings piled inside her and blended together until her stomach swirled with anxiety. Leena exhaled completely to calm her insides.

The trees were massive. Dad had told her stories but she always assumed he exaggerated! He had not! This magical and mysterious place stood real and right in front of her. Leena hesitated at the edge. What would she find in there? Who would she find? She closed her eyes and took another deep breath. Then stepped in, not knowing, but trusting.

A strange feeling pricked her insides. Her mind reached deeper into the forest, and she sensed a heartbeat among the trees. Leena could feel the breath of the Life Breather that lived here. It was him. She knew it was him. A boy around her age, living alone. His presence strengthened her, and a surge of love for this human flooded through her body. Leena placed a hand over her chest, and their heartbeats blended for a moment in the stillness of the evening. She wondered if he felt it, too. Did he know she was coming for him?

Leena cautiously continued on the path that led through the trees, looking over her shoulder every few minutes, imagining the boy following close behind her, but he did not appear. The crowded, cramped feeling of the forest, with so many trees surrounding her, felt so different from the open space of the meadow. If everything didn't look burned and dead, she imagined it would feel quite cozy here. Ferns grew abundantly throughout the forest as a ground cover. She sensed that the same sadness covering the forest now was the same sadness that covered Leena's heart all those years in the meadow.

The dusk light faded into night, and Leena found it difficult to see her surroundings. The light of the moon peeked through the trees. Leena found a small spot of soft black moss and she ran her fingers along the ground letting the moss know she wanted to help. With a straight back, she sat relaxed and looked up at the sky through the branches, night closing in around her.

Gently close your eyes. Choose a comfortable position with a tall back, palms facing the sky and relaxed in your lap. Feel your breath. Take in a deep inhale through the nose and exhale completely and slowly through the nose. On each inhale, say the words in your mind 'I have a purpose. I am needed.' And on each exhale say the words in your mind 'I am loved. I am one with the earth.' Continue to breathe in and out deeply through your nose. As you exhale, feel your body soften and relax. Your mind is a powerful place and your breath combined with your mind will bring your body and spirit together and you can accomplish anything.

Leena visualized the moss in her mind. Glowing green and alive with color, soft and welcoming as a place to rest in the forest. Like the familiar feeling she had experienced before, she felt the moss underneath her take a breath. Leena and the forest floor inhaled and exhaled together in a steady rhythm.

Unaware of how much time had passed, she opened her eyes.

Through the light of the moon shining through the trees above, she saw a lush green bed of moss underneath her legs, covering the ground. Tiny white flowers glowed like tiny white lights in the moss. Leena stretched out onto the ground hugging the earth and breathing in the moss. Her hunger pangs were swept away with exhaustion, and now she needed sleep more than food.

Just as her thoughts drifted into dreams, an icy shiver floated through the air. A darkness watching, waiting, wanting. Leena gripped her stomach wrapping her arms around herself in a comforting embrace and closed her eyes tightly.

Gently close your eyes. Relax the muscles in your shoulders. Soften your face. Drop your jaw slightly and be still. Slowly and smoothly breathe in and say in your mind I am a Life Breather. Slowly, steadily breathe out and say in your mind I am safe. I have a purpose. I will fulfill my purpose.

The icy air thinned, and a warm breeze billowed softly in.

A voice. Leena woke up with a jump when she heard talking in the distance. She had slept all night and deep into the next day. Immediately she scurried behind the closest tree and crouched down, listening hard to hear the chatter.

"Then you'd never guess what happened next. Do ye have a guess? I didn't suppose ye would. I'll tell ya. The rain be comin' down so hard that it turned into a mudslide! And we floated for miles down it! It was the most fun I've had in me life! Covered in mud I was for weeks! It was fantastic! If it would rain like that day again, I'd be...I'd be...so happy." He sighed and his voice trailed off, going from excitement to sadness abruptly.

He spoke like a young boy but had the voice of a teen whose tone was in the process of maturing awkwardly into a man. His thick accent made him hard to understand. Hope fluttered in her chest. The boy she'd been searching for was right in front of her, but who had he been talking to? Leena thought for sure there were no other humans in the forest.

Leena peeked around the tree trunk to get a closer look at him. His shaggy blond hair and tall thin body fit his voice to perfection; in between boyhood and manhood. Dirt covered his pants, hands and face. His clothes were torn and tight. All alone, having a conversation with himself, holding a handful of sticks, he chattered on. This was the first human Leena had seen since the day she turned seven. Leena froze and could not find it in her to step out and introduce herself, feeling shy and oddly unprepared.

The boy passed by Leena and did not notice her hidden behind the tree. He continued to walk casually through the ferns with his handful of black sticks and he chatted about toads and wild strawberries. "...ya see that? I thought to meself, it must be a moose but nah I haven't seen a moose here in years, maybe even decades. But then I seen it more clear and it was nothin' but a log, with branches lookin' like an antler on its head. So disappointin'..." He continued to talk, no longer in earshot of Leena. She followed him.

Leena, driven by curiosity, followed the sound of his voice, careful to stay far enough behind so he didn't hear her. He continued to talk the entire time almost without pausing for breath. Recalling the daily conversations she had with her daisies made Leena's heart sink, thinking about how far away they were now. Leena understood what it felt like to be alone. He must have made friends with the sticks he held on to because every so often he would look at them and ask, "are ya payin' attention? Did ya hear what I asked ya?" Leena couldn't help but giggle to herself at his odd behavior. But he also seemed adorable and genuinely kind.

The boy stopped when he arrived at a small clearing where Leena could see a skinny track from high up in a tree that curled around in a circular shape like a ringlet of Leena's hair down to the ground like a slide. The boy climbed the tree like a squirrel. Leena wondered what he intended to do. He could not fit in the slender track. She watched him waiting in suspense.

From up on a high branch he pulled out a few curiously light blue rocks and sent them down the top of the track one at a time. The rocks glowed in comparison to the blackness of the wooden track. Leena had never seen anything like this. She had to catch herself from gasping out loud. When a rock would roll all the way down the tiny track to the forest floor without getting stuck, the boy would call out, "Nice roll!" speaking to the rock as if they were teammates in a game. But most of the rocks got stuck in the middle of the track. He rolled his eyes and shook his head and yelled out, "Ehhh come on! Get goin! Whatcha doin'? Get a roll on! Yer holdin' up the line!" But never in an angry tone. Always joking and teasing. He raced up and down playing with his creation.

Leena wondered how the rocks had kept their striking pale blue color through the day of destruction. Her Dad never mentioned stones from the forest, and she had never seen the color blue glow quite like the boy's marble stones.

Fascinated by the game he played, she watched intently. The boy found entertainment out of everything and out of nothing at all, building and creating his whole day out of sticks, rocks and bark. How did he do it? Leena admired him already, his creativity, his funny charm, the kind way he treated everything around him with gentle teasing fun.

Eventually he led Leena to his home, a small cabin, nestled among the trees. Outside the front door were two stumps that came up to his knees. On one stump sat seven tiny chairs and a tiny table, beautifully crafted out of nature. Leena stayed hidden and watched him closely from behind a bush. He set his handful of sticks down carefully one at a time and placed each of them in a tiny chair around the tiny table. The forest boy sat down on the other stump.

"What's for dinner tonight? Ahhhh yes, tonight I went huntin' and got meself a toad." He pulled out from his pocket a piece of black bark and carefully broke it into pieces for each stick then one larger piece for himself. "And tonight? Dessert! Strawberries and fresh cream! Who be wantin' some?! It's goin' to be delicious." He again brought out a piece of bark from his pocket and a blob of black mud. Gently breaking off a bit of dessert for each stick and sharing what he had with the others at the table. Leena watched in amazement. Did he really believe the sticks were alive? He finished every bite, licking his fingers with satisfaction. Leena wondered if he'd ever eaten a slow roasted 'shroom, the kind her Dad would bring home from his trips. She figured this boy would go wild for some real mushrooms. After the boy finished his meal with his stick family, he collected them up into his hand and took them inside his cabin.

The words of the riddle repeated in her mind. *The soldiers with many arms stand guard hiding the fungi under their beams.* The mushrooms are hiding under the logs. She could see them clearly now. A smile spread across Leena's face and she began searching.

6

Mushrooms

"What do you do when you feel bored?
You are a creator. Go create something."

Some mushrooms look beautiful with their red caps, but Dad's words rang in her ears. *Never eat the red capped ones. They're full of poison. The smooth brown cap mushrooms that are thick at the base and get skinnier towards the cap are the best for roasting,* he would say. *And the golden-yellow mushroom with wavy, upturned edges are scrumptious. The stalk is shaped like a trumpet and it thickens where it joins the cap.*

Dad knew everything there was to know about mushrooms, but how would Leena know delicious from poison when everything looked the same charred black? Leaving the path, she searched through the trees that were closer together. Her eyes hunted around the base of every trunk and along every fallen log.

The log that the boy had referred to in his jabbering—the log that had antlers that looked like—what was it he called it? A moose? —lay in front of her, looking like a large, sleeping animal. As she examined it more closely, she could see just underneath it, a grouping of stout black mushrooms. Rounded tops and strong thick trunks, about the size of a small apple but grouped together in clusters growing out of the side of the moose log.

Leena's face lit up. Carefully she examined and plucked each black mushroom off the underside of the log. Hunger filled her insides. After gathering, she found her way back to her little mossy meadow, and started making a plan.

"Perfect," she whispered. Using her breath, visualization, and focus, she brought them back to life. As the mushrooms took their first breath, the tops shed their black skin and underneath showed a lovely golden-tan color. The perfect gift for the forest boy. Taking a bite of the soft, mild, mushroom reminded Leena of her childhood. Of course she didn't have fire to slow-roast the mushrooms, and they definitely would have tasted better popped and toasty, but bringing back fire to the world remained something she had not been able to do.

Fire, extinguished from the earth like everything else on the day of destruction, remained breathless. Leena had tried several times to start a fire in her wood stove back in the meadow, like her Dad used to, but she could not.

The next morning Leena woke up to the sound of whistling. The boy made his way through the forest, skipping along. His long legs looked even longer than usual as he hopped around, this time with no little sticks in his hands. She could tell by the way he swung his arms and collected things as he walked. Her fondness for him grew as she watched his cheerful attitude and love for life.

Leena sneaked off to his cabin and carefully placed three large golden mushrooms on the little stump, sitting outside his front door. Her water jug, she placed in the center of the stump. Then she stared at the front door, curious about what it might be like inside the little black cabin. Trying to resist the urge, she hesitated, but her curiosity won. The door pushed open easily, and when she poked her head inside the humble home, Leena saw how tenderly he cared for his little family of sticks. The sticks lay on a small side table next to a long couch. Each stick rested comfortably with a black leaf blanket. Leena's heart sighed and melted a bit.

He must have been so young on the day of destruction. A large table, with seven chairs around it, sat in the main area of the cabin. She didn't want to go all the way inside without an invitation, invading his privacy, so Leena gently closed the door and hid around the big tree a ways off, so she could wait for him to come home for lunch.

Sure enough, around lunch time, the boy came trotting along home on his familiar path.

"So ya see, if I wanted to, I could climb that tree and prob'ly make a great bridge goin' from that tree to the other one. It would take me a while but…" He stopped talking as he approached the porch. Leena could not see his face but the fact that he had stopped talking was enough to tell her that he had seen the golden mushrooms on the stump.

"Whaaat?" he said slowly, "… wha' is this?… Wha' be 'appenin'?.. How?… Who?" He flung his head from one side to the other then his voice choked, excitement mixed with tender emotion and confusion. He picked up a golden mushroom and held it in his hand like a treasure. He spun around looking for anything out in the forest that might explain this miracle. Then he began to laugh and cry simultaneously.

"It is magic, it is! Magic! And wha' is this?" he asked himself, picking up the jug of water. "It cannot be. Water. Clear water fresh fromma stream!" It looked as if at that moment he truly felt thirst for the very first time.

Then he did something unexpected. He did not stuff the mushroom into his mouth or guzzle the water like he clearly wanted to. Instead he flung the front door open and ran inside. Delicately scooping up the seven small sticks out of their leaf beds, he brought them outside to the porch with him.

"Ya see! I ain't jokin! Look at 'em! Mushrooms! I dunno how this happened but it is the greatest gift and the greatest day! Better than any old mudslide! Better than th'Founding Forest Feast!"

He placed the sticks all around the stump in their wee little chairs and divided out the mushroom, just a tiny bit for each one then the rest he placed in front of himself. Staring at the mushrooms, still amazed and grateful, the boy closed his eyes and took in a deep breath through his nose and released it through his nose. A breath of gratitude. Leena had never seen him do that before, but she could sense his immense thankfulness for whomever provided this meal for him.

"Dig in!" He picked up the largest mushroom and took a big bite. Then followed it with a long swig of water. Leena remembered what it tasted like to eat bark and mud. And she remembered the taste of her first bite of real food again. This had to be the most satisfying experience of her life so far, watching the forest boy eat his meal with his stick family and not knowing who provided it. As much as she desired to introduce herself, the time didn't feel right yet, so Leena quietly made her way back to her moss.

When night came, she fell asleep easily. As she slept, she dreamed about the boy but he was not tall like now. He was small, very small. Same shaggy blond hair and big feet, but a little boy.

"Mama, I gonna get down the hole today? Is it me turn? Imma find so much stuff in the tunnel today! And now I five years old and I could go down by meself and get a load of goods. Them shiny round stones that Cliff found, I could do it now!" he said in a small raspy voice, thick with his forest accent. In Leena's dream she saw his mama, and she answered him.

"Yes, Fife, it's your turn to be a big boy like your brothers and work. They're busy choppin' wood today to prepare us for winter so it'll be up to you to find th'stones. It'll take hours though. Can you be in the tunnel for hours?"

"I can! I can!" Fife answered back with confidence.

Leena watched him kiss his Mama goodbye then go through a hatch door close to a tree, holding a lantern and a satchel. Such a little thing with such a strong spirit.

Her dream shifted, and she saw his four older brothers chopping wood in the forest by their home. Without warning, the clouds rolled and turned black as night, and the sound of thunderous sticks thumped on the earth like drums beating the ground, getting closer.

Fife's Mama ran frantically to them carrying a young girl, and another young girl ran close behind her.

"Get to th'tunnel! Get to th'tunnel!" she yelled, sweat and panic all over her

face. The boys quickly obeyed. But they never made it to the tunnel. The black cloud found them, and they were gone. The forest lay silent and black.

Hours passed in Leena's dream and finally Fife came out of the hatch door, finished with his day's work collecting a satchel full of pale blue glowing stones.

"Mama! Mama! Look what I found! Look how many—" His small voice stopped abruptly. Not knowing what had happened earlier in the day, he looked around at the blackened earth and black trees. The frightened little boy was left alone in the forest.

In the silence of the forest, he screamed.

Leena forced herself awake, refusing to witness the terrible scene any longer. She buried her face in her hands and resisted the urge to pound on the moss and cry out in anger. Her heart ached with compassion for Fife. He needed to know that he no longer had to be alone in this world. Leena would be here with him from now on.

Without hesitation she sprinted to his cabin. Breathless she ran up the porch steps and beat on his door. No answer. She had no idea what she would say to him when she saw him but her desperation consumed her. Cupping her hands around her eyes she peered in the front window. No sign of Fife.

Leena ran through the forest, longing to call his name, but instead stayed quiet and ran until she saw him in the distance. She stopped, breathing hard, her lungs sore from running.

Fife scraped and sanded the arms of what looked like a rocking chair with rough grit on some sort of homemade wheel contraption. Though it had no deep brown wood color, only black, the craftsmanship truly amazed Leena and she stared at him working on his chair with her mouth open in awe. Her desperation returned with the remains of the dream still clinging to her mind and she could no longer hold herself back.

"Fife!" Leena called to him, sure of his name after the dream she had, but at the same time slightly worried she might be mistaken. Fife turned, his eyes wide and wondering. He stood up, and Leena could tell he wanted to run to her, but he caught himself.

In a choked voice he called out, "Oye! Are ye real? Or are ye in me imagination!" He looked down and shook his head and said, "Bless me soul." He paused as if words raced through his mind but couldn't find the right path to his mouth. He looked up and let out a giant laugh and tears came at the same time. His legs took off in a full sprint towards Leena, and then he stopped right in front of her. Now that he stood so close, she could see his blue eyes and slightly crooked front teeth. They stared at each other without speaking for a moment. Then with his long arms he reached out and grabbed her arms and pulled her into his chest, hugging her. Leena had forgotten what it felt like to be hugged so warmly. A flood of emotion swept through her, and she wanted to cry, but she didn't.

"It was you leavin' me mushrooms, all fat and delicious!" Fife released the hug but continued to hold her arms tight in his hands. He stared at Leena with his eyes still wide and a big grin on his face. Leena gave a warm smile.

"Yes it's been me." The words barely squeaked out of her mouth. All the thoughts she wanted to say seemed to run away from her and hide. He now stood in front of her, looking right at her. She paused as the reality set in that she had revealed herself, and that things were now set in motion.

"My name is Leena." She swallowed hard and steadied herself. "I've come from the meadow. Three day's travel away." She gripped the sides of her dress with her sweaty hands, feeling suddenly aware that her hands had nowhere to go and then shoved them into her pockets and continued. Fife just stared at her and listened. "I've lived there alone for ten years and I came searching…for you." She paused, taking a slow breath. "I think if we work together… we can bring life back into your forest and eventually into the world." Fife looked like he wanted to say a million things and ask million questions, anticipation building on his face, but he quietly listened, which she had not expected, so she continued to talk faster now as the words formed clearly in her thoughts and began to spill out of her. "My Mum and Dad and baby brother disappeared on the day of destruction. I was seven. It took me years to recover from that day, but I found my breath and learned how to use it to heal."

"How did ye know I was here? I dunno how old I am. I dunno how many years have passed neither." His eyes darted around quickly as he processed all the new information. "If ye say ten years, then that makes me fifteen. I don't even know what 'appened on that day. I just came out the tunnels and everyone…and everythin'… gone." Tears crowded into his blue eyes unexpectedly, and then he blinked and the tears slid down his cheeks, but he didn't seem to notice or care that he'd shown emotion. Compassion filled Leena as she looked into his face—a face still so much like the little boy in her dream, though his hair was now matted and rough, not soft like when he was younger. Leena desperately felt the need to take care of him. The longing inside her to teach him everything about breath grew.

"Do you want to see something?" Leena asked with a smile curving up to one side.

"Is it more magic? Like th'mushrooms comin' back to life?" he asked.

"I suppose maybe it is like magic, but it's so much more. If you let me, I can teach you." She waved her arm forward to lead him in the direction of the mossy clearing. When they could see the moss in the distance, Fife gasped with excitement and grabbed her hand, squeezing it.

"Whoaha!" he called out as he took off in a full run. His long legs charged through the black forest until he reached the emerald moss. Immediately he flung himself onto the soft bed of green velvet and rolled on it like a child. "You're amazin', Leena! You done this? You bringin' it all back, th'way it was? But how? I want t'learn. Teach me! I can learn anythin'!"

Leena, out of breath from chasing him, laughed as she caught up with him.

"Yes! Yes! But you have to slow down!" She flopped down beside him. They sat laughing and running their fingers through the moss, talking for hours as if they'd known each other their whole lives.

Fife told Leena all about his family. How his papa had died when he was only three, and he barely remembered him. He told her about his mama and her long blonde curls and how she made the best potato soup. His four older brothers, Cliff, Jack, Paul and Ron and his twin sisters Lil and Rose, who were two.

Leena told him every sad detail about the day of destruction and how she struggled to want to live and then how she smelled the lavender and remembered life. She told him about her gift of breathing and how she could meditate and breathe life back into nature, the stream, the tree, her daisies, all of it.

"You are a Life Breather too, Fife," Leena said, and their eyes met.

"I dunno what that means, Leena. I ain't never breathed anythin' back like you."

"I had a dream about you," Leena continued, "…before I came to find you. You are a Life Breather, I know it. You were very young on the day of destruction, and maybe no one ever taught you, but your life was spared for a purpose. I can teach you how to use your gift."

Fife gazed at Leena, listening intently. "I'd like that. I'd like that very much."

The two of them talked until the sun had nearly gone down. After they had both said everything they could think of, there was a moment. A moment when they looked at each other and they both knew that this was one of those moments that is captured inside the heart and can never be erased. Friends. They were friends. Leena had a best friend and Fife had a best friend.

7

Amazonite

"Have you ever thought about the life of an earthworm? Digging and digging blindly in the darkness?"

Leena woke early. She rummaged around in her pack and pulled out some strawberries.

"Is that wha' I think it is?" Fife sat up. His sleepy eyes looked as big as the berries. "That be a strawberry!"

Leena handed him a few and smiled. "Alright, Fife. This morning we will begin breathing life back into the forest. Are you ready?"

"I was *born* ready. I can learn anythin'," Fife said confidently, rubbing his hands together. His hair was even more wild than usual first thing in the morning, and his eyes were still puffy from sleep. Leena giggled at the sight of him and nodded her head.

"We have a lot to do. There's so much I want to teach you, and we don't have much time." "Why don't we have much time?" Fife asked innocently.

Leena took a deep breath remembering the icy shadow that fell upon her the previous night, and she shivered, knowing the Destroyers kept a close watch on them. "Because we have to find the three others who survived the day of destruction and breathe life back into the earth…all before…" Leena paused and pulled the book of riddles out of her pack.

"Before wha'?" Fife looked at her confused.

"The Destroyers will return. I don't know when, but we need to find the others and be ready."

Fife looked as though the wind had been knocked out of him. "I dunno who the Destroyers are or anythin' about 'em. But I never thought the destruction could be comin' back."

Leena remembered the dream and realized Fife never knew a thing about what happened, why the earth turned black, where his family had gone, why he had been spared.

All the stories Mum told her came flowing out of her, and Fife listened intently. She told him about Grandmother Lacey, the early snow, and late daisies on the day of Leena's birth. As she told him the legend of the Life Breathers, Fife looked as though he mentally prepared for battle with each word she spoke.

The book of riddles lay in her lap.

"Wha' is that?" he asked.

Opening the book she flipped through the pages and shared with Fife the riddle about her birth and also the riddle about the forest.

"Do you like riddles?" she asked.

"I ain't never done a riddle."

Leena held the book sideways to read the writing scribbled along the margin. "It says sodium, magnesium, potassium, calcium…I'm not sure what that means."

"Them are minerals."

"How do you know that?" Leena asked, surprised.

"Mama use t'sing a song while makin' her soup as she tossed in the salt, and it had all these funny names of th'stuff in salt. I dunno it's a catchy tune though." Fife started humming and pretended to stir the soup and throw in dashes of salt. "A little bit'a iron a little bit'a zinc, calcium and don't forget magnesium." He chuckled, thinking about his mama singing and making soup.

Leena couldn't help but be amused. She watched him and laughed.

"The riddle by it says, *I have no beginning, no end, and no middle. I smell like minerals in the breeze. I am equal to the sky. Find me.*"

"Find me?" Fife repeated. "Find who?"

"The riddle is guiding us towards the location of the next Life Breather that we need to find."

"Ahhh, right. Hmmmm…well I'd be thinkin' it sounds like the sea to me."

"The sea?" Leena asked, squinting her eyes.

"Yeah I mean it talkin' 'bout salt in the breeze and stuff. That's what th'sea smells like. Salt."

"Oh, I've never been to the sea. What is it?"

"It be water. Lots and lotsa water. And sand. I ain't never been there, but Mama use t'read me a book 'bout it."

"Is the water really equal to the sky like the riddle says?" Leena asked.

"Th'pictures in th'book looked like it but that's all I know."

"Well that's a lot more than I know about it." Leena sighed, relieved. "I think we'll make a good team, you and me." she smiled.

"Alright, let's begin." She sat cross-legged and placed her hands, palm facing the sky, resting gently on her knees. "I'm going to show you how to use your gift of breath to help the earth heal. First you find a comfortable position where you can relax, but keep your hands open facing the sky."

Fife shifted around trying to get comfortable. Clumsily he forced his legs into criss-cross but his long legs made his back hunch over awkwardly. The inflexibility of his legs created a problem.

"You'll need to have a straight back with your spine aligned so your breath can be as free and open in your body as possible. Hmmm…" Leena looked around trying to think of another position Fife could be more relaxed in. A stump round sat just a little ways off. "Let's fetch that stump and see if that might be a good chair for you to use."

Fife jumped up and quickly rolled the stump over to the moss. He sat upright on the stump with a straight back and his feet, flat on the ground. Leena gave him instructions on how to place his hands, gently and relaxed on his knees.

"Comfy now, Fife?" She tried not to giggle. "Make sure your feet are grounded to the earth, and close your eyes. Breathe in slowly through your nose, then breathe out slowly through your nose. Do that three times. Nice and deep and slow. In….and out. This will bring your spirit home to your body and will focus your thoughts."

Fife took one big breath in, wrinkled his nose up, and said, "The smell of me own skin is makin' me think I be needin' a good hot bath."

Leena's concentration broke unexpectedly, and she stared at him curiously not knowing how to react. She laughed.

"Yes you do, we will take care of that very soon," she said with the confidence that he would be cleaned up in no time.

They sat breathing in and out for a few minutes and then Leena began to guide him through the thoughts he would need to be able to breathe life back into the trees around him.

"Imagine you are on the edge of the forest looking at all the trees in front of you. Continue to breathe deeply, in and out through your nose. See the green on the trees. See the brown pine cones alive on the branches and scattered on the forest floor. Can you see them?"

"I can see the trees jus' fine, but they're still all black and dead. I can't remember what it looks like for them t'be all green," he answered.

"Keep trying. One of the most important things about giving breath back to nature is to quickly forgive yourself if it doesn't work right away, or if you get distracted or out of focus. Give yourself patience and grace. Having self-compassion is key. Do you under-stand? Forgive yourself and move forward. See in your mind the green of the moss. Then use your imagination to lift it off the ground and dress the trees with it. Your mind will find it. Keep trying."

They sat in the mossy spot for an hour, trying to breathe life back into the trees around them, but Fife kept getting distracted and asking questions.

"How long this gonna take? When do ye know if its workin'? Did ya see that log over there? Lookin' like a slug?" On and on Fife chattered and rambled with questions and observations. Leena sat patiently, giving words of encouragement, but inside she feared she may not be able to teach her gift of breathing to him. Her heart sank a bit.

"Let's start very small," Leena suggested, rethinking her method. "That chair, that rocking chair you were building the other day. Let's go to it. I want to try something."

Without questioning, Fife got up from his stump and nodded his head. They walked the forest path until they reached the place where Fife had been working on his chair. Intricate carvings lined the back and arms of the chair that Leena had not seen before because she had been so far away.

"It is lovely. May I sit in it?" she asked politely.

"It'd be an honor if ye did." Fife looked pleased.

Leena sat in the chair, closed her eyes, and rocked back and forth. The rocking reminded her of the porch swing, and she remembered the moment she felt life again with the scent of the lavender bush. Fife had worked so many hours on his special chair, making it just right. The chair deserved some living color. Leena stopped rocking and opened her eyes.

"Alright, Fife. I want you to sit in your chair. I will guide you through the breathing, and you focus on your beautiful chair. Can you remember what the fresh-chopped wood smelled like that your brothers used to cut?"

Fife breathed in through his nose imagining the aroma. "Yeah, yeah I do. That fresh cedar scent that opens up yer nostrils and fills it with the goodness of th'forest. Awwww." He sighed at the thought.

"Yes! Think of the cedar scent!"

Fife sat down in his rocking chair and rested his arms on the arms of the chair. Leena took his hands and turned them over to face them palm up in a receiving position.

"Now then, now that you are comfortable, close your eyes gently. With a straight back, think about a golden thread coming out of the top of your head and connecting you to the sky. Breathe in hope and light. Fill your lungs completely, and then breathe out fear and sadness. Let it go. Feel the rhythmic rising and falling of your chest and your belly. Your mind and body are now connected. No longer separate." The lightness in Leena's voice soothed the air around them. "Visualize the tree that provided this fresh wood so that you could create this chair. Continue focusing on the smell of the wood. It is clean. It is good. It is alive. See the fibers in the wood grain. See the luster of the woods shine. Feel the wood. Breathe in and out. Feel gratitude for the tree that gave you the wood." Leena could see that Fife sat fully focused and relaxed. "The chair wants to live. It wants to breathe, and only you can bring back its beauty. Say in your mind as you breathe in, *there is life all around me*, and as you breathe out, *there is life in me, there is life all around me. There is life in me.*"

Fife sat in his chair and focused on his breathing, using visualization to see. The chair vibrated and took its first breath. The vibration pulsed again, and Fife opened his eyes, astonished. The chair changed from dark charcoal to a light pinkish-red. The scent of the cedar swirled around Fife and landed on his skin and, like a ripple down his body, washed him clean.

His rugged blond hair became soft and light. His long fingers that had dirt embedded under the nails were now well groomed and trim, leaving behind no trace of mud or filth—completely manicured from head to foot. A clean pair of navy-blue pants emerged from the old tight ones, a fresh tan shirt, and a proper pair of shoes slid onto his feet. He looked quite handsome. Leena did not expect him to be nearly so…so…she could not think of what she thought of Fife all clean. But she admitted to herself, he looked attractive.

He opened his eyes. "Wha' in the world jus' 'appened!" he said not in the form of a question but an exclamation. "I…Imma…new, clean man! And me chair! It's so beau'iful!" His hands rubbed the fine finish of the fresh cedar, and he got his nose down close to the chair and breathed it all in. Leena clapped her hands with joy, and they hugged at the sight of the new life he had brought back.

With Fife being a hard worker and having a great imagination, once he found his focus, breathing life back into the forest came easily. They worked on it together, and life bloomed all around them. Delighted, Leena discovered that even though they were still tired after breathing the forest back to life, it wasn't as exhausting as when she worked alone. Working on it together took less of her energy, and they were able to work twice as fast.

After working for days, Leena and Fife had brought back the trees, the pond, the ferns, the forest flowers, and all of Fife's amazing creations. All of the things he'd built around the forest, like his miniature table and chairs for his sticks, the rocking chair, and the stone rolling track, were now alive and full of color. They brought his cabin to life with all the wood back to a deep brown.

One afternoon as they hunted for mushrooms, Leena asked mischievously,

"You know what we need?"

"What's that?" Fife asked with a sly smile. Leena answered his question with a riddle she remembered from her Dad. "What grows when it eats and dies when it drinks?"

Fife looked puzzled. Keeping his curious smile, he squinted his eyes.

"Fire!" Leena said, wapping him in the shoulder and laughing. "We need some fire."

"Fire?" asked Fife, slowly side-glancing Leena.

"Yeah, fire. You know, it eats the wood and gets bigger, but if you put water on it, it dies. We need it so we can roast some of these mushrooms," Leena said, holding up a bowl and shaking it a bit. "Fire is alive. It was destroyed on the day of destruction like everything else, but I've never been able to get it to breathe again. At least not on my own, but I think maybe if the two of us…"

"I can't," Fife got up from where he was sitting and paced. "I ain't ready."

Leena frowned. There was silence for a few minutes before she spoke. Fife must have a good reason for his response to her mentioning fire, but for the life of her she couldn't think what it could be.

"What is it, Fife?" she asked quietly. "Why don't you want to bring back fire?" Fife did not answer. "Will you help me understand? We will need fire eventually. Please can we at least try?" she pleaded.

Fife stopped walking and looked at Leena. Then looked down at his feet and took in a deep breath.

"Me first memory was 'round the campfire. Me family tellin' stories 'bout far away places and magical lands. We're fallin' asleep to th'sound of crackling wood. Th' burnin' embers glowin' in the fire pit 'til the wee hours of the night. Papa scooped me up in his big arms and carried me to bed." He paused for a few seconds, then looked Leena in the eye. "But them fires betrayed me," he said even softer. Leena's heart felt like it stopped beating.

Fife looked out in the direction of the big clearing inside the forest a ways off. "When I was three, the fires took my Papa. I could see th'smoke and hear the cries of them families trapped in the fire. Papa ran to help and saved three others before he got…trapped… and couldn't get out."

"Fife, I'm so sorry. I didn't—" Leena stopped short and couldn't finish her thought. Fife looked lost in thought. She could see that he was replaying the terrible memory over and over in his mind.

Finally he spoke. "It'll be alright Leena. I know ye didn't know. Mama didn't talk 'bout it much, only to tell us Papa was a hero." Fife gave a faint smile. "And he was. But we never be havin' campfires again after that." There was a long pause. "There somethin' else though, Leena. I'm thinkin' maybe it be me that started th'fire that day." He looked at her with shame in his eyes. "Me Papa, he had me help with the campfires b'cuz I could start'em real fast. I dunno how I did it. I would jus' look on the wood and imagin' it aflame, and it'd come to life right there like I be talkin' to it."

"Fife, you didn't start the fire that took your Papa. Don't you see? You have a gift to bring things to life. Even when you were little. You were using your gift, and you didn't even know it. You are a Life Breather. You were born a Life Breather. Your gift can never *take* life away. It can only give."

Fife pondered what Leena said. "Never thought 'bout that." He rubbed his forehead. "Bein' so young I jus' didn't know how to explain any of it. Then I be puttin' it outta me mind so I never had t'think 'bout it again. But here I am, thinkin' 'bout it." He gave a soft laugh through his nose that resembled a sigh.

Leena didn't ask about making fires again. She knew when Fife felt ready, he would. And if he never felt ready, that would be okay too. She understood.

Early the next morning Leena woke up to the sound of thumping outside the cabin. For a brief moment in her sleepiness she thought she might still be wrapped in a dream. But as the thumping got louder and closer, her heart raced in her chest. The familiar sound rooted deep in her memory terrified every inch of her. The Destroyers. She scrambled out of bed. Fife's bed lay empty.

"Fife! Fife! Where are you?" she yelled through the cabin.

She raced out the front door and called for him again, desperate to see him safe. When she looked out the door she saw something she did not expect. Fife sat on his stump with a straight back and a small deer ate a strawberry right out of his open cupped hand as it rested on his knee.

From panic to peace, she let out a sigh and covered her mouth with her hands.

"How can this be?" Leena whispered to herself. She had not believed in the possibility of bringing animals back to life. What did this mean? Could all life be brought back? She shut the thought down and pushed it away, not allowing herself to hope. "Fife! You are working your magic! You brought back a deer?"

He turned around and with a big grin didn't say a word. Just smiled.

Leena approached cautiously so she wouldn't scare the fawn away, but the fawn did not appear to be a bit afraid and approached Leena easily. "Oh my goodness, she is beautiful." Seeing an animal reminded Leena of her animals. Her goat. Her sheep. The chickens. The kittens. An entirely new level of life entered in with bringing back animals. Leena's heart swelled.

"How did you do this?" she asked with wondering eyes.

"I jus' be sittin' here on me stump and sayin' in me mind the things you taught and I started seein' her. The fawn. I could see her clear in me mind. Then I heard a bit of rustlin' in the bush and out she comes. Wobblin' and shaky like a new babe. Within the hour she's been runnin' and jumpin' all over the place!"

"Fife, you are incredible! This changes everything! Don't you see? You can do this without my help, and you have powers that I don't have—" Leena stopped talking when she heard something in the distance. They both looked in the direction of the noise. This was not the sound of deer running. This was bigger. This was the sound that she feared most of all. The sound of sticks beating on the ground, embedded in Leena's mind. Leena's heart froze and her eyes stared blankly in disbelief. Feeling numbness crawl over her, she buried her face in her hands.

"Oh no. It's them. How are they here? They've come back." Her voice sounded fragile. "I never thought they'd return so soon. This is not right. This is not…" It did not sound like thousands marching toward them, only a few. They were getting closer. The sky stayed blue and calm, no blackness in sight.

Fife looked at her with urgency, and said, "We have to hide. Now."

Fife grabbed hold of Leena's hand, and they ran for the hatch of the tunnel. Leena had never been there so she followed his lead. Fife kept hold of her hand and guided her as they ran. The fawn ran close behind them until they reached the hatch door. The handful of Destroyers got closer. Leena could feel their venom pressing behind her, desiring her most prized possession, her breath. Leena's normally quiet mind raced, and the pounding of the sticks matched the pounding of her heart.

Fife knew exactly what to do. He opened the hatch. The three of them piled inside and traveled down the corridor. The steep steps leveled out onto a tunnel path. In complete darkness, they traveled, slowly feeling their way through the slender underground hall. Leena's breathing was ragged.

"Stay close, Leena. It'll be alrigh'."

Once they got to the end of the tunnel, Fife's hands searched around for a lantern. Fumbling in the dark, he grabbed the metal handle and picked up the old lantern that had been down there for all these years.

Sitting in the darkness near the end of the tunnel, deep under the ground, they could no longer hear the sticks beating the earth. They had no way of knowing when it would be safe to come out. So they waited in the pitch dark. Leena sat shivering quietly as the memories of that day so long ago crept into her mind. Fife wrapped his long arm around her, and she leaned on his shoulder.

"It'll be alrigh'. That be a promise. We're together now. They can't harm us down here," Fife said.

Leena tried hard to focus her mind but fear controlled her thoughts. She shook from the cold temperature in the tunnel combined with the panic flooding through her. Closing her eyes, she attempted to put her mind in a different place.

"Mum, look at Aaron!" Leena called out, pointing at her baby brother. Mum who was pulling weeds out in the carrot patch turned her head in Leena's direction. A smile spread across her face, and her eyes lit up. "He thinks the bumble bee is like a kitten, and he wants to pet it!" Leena said giggling.

The bumble bee had landed on the lavender bush, and Aaron with his chubby little finger reached out and gently stroked the fuzzy bee. As the bee gathered the pollen, it didn't seem to notice Aaron stroking its back. But then, Aaron tried to scoop up the bee with his cupped hand and said, "My beebee." But the bee quickly hummed and flew away. Leena and Aaron watched as the bee flew up higher and higher. And then Aaron began to cry.

"My beebee!" he sobbed. His face scrunched up, and tears poured out of his big blue eyes.

"It's okay, Aaron. Beebee will come back. But we can't hold it. It wants to fly home."

Aaron reached for Leena. She gathered him onto her lap and wrapped her arms around him, gently patting his head just like Mum would do. Within a few minutes, Aaron bounced off her lap, ready to find something new to play with.

Leena remained quiet, even though she wanted to burst into tears remembering her little brother. The lump in her throat pulsed and ached as she held in her tears. Aaron would be eleven years old now. The thought of him being older only made her miss him more.

Fife held her close. The fawn had settled down finally and calmly lay beside Leena. Leena's heart slowed down as she felt the rhythmic breathing of the fawn. The ache in her throat eased.

After sitting in darkness for what felt like hours, Fife inhaled a steady breath through his nose. He had come so far in his breathing gift in such a short amount of time that when danger came, his first response was not to panic, instead he responded by sitting calmly and breathing. He took in and released three slow smooth breaths. As he held the lantern in his lap, he began to repeat out loud.

"I can see. There is light all around me. I can see. There is light all around me."

His voice, so clear and steady. Listening to him soothed Leena's heart, and her mind stayed calm. After a few minutes of his deep breathing and calm speaking, a tiny flicker of light sparked inside the lantern. Just a small burst of light, but the flame showered light through the whole tunnel brilliantly.

"Fire," Leena whispered. "You did it, Fife."

Fife looked at Leena in surprised satisfaction. Both of them, speechless. The flickering light from the candle in the lantern made spots of pale blue lights glow along the walls. Hundreds of small glowing blue rocks fixed into the sides of the burrow breathed life.

"Holy hot slippery jumpin' bugs," Fife exclaimed under his breath. "This be the biggest load of glowin' rocks we ever had here. This be a miracle load."

"What is it?" Leena wanted to shout, but it came out as barely a whisper.

"These be amazonite gemstones. It's th'most precious stone in th'forest. It takes years to get this many of'em." His mouth opened wide, and his eyes were as round and blue as the stones. He held up the lantern to the sides of the walls and the stones glowed a brilliant pale blue. Leena noticed that Fife's eyes matched the blue of the amazonite and the blue of Aaron's eyes.

They collected the glowing rocks, admiring each unique gemstone before they put them into their pockets. Then they waited. After another hour, they made their way back through the tunnel.

Leena feared what they would find above ground. Would the

Destroyers be waiting for them? Slow breathes. Would all the life they brought back to the forest be destroyed again? She continued to reassure herself that they would be kept safe—that they were spared before and would be spared again, but the trauma of the Destroyers returning, even if it was just a few of them, seemed too much to process just now. Her worst fear had happened. Now what? What happens when the thing you are afraid of most happens and you survive it? Then what? Then, Leena supposed, there is nothing else to fear.

Cautiously Fife opened the hatch, and they listened intently. Silence.

"I didn't know they still be alive and wanderin' about the land. I never heard 'em or seen 'em those years ago. Do you know what they be lookin' like?" Fife asked as they crawled out of the hatch hole. He reached his arm down to help Leena out. Then gently bent down and lifted the fawn out after her.

"I've only seen them in a dream. They are covered in black and are very tall and thin, and slightly hunched over, holding long sticks that they beat on the earth. Their sticks extinguish any life they touch." A chill crept over Leena's shoulders as she thought about them. "They have no faces. And they have no souls." Leena squeezed her eyes shut. "We have got to finish our work here and move on. "

They made their way back to the cabin through the darkness by the light of the fire-lit lantern, holding the glowing rocks in their pockets. The amazonite rocks.

"What do you know about these stones?" Leena asked curiously, rolling them around through her fingers.

"Mama called them harmony stones. They be givin' hope when all feels lost. These're the same rocks I built th'track for. Them rocks gave me hope to build it and helped me feel happy and confident, like I had a purpose buildin' it all those years ago. I needed some-thin' to keep me goin'. Since I made it, I've built lots a things 'round the forest. But the track was me first. It helped me heal. I talk to me stick family a lot and would bring'em to the track to watch the races." He paused, then said in a softer tone, "I was so lonely."

"I know," Leena said, meeting his blue eyes. "I felt it, too. I understand. My sadness stayed with me for years. A sadness beyond crying. My tears were gone. To lose everyone we loved in an instant…" She didn't finish her thought. She knew they both understood.

They continued to walk along the path toward the cottage, the deer following closely beside them.

"What made 'em come back do ya think? Why after all these years?" Fife asked.

"I don't know. The only thing I can think is that when you brought back the deer, they sensed a new life and came in search of it."

"Yeah, but what about the life a th'trees and plants and stuff? They be breathing, too, and they didn't come back in search for them," Fife said, churning through the information in his mind trying to make sense of it.

When they reached the cabin door, Fife turned to Leena and asked with a smile, "So do we let the lil' deer inside? Mama never let us bring the animals inside th'home, but I think she'd be okay with it under these circumstances." He couldn't help but laugh at the oddness of the whole thing. Leena quickly agreed that the fawn should come inside. And they opened the door wide. The fawn bounded in, making herself comfortable on a soft rug, curled into a ball, and fell asleep.

Fife eagerly got to work on filling the empty fireplace with wood.

"T'night we be havin' a fire in this place." After the long day in the cold dark tunnels, that sounded amazing to Leena.

Fife sat in his chair and breathed in and out slowly and controlled.

Take in a deep breath through the nose. Now exhale though the nose, slowly releasing all the breath inside you. Close your eyes gently and continue to breathe. In your mind, see the light. See it burning brighter and brighter. Keep breathing deeply. In and out. Feel the warmth on your face. Feel the life of the fire burning inside you. Feel the fire breathing. The embers glowing beneath it. The crackle of the wood as it bursts and pops. Chatting and laughing. It is alive.

The fireplace came to life with a glorious flame. Fife stood up, and Leena put her arms around Fife and squeezed him tightly around the waist. She had always wondered what it would be like to have a friend you loved so much that you couldn't imagine not knowing them. Now she knew.

"You are brilliant. You know that?" She rested her head on his chest.

"I am pretty amazin'. You are right 'bout that." He winked and hugged her back.

Then her smile widened, and she said, "I'm starving." Leena looked at Fife.

"What are you smilin' about?" Fife asked curiously.

"This calls for a celebration." Leena grinned as she unpacked a bundle of mushrooms from her pack. "Slow roasted 'shrooms." She grabbed two long sticks from outside. Poking the stick through the middle of the mushroom, she handed it to Fife.

"Now, you have to twirl the stick to get the mushroom roasted evenly on all sides," Leena instructed.

After a few minutes of roasting and twirling, a popping sound shot through the air, puffing the mushroom up to twice its size!

"Holy hot poppin' pockets!" Fife could not contain his excitement! With his stick still in his hand he leapt in the air in celebration. They both laughed and laughed. The outer shell had a crisp crunch to it and the inside tasted airy and light.

"Mmmmmm. This is spectacular! How'd you know how t'do it? That flavor jus' exploded outta that thing!"

"My dad used to bring mushrooms home from market, and we would roast them the first night he returned. It was a tradition." Leena cooked up one for herself. It popped and expanded. More laughter and leaping followed. As she took a bite, memories of her family came flowing into her mind.

"First one is for my beautiful queen. Watch out, they are very hot right out of the fire." Mum pulled the slow roasted 'shroom off the roasting stick that Dad held out to her bowing, as if presenting her a bouquet of flowers. Mum blushed, and Leena watched the sparkles in her Mum's eyes.

"Me next! Me next!" Leena squealed looking at the fat toasted treat in Mum's hand. Four-years old Leena looked just like her Mum. Fair skinned and

dark hair. Except of course for Leena's ringlet curls. Mum's hair hung long and straight down her back, held back with a ribbon.

"Yes and you! My Princess Leena! Here is a 'shroom for my favorite little honey pie princess." Dad handed his darling daughter a hot mushroom and then kissed her on the nose.

Inside her mind, Leena sat around the fire with her family again, feeling all the love as if they were right there with her.

"I'm proud of you, Fife."

"Proud? Of me?" He looked surprised.

"You overcame a deep fear today, bringing the fire back. You are healing." Leena smiled and reached for another mushroom. Fife stared into the fire and nodded his head.

"Leena, I think you're right. I think I am healin' a bit."

Leena and Fife ate as many slow roasted 'shrooms as they could fit in their bellies, popping at least a dozen each. Magic filled the air as they fell asleep by the fireplace that night.

Leena dreamed of the sea.

MEDITATION MOMENT:

Sit up straight in a comfortable position.

Imagine in your mind you are sitting in a smooth cedar rocking chair.

Breathe in through your nose, slowly filling your lungs. Breathe out slowly through your nose, completely releasing all your breath.

Breathe in the cedarwood.

Say in your mind as you breathe in, *I am creative.* Say in your mind as you breathe out, *I am a problem solver.* Say in your mind as you breathe in, *I am compassionate.* Breathe out. *I am grateful.*

8

Market

"The sun will be your guide."

Black sand stretched across the earth as far as she could see. Leena heard crashing water, grand and majestic. The massive waves rose higher and higher and then crashed onto the sand, immediately changing their mind, calmly running up to greet the sand and then rushing backwards, only to rise up and do it all again. Leena had never witnessed a more beautiful sight, the wild rhythmic motions so calming and hypnotic; waves rolling in and out of the sea. The sea. This was the sea. The water, as blue as the sky, clearly breathed life continuously, but the sand, seashells, and driftwood were still black and had no breath. But just like in the forest, she felt a life there. A life that called to her and needed her help.

The waves ebbed and flowed, gathered momentum and crashed hard—she could hear it calling her name.

"Leena. Leena. Come to the water. Come find me. I need you."

By the water, a girl stood in a white dress. The white ruffle of the dress rested just above her knees, and the sleeves billowed in the wind. Her skin, browned by the sun, complimented her yellow waist-length hair that flowed wildly down her back.

Leena stood far away from her, but she could see the girl's bare feet in the black sand. The girl reached her arms out towards the water, but didn't move her feet. The sand moved slowly, and as it moved, the girl's feet sank little by little into the sand. Deeper and deeper until her toes were covered, then her ankles. Her feet sank deeper, but she did not try to escape, allowing the sand to take her as if she didn't care or didn't know. It happened so slowly that the girl didn't recognize the danger. She reached for the water, with longing in her face.

"I'm coming!" Leena called, and she ran to the girl.

The thick sand made it difficult to run. Leena's lungs burned. She called out again but the girl didn't look up and didn't answer. The girl stared at the sea, wanting to be part of the water. Out of breath, Leena kept running hard across the heavy sand. Her legs ached, pushing her to go faster. The sand covered the girl's knees now. As Leena got closer she saw that the girl looked about her same age. The wind whipped her flowy white dress, the ruffle now even with the sand. The girl bent down and wrote in the sand with her finger. J-i-l-l-i-a-n. and drew a circle around the word.

Leena now stood right in front of her, but the girl's eyes were glazed over, lost in the sea, and she could not see Leena.

"Jillian," Leena said. "I'm coming."

Leena woke up, disoriented. She rubbed her blurry eyes then looked around wildly.

"We need to go to the sea!" Her words stumbled out of her mouth without thought, hands shaking. "It's time!" She pushed on Fife's shoulders to shake him awake. "It's time. We have to find her," she said in a voice more alarming than she had intended.

Fife opened his sleepy eyes and let out a yawn. He sat up. With his hair scrunched up on one side and in a gravelly voice said, "Who? Who're we findin'?"

"The girl by the sea! Her name is Jillian!" she said, out of breath. "She's a Life Breather, and she's alone… and she's sad… and sinking in the sand." Leena's voice sounded far away like her mind had stayed in the dream.

Fife cleared his throat, and his long legs stretched out of the warmth of his blankets and onto the wood floor. Fife glanced around his little home. He let out a sigh and nodded his head.

"Well, then. Let's be goin'. But I never been outta the forest. I dunno know the way."

One thing Leena most admired about Fife is he never hesitated. He didn't overthink things. He just got to work. Always ready to do whatever needed to be done.

Leena didn't know the way either but said confidently, "We need to ask the earth for guidance. I know we will be led to the sea if we are listening."

They ate breakfast quickly so they could catch the sun at first light. With their stomachs full of berries they made their way down the path to the mossy clearing in the dawn light. The sun emerged steadily while they waited quietly on the moss, now surrounded by the trees that were alive and full of color. One sunbeam at a time filtered through the forest creating marvelously straight rays through the majestic trees. Perfectly quiet, with mouths slightly open, they sat in awe of the sight. The sunlight dappled through the pine trees in its purest form.

The quiet beauty created by nature was the real magic. And this sight was beyond any magic Leena had ever seen. Cotton floated through the air, blowing off the cottonwood trees like snow, but instead of falling to the ground, it blew easily and gently in all directions. It reminded her of the wisps on the wish flowers blowing smoothly in the breeze.

Fife and Leena sat in meditation. Leena on the moss and Fife on his stump. Straight backs and open palms.

Breathing. Connecting. Asking. Focusing. Listening. Waiting. Receiving.

Allow your eyes to gently close, and take a moment to connect your spirit with your breath. Breathe in deeply through the nose. Inhale peace… and exhale fear. As you breathe in, feel the calm of the forest around you. Allow your face to soften. Continue to breathe. Feel your arms gently resting by your sides. Allow yourself to be at peace in complete relaxation. There is no hurry. Be in this moment. Breathe. The sun is your guide. Look to the sun, and you will receive the answers you seek. Take as much time as you need. Continue to breathe in and out. How does your body feel?

Your body is at peace. Your mind is at peace. Your spirit is at peace. You will receive answers. The sun will guide you to the sea. Be at peace, and go with hope.

Leena saw the clear path to the sea like a map in her mind. The rays of the sun that beamed through the trees created the answer. *Follow the sun.* She stood up, and with the momentum of hope fresh in her mind, she said reverently to Fife, "We will follow the sun to the sea."

"I seen it. The sea. In me mind. All that water. It's beau'iful, it is," Fife said in a soft voice. Looking at Leena he said, "Thank you Leena. For comin' and savin' me. Thank you for seein' me in your mind and leavin' your home to help me. Let's go and help Jillian. She be needin' us now."

She reached her hand out to Fife, and he took hold of hers, giving a quick squeeze. The sun shone fully through the trees now, and the warm air matched the warmth Leena felt inside.

Together they gathered the amazonite stones they had collected from the tunnel. Fife put a handful in his pouch. Leena added the amazonite to her collection of amethyst inside her special box. They placed some of the amazonite stones around the forest. These stones, just as they had protected Fife's life under the ground on the day of destruction, would now protect the forest floor from any Destroyers that might come back. The forest would never again lose its breath.

Fife pulled off a sheet of moss covering a fallen log and carefully wrapped his seven sticks into it like a blanket. He rolled them into the moss and gently patted the bundle, placing them in his satchel. Searching around on the forest floor, Fife found a small fresh cedar stick and rubbed the bark off, showing the smooth wood underneath. The scent radiated out of it. Taking a deep breath in, the scent of his precious cedarwood filled his body, and he visibly relaxed. He added the cedar stick to his pack of special things from the forest.

"I'll be comin' back, don't ya worry," Fife promised as he brushed his hands over the rocking chair that now rested on the front porch. The little fawn laid down beside the chair, looking at

Fife, a hint of sadness in her eyes. The fawn wanted to stay in the forest, and the forest needed her here.

With a long breath in and a deep sigh, Fife turned to face the direction of the sunlight. "Time t'go." The sun streamed through the trees showing them the straight path that would lead them out of the forest and eventually take them to the sea.

As they journeyed through the forest, they continued to breathe life into everything they passed by. Streams and plants. Trees and berry bushes. Fallen logs and mushrooms. All that had been taken from the forest, now given back breath. Alive, breathing, and protected.

Leena and Fife stopped at the edge of the forest. The dirt path evolved into a pebble road. The edge of the forest appeared nothing like Leena had imagined. Without warning, the towering trees ended abruptly, and the forest opened up to a large stretch of bare land. About a quarter mile ahead lay the village. They could see the houses lining the streets in the distance. Leena had never in her life seen anything like it.

"Oh my goodness! It's the village! Look at all those houses! So close together!" Leena said with excitement. And then remembering all the life that once breathed in the village, now gone, her excitement faded. Countless carriages over the years had passed over this road. Including Dad's.

Blackness covered it all, just like the meadow and the forest had been. All the streets, homes, and shops, frozen in the exact place as the day they had been destroyed.

Leena thought about Dad, driving his carriage, Doveton the pony pulling it along slowly through the forest on the dirt path. Then onto the gravel road that led to the village, and through the village on the cobblestone streets, the back of the carriage stuffed full of goods to sell.

As Leena and Fife silently approached the village houses with their packs slung over their shoulders, looking at all the wonders of the village. The village rested on a slight hill, so after they wandered through the streets, they needed to stop and rest.

"Did you ever go to market?" Leena asked Fife, leaning against the black brick wall of a small flower shop.

"No. I was too lil' to go. And after me family disappeared, I's too afraid to leave the forest. I didn't know what I'd find if I left."

"I felt the same. I wanted to stay in the meadow. I didn't know anything about the world or if I'd be faced with the Destroyers again. I guess I never felt strong enough to leave on my own, nor did I have any desire to, but the loneliness..." Leena shielded the sun from her eyes with her hand and looked at Fife. "Not until I dreamed about you and the other Life Breathers. Then I knew I needed to leave, and my heart changed. I wanted more. I wanted you" —Leena paused and smiled— "and the others to be with me so we could help each other, but it was still hard to leave."

They stood in silence for a few minutes, looking at the colorless homes and shops that lined the street.

"My goodness, though, I never ever could have imagined this village. Even after all my dad told me. Some things you just have to see for yourself. You know?" Then she blinked and looked at Fife. "Fife, I think we need to bring life back to the homes here before we find the sea." She looked at him hoping for approval. "I can't bear to leave it destroyed and left in darknessness. But if we do, then we will have to stay...I'd say at least a few days. But I feel like we need to. *I* need to. I feel like there's something here for me. Though I don't know what it is."

"Leena, I hope ya know by now that I'll be followin' you 'till you say 'stop followin' me'." He laughed softly. "Whatever you say, I'm there."

Leena smiled, stood up, and looked around. "I wonder where the marketplace is."

Fife shrugged his shoulder. "Dunno."

Now that she had seen all the houses and streets, she could imagine the bustle of market time. Everyone with their carts of fine things to sell. All the various smells of food, like bread baking, fresh fruit pies, and cinnamon candies. The beauty of fine jewelry and candles. Dresses and shoes. The sound of chatter among the sellers and the buyers. The clomping of horses and ponies up and down the cobblestone streets. She could see it all in her mind, and it looked marvelous.

They searched through the streets until they rounded a corner and came to a place where the ground completely leveled out. On the other side of the street, hundreds of carts were set up in a grassy clearing. Everything stained black, looking eerily like a ghost town. What lay in front of her looked like a shadow of a forgotten time.

Without thinking, Leena began running through the market carts. An instinct erupted through her that she couldn't explain. Her insides flared. Driven and impulsive, she didn't know what she searched for, but she chaotically picked up trinkets off the carts, looking for something of significance. Then, at the far end, she saw something she had not known she was searching for: A faint purple glow.

Leena ran across the clearing as fast as she could toward the cart with the purple stones glowing on it. Shaking, she grabbed hold of the cart and fell to her knees, covering her face with her hands. Dad's cart. Tears of sadness and anger raged in her eyes. Without even trying to hold the tears back, she sobbed loudly. Her body shook, mourning his loss all over again. Sorrow filled her as she thought about the Destroyers and all they took from the earth. Why? Why had they done this? How could such cruelty exist? Her biggest fear still lurked in her thoughts like a menace; what if she wasn't strong enough to defeat them all and save the earth. How would she defeat them? What if she failed to do what the earth asked of her? So many questions still unanswered. Anguish grew inside her, and as she cried she grabbed a small handful of the remaining stones, holding them close to her.

Fife came running.

"Leena! Leena! What is it? Are ye alright!" In one motion, he bent down and scooped her up in his arms, holding her as she cried, rocking her back and forth.

"My dad…this was my dad's," Leena said through broken sobs, tears flowing fiercely. She laid her head on Fife's shoulder, and they sat together in the strange stillness of a marketplace that had been dead for ten years. Having Fife there with her through her grief helped ease the pain. He didn't ask questions that she had no strength to answer or try to talk her out of her pain that she wanted to feel, he just held her.

"I'm sorry. I'm so sorry," Leena said vulnerably through her tears.

"Ain't nothin' to be sorry 'bout, Leena. It's okay t'cry. It don't mean you ain't strong. You be the strongest person I know."

Leena let out a small laugh without meaning to.

"I'm the only person you know, Fife," she said, wiping her eyes.

"Yeah, I know that," he said. "I'm bein' serious though. Ye don't gotta apologize for cryin'. Ever."

Leena nodded. Even as a young girl, she never wanted her family to see her sad. And definitely didn't let them see her cry. It made her feel weak. And she did not want to be seen as weak. After-all, she is a Life Breather, strong and in control of her emotions, but now she could see that sometimes it takes strength to cry. It takes strength to acknowledge sadness and fear and all those other tough emotions. That's the real strength, not burying it and pretending it doesn't exist.

Wiping her tears with her scarf, she looked around at Dad's cart. Most of the things he brought to sell were gone, sold long ago, but there were a few things remaining. Two of Mum's pies sat on the cart shelf and three scarves. The pies were black like everything else, as if they had been cooked for sixteen hours in the oven. Picturing a burned black pie that had cooked in the oven too long made her smile.

She held up a pie.

"Are you hungry?" she asked Fife, unable to keep from laughing, her face puffy from crying.

"Always." He laughed back.

Carefully, she unhooked the three scarves that draped over a pole hanging off the side of the cart. Even though they were color-less and lifeless, she hugged them reverently and breathed in the scent. Nothing. No scent. But it comforted her to have Mum's scarves with her.

Leena handed a pie to Fife and picked up one for herself.

"Ready? Because I am starving," she said, wiping the tears from her cheeks and eyeing the pies.

Fife looked down at the ten-year old pastry.

"Are ya sure we should be eatin' these? I mean, I be believin' your mum is a fantastic baker and all, but….ya know…it's been here *a while*."

Leena giggled. It felt good to laugh after feeling so sad and angry. Fife knew how to make her laugh.

"Trust me. I want to try something." She looked down at her burned pie. "I think this one is cherry. And yours…" She peered over to the pie Fife held. "Yours is apple, I'm pretty sure. Mum made the best apple pies." She closed her eyes and breathed in, remembering the smell of the apple tartlets on her seventh birthday.

Fife scrunched up his face, indicating he may not be up for eating a decade old pie that looked burnt to a crisp.

"What?" Leena demanded in a mock tone. She smiled and punched his arm. "Let's bring this pie back to life. As much as I love mushrooms, I need some pie right now. Do you agree?" she asked, raising her eyebrows.

Fife answered slowly. "If we can turn this back into a pie? Then we can truly do anythin'. I'm ready."

Leena climbed up into her Dad's carriage. It felt a little rickety, the same as she had remembered. The seat creaked as she sat down, same as she remembered. It felt like home.

"Come on up, Fife," she said as she patted the wooden bench, inviting him to sit beside her. Fife joined her and they both set their pies in their laps. Sitting with their backs straight, they closed their eyes at the same time, hands resting in a palm open position, relaxed on the bench.

They took in three deep, smooth breaths in and out through their noses. With each breath they pictured the market scene as it stood ten years ago.

"I'll give you two gilders for that scarf." A plump man pointed at a royal blue colored scarf hanging on a pole off the side of the cart.

"The price is seven, not a bit less," said the seller in a calm voice. "The lovely hands of my wife made this scarf, and I know it's worth ten gilders at

least." The plump man shook his head, but the seller continued to speak. "The wool from this yarn, spun from my prize sheep—softest sheep in the land. And the weaving, dyed blue with the cornflowers grown in my own garden by my own hands. You'll not find finer, softer yarn anywhere."

"Ehh!" the man grunted. "Not worth seven but how about three." His tongue rolled.

"I'll pay eleven," a new softer voice spoke. "I know skill when I see it, and this is the finest I've seen. It will be perfect for my son here as we head home for the winter."

The man selling the scarves turned his attention to the new customer. They smiled at one another, and the new customer bowed looking at the ground.

"Well that would be very kind of you, sir. And you," the seller added as he looked at the young boy that stood by the new customer. The young, dark-haired boy, probably nine or ten years old, bowed in respect and smiled. His deep-brown eyes that matched his dark hair stared at the blue scarf in excitement. The seller unhooked the royal-blue scarf from off the pole and handed it to the man in exchange for eleven coins.

"Thank you, my friend," the customer said as he bowed again.

"And thank you. My wife thanks you, too," the seller said with sincerity and he tipped his cap. "Safe travels as you head back home…where are you headed?"

"The mountains. We live in the mountains," the man answered.

Leena opened her eyes. What had just happened?

"Did you see that, Fife?" she asked with round eyes. "Did you just see what I saw? The selling of that blue scarf?"

Fife opened his eyes and looked at Leena. "Yeah, I did! Who were they?"

"That was my dad," she said, gazing at the pile of scarves. "I don't know who the others were, from the mountains…" Her voice trailed off, getting caught in her throat.

"I miss him. I miss my dad. I don't think I'll ever stop missing him. He feels so close right now." She blinked a tear away, stopping it before it could fall.

After giving herself a few seconds, she readied herself to try again. The pies still sat black on their laps. Leena's empty stomach did not give up easily, even more determined now to give the pies back some life.

"Alright, let's begin," she said.

Once more they softened their bodies and relaxed their minds. Inhaling and exhaling slowly. They envisioned the pies. Everything about the pies. The fruit that supplied the filling. The trees that provided the fruit. The hands that worked the dough. Breathing in gratitude for all.

Calmly they waited with their eyes closed, and they breathed. Fife's nose twitched. Without opening his eyes, he said, "Do ya smell that? And do ya feel that?" Heat clung to their thighs as the pies cooked on their laps. But he kept his eyes closed.

"Yes I do, and yes I do!" Leena answered, smiling but kept her eyes closed. "It's working!" she whispered in excitement.

When the pies reached an uncomfortably hot temperature on their laps, they opened their eyes and stared down at the bubbling dessert. If there was ever a time in all of history that a pie was appreciated and anticipated more than any other, it was this time. They were both so hungry, and the smell of the cherries and apples cooked in a homemade crust seemed to be the most delicious fragrance that had ever reached their noses. Mouths opened, they turned to look at each other in awe. Then laughter erupted from deep inside their bellies as they carefully took the hot pies off their laps and set them on the bench beside them.

"Leena, look!" Fife pointed at the pile of scarves on the floor of the carriage that Leena had taken from the cart pole.

A pastel blue scarf, a white scarf, and a gray scarf sat lumped together in a heap by Leena's feet.

"They're alive," she said and picked the scarves up carefully, handing the light blue one to Fife. "This one belongs to you now. From my mum."

9

Taffy

*"When the earth gives you something, say thank you.
Gifts from the earth are the earth's way of wrapping its arms around you.
Feel the gratitude fill your body and you will be given more and more."*

The pies tasted like a carefree summer afternoon when all is right in the world and life is warm and good. The taste of the pies filled them up with memories and settled into their stomachs just right.

That night Leena and Fife slept on the empty carriage and looked at the stars until their eyes naturally closed, comfortably wrapped up in blankets they found from another cart shelf.

When they woke up the next day, the sun shone brightly, already halfway through the sky. They ate a few bites of leftover pie for breakfast and looked around for a place to begin their meditation for the day.

"Where d'we start?" Fife asked, looking around. "I'd vote the market. I'm wantin' to see all the treasures that're here. And I mean, I'm still a bit hungry, so I wouldn't be turnin' down any breads or candies if they come back to life." Fife chuckled to himself.

Leena nodded but her thoughts were not on food. Thoughts of Jillian and the sea kept circling back to her mind.

"We need to ask the earth what is needed most so we know where to start."

They found comfortable places to sit and closed their eyes.

"Prepare yourself by relaxing every muscle in your face. Drop your jaw slightly. Soften your eyelids. In your mind, see the clouds in the sky. Sweeping clouds spread along the blue sky like cotton and puffy clouds that billow like white sheep floating through the air. Breathe in, and the clouds come close. Breathe out, and the clouds are pushed further out into the sky. Breathe in… Breathe out… Think about the clouds. Moving and changing pleasantly with the breeze. Your whole body is relaxed, like a cloud."

As they meditated, the stillness of the marketplace was interrupted by a slight breeze. Windchimes hanging on a cart nearby made a tinkling sound in the calm wind, a lovely song that filled Leena's heart with peace.

It had been a very long time since she heard the delicate sound of the chimes. They paused their meditation and listened to the sound of the breezes blowing through the small wooden and metal pieces, like a lullaby. The windchimes sang quietly together, the wiggling reeds of wood dancing on their strings as they bumped into one another. And the thin metal tubes dancing from their strings answering back as loud as they could, but still created nothing more than a tinkling whisper.

"Oh, that's a nice sound," Fife said without opening his eyes.

They continued to breathe the clouds in and out. Their bodies, like clouds, floated and relaxed in the breeze, peaceful and calm.

The breeze evolved into a wind. A gust blew Leena's hair whirling it around and her curls flopped onto her face. Wind whipped through the carts, blowing things here and there. Fife's hat blew off his head and across the clearing. Leena and Fife's concentration broke, and they opened their eyes.

Curiously, Leena listened. The air breathed messages that something extraordinary stirred in the market. Leena waited, holding her breath in anticipation.

Without warning, the light-gray clouds above banded together and covered up the blue sky. Fife brought his hand to his cheek.

"Wha' be this?" He wiped a droplet of water off his face. One by one, drops of water fell from the sky, sprinkling down on them. Soon a downpour of rain fell onto the marketplace, as if an artist painted a watercolor scene and dipped an invisible brush into paint, spreading the flow of the water all over the black scene. Like droplets of paint falling from the sky, Fife and Leena watched as the blackness that had covered everything began to breathe in color. Everytime a drop landed, whatever it touched came to life. And soon, the whole market place vibrantly showed a rainbow of colors.

Leena's hair fell drenched with water down her face, but she didn't notice. They both jumped off the carriage and twirled in the rain. Just as quickly as the rain began, it trickled to a stop, like a water spigot being shut off.

"Wow! I ain't never seen a rain shower like that before!" Fife said, his blond hair clinging to his forehead and neck. He shook his head from side to side, flinging water in all directions. "There's been no rain since I was a lil' guy! Since before the blackness!"

"I know! It's brilliant! Like a masterpiece! This place has more color in it than a garden! Look at those blue candles and that red blanket!" Leena said pointing.

"And th'candies!" Fife shouted, running full speed to a cart across the clearing.

"How can you even see that far away?" Leena called out after him as she ran, because she, too, wanted candy.

Fife did not answer. He just kept running until he came to the jars of goodies.

"Is it stealin' if we eat'em?" he asked, panting, holding his hand out over the goodies, hesitating before he picked up a green taffy.

"I don't think so." Leena giggled like a child and grabbed an orange taffy from the jar, unwrapping it carefully and popping it into her mouth. The soft, sweet taste of tangerine melted on her tongue.

They both sat on the new green grass, eating taffy and laughing about the funny shapes they were making with it, twisting and mixing colors to make crazy animal figures. They stretched the taffy out as long as they could, watching the strings get skinnier and skinnier like a thread.

"Oh my. Th'pie and now this," Fife said in a dreamy voice. "I think we could be livin' here quite happily, Leena. Pick a house. Grow food. We would have the finest treasures from all these carts. If ye ask me, I say we stay here," Fife said partly joking but with a hint of seriousness.

Fife could be right. She could be happy here with all the fine things of the village. The comfortable clothing, beds, a home, her best friend Fife with her. What more did she need?

Leena lay in the grass, daydreaming about staying in the village. If they stayed, she would have hundreds of dresses to choose from. And jewelry. Such beautiful jewelry. Hats and shoes and perfumes and spices. So many things that Leena wanted in this moment, that only days ago she had never thought about, but now that it was all right in front of her, she desired it.

A knot formed in Leena's stomach and slowly crept up into her throat. Is this what she wanted? What did she *want*? Leena stared out to the land beyond the village without blinking.

"What is it?" he asked. It took a few seconds for Leena to answer.

"I know this place is wonderful, and I can't deny part of me wants to stay here with you and never leave." Leena closed her eyes, taking in a breath through her nose and exhaling through her nose. "But we need to gather food and supplies from the market and continue our journey. We need to get to Jillian as soon as possible. We need to work quickly here." Leena took in another breath. "Everything has life inside it. A scarf. A pie. A house. A chair. We need to bring it all back, but we can't linger any longer than needed here. The village is charming, and I want to stay, but Jillian…"

"Yes, Jillian…she be needin' us." Fife finished her thought.

"And" —Leena hesitated— "and I keep having the terrible feeling that the Destroyers are preparing to return. Soon. Sometimes I even feel like they're watching us, waiting." A heavy throbbing pounded inside her.

Fife looked serious. Leena continued.

"I mean, they know we have begun. They know who we are, I can feel it. I felt it in the forest when we ran and hid from them, and I've been feeling the same way here. Like they're watching us. Following us. Waiting for us to bring it all back so they can steal it all from us. They are waiting until we have done the work of bringing life back, and then…and then they will come for us again."

"And when they be comin', we'll be ready for 'em," Fife said. "But righ' now, they are waitin' on us t'finish what we set out to do. If they come back now, they won't get much breath at all. I think you're right. I bet they be waitin' for the animals and all the land to breathe. That's when they'll get th'most breath, right?"

Leena looked at Fife and nodded. Then she said, "So with each day that we breathe back more life, the closer they are to coming for it." She closed her eyes and shook her head slightly. "Sometimes I feel so strong. So powerful. Then other times I feel weak and small. I'm just a girl. You're just a boy." Her confidence once again sank inside her.

"Leena, ain't you learned nothin'?" Fife said softly. "You ain't just a girl. You be savin' things all around you one breath at a time. Just one breath at a time. That's all we gotta do. Nobody's askin' us to do more than that. One breath at a time."

Her thoughts slowly melted into memories of her meadow. All the miracles she had brought back to life like the stream, her tree and her daisy patch. Leena knew that she could never be truly happy if she stayed in the village. They had a duty to the earth. A gift had been given to them and they had a responsibility to bring back *all* life. She realized she didn't want all the things the village had to offer. For the first time she allowed herself to want something bigger.

She wanted her family back.

Bringing other humans back to life brought a thought she had never allowed herself to ponder too deeply. The hope that she could bring her family back somehow seemed too painful to think about. If she set her hopes too high, and she couldn't bring them back, it would be like losing them all over again. If they could breathe life back into the earth, plants, objects, and Fife could bring back fire and animals, then could they not bring back what ultimately is the gift most precious to them all? Their families?

Feeling a glint of courage she asked Fife, "Do you think we could ever…"

She stopped herself.

"Wha? Ever wha?" Fife said, looking into her eyes He chewed his taffy, looking like he still half hoped she'd accept his offer to stay in the village.

"Do you think we could ever bring life back…to our loved ones? Our families? I mean, do you think they are still out there, waiting for us to become strong enough in our breath to…bring them back?"

Fife put on a thinking face and looked serious, slightly raising an eyebrow and pursing his lips together thoughtfully.

"I was hopin' you were gonna ask me an easier question than that. I dunno. I mean, that would be the greatest thing ever. But I dunno know if we're *that* powerful."

"But what if we could be. With the help of Jillian and the other two. What if together we could be powerful enough to bring it all back? All of it, Fife." Then she fully allowed herself to hope. "What if I could see my mum again?" The pitch of her voice got higher. "What if you could see your brothers? Is it worth it for you to hope? It's worth it for me to hope, and I believe it's worth it for us to try. We have to keep going on this journey, Fife. We have to go to the sea and find Jillian. I know she has a part to play in our lives. If we get comfortable and stay here, with all the easiness of village life, we may never know what we are capable of. We have to at least try. We have to keep going."

"I know you're right. You're right. I shouldn't've asked ya to stay. I will of course follow you," Fife said, nodding and resolute. Leena looked around. The rain had brought back life and color to the market, but the village homes, shops and streets remained black.

"We leave for the sea as soon as we breathe life back into the village. We need to work quickly. Jillian needs us."

Leena and Fife worked tirelessly on the village. It looked spectacular. The streets were paved in gray and tan cobblestone, and the village houses and shops looked magical and alive. It felt empty though, without the townspeople there to create the movement and rush of city life, but the homes were now colorful, friendly, and clean.

Working so quickly took every ounce of energy from both Fife and Leena, and with a long journey ahead, they needed a full day to rest.

The morning they were set to leave, they walked through the village to say goodbye to the homes they had brought back to life. They placed a few of the amazonite stones they had brought from the forest, and amethyst gemstones that were on Leena's Dad's cart around the homes as protection against the Destroyers.

"If we *were* stayin', I'd live in this one." Fife pointed to a house on the edge of town. "That way I could keep an eye on me forest and still be close enough to the bakery across the street. Or maybe I'll be the baker. I'd be bakin' pastries, muffins, breads, scones, and pies!"

They both laughed at the thought of Fife being a baker. Leena could easily imagine him in an apron and a tall bakers hat. What a sight he would be.

Inside the bakery, the fresh doughnuts and snack cakes filled the trays on every shelf.

"Well my boy, we better stock up and bring some of these for our journey. I have no idea how far away the sea is, and we might be walking for a long, long time." Leena handed Fife a jelly roll.

Carefully, they packed a sack full of pastries and headed up to the market. Leena and Fife both found new sturdy burlap bags from a cart at the marketplace and filled the bags with essential supplies for their trip. Leena found a purple sweater that matched her dress and scarf and tucked the two extra scarves into her bag. Fife wore his light-blue scarf and his tan cap. Leena had grown fond of the little town, but the excitement coupled with the urgency to find the sea and Jillian filled Leena with purpose, and pushed her onward.

"Let's take a minute and breathe in gratitude for our time here," Leena said.

Fife agreed. They went to her Dad's carriage one final time and sat in the front bench. With straight backs and their hands resting gently on their legs, they closed their eyes.

Visualize colors. See the red of the cherry pie in your mind. Through your nose breathe in gratitude for the color red. Exhale gratitude and send your grateful heart to all the red that lives in the village.

See the color of the green taffy. Take another soft breath in through your nose. The green grass. The green rooftops of the village houses. Breathe out, thanking the green for surrounding you with sweetness and serenity.

Continue to relax your mind and your body, and think about purple. Breathe in gratitude for the purple gemstones. The purple flowers in the window boxes of the shops in the streets. Feel the peace of the color purple. Breathe out through your nose gratitude for everything purple.

Fill your mind with yellow. The sun. Breathe in the warmth of the yellow sunlight. The marigolds and cornstalks. Breathe out gratitude for yellow. Sending love to everything yellow.

Thank you, orange, for all you do. You give vibrance and life to everything you touch. Breathe in a grateful heart to the orange flame of the candle and to the orange taffy, sweet and soft. Exhale through your nose. Breathe in the tangerine scent of orange and breathe out gratitude.

Now see the blue. The blue of the scarves and the blankets. The blue of the dresses and bags that hang throughout the marketplace. The blue sky. Thank you, blue, for being so beautiful.

Breathe in and out. Grateful to all the colors of life. We need you. We are grateful.

Leena and Fife took one last cleansing breath and opened their eyes. They hopped down from the carriage, grabbed their sacks full of supplies, and waved goodbye to the village, hoping with everything in them that they would return someday.

10

The Sea

"Think a happy thought, create a happy feeling, do happy actions, enjoy happy results."

Nothingness covered the land beyond the village. They continued to breathe life into the nothingness, but Leena struggled to convince herself that they should use their energy on it. Eventually, the dirt became grainy, and the trees thinned. No more grassy meadows, thick forests, or charming villages. These lands were forgotten, no longer a clear path, just dusty ground in every direction.

"We've been walking for thirteen days. I'm not sure we're ever going to get out of this wasted land," Leena said one morning, kicking a pebble in her path. Hopelessness piled inside her the longer she walked. "Are we even going in the right direction?"

"I'm bettin' it ain't much further to the sea. I mean…looks like it probably will be but I dunno…how it could be." He stopped walking and looked around. "This is real pretty though. I mean, you never seen any land like this before, right? Dust and rocks and… yeah, that's 'bout it, dust and rocks." He picked up the pebble Leena had kicked only seconds ago. "But it's got a beauty of its own." Fife looked closely at the small rock in his hand, tossed it in the air, and then pocketed it. "It ain't so bad."

Only three pastries remained. When Leena bit into one earlier that morning, it was dry like toast. Water became harder and harder to breathe back to life since the streams and ponds had no place here. Leena ached for home. Fife carried on, looking on the bright side, continuing to find the good in every situation.

Once a day, he unpacked his family of sticks wrapped in the blanket of moss. He'd tell them all about the day's journey. Which meant sometimes there was not much to tell, but he would create entertainment out of the very mundane adventure they were having. After climbing a steep hill, Leena rested on the dry ground and overheard Fife chatting to his family.

"So *then*, we walked up the dirt hill. Huffin' and puffin'. Rocks were slidin' down with every step, b'cause the dirt was so thin and slippery-soft. We're hungry but we don't care because we know we've almost made it to the sea. Can you believe it? Me goin' to the sea! Your lil' forest boy out on an adventure. This is the life, I tell ya. Happiest I ever been."

Leena lifted her tired head and looked over at Fife. Fife, so happy to be alive, so grateful to be breathing. Even through this bleak, seemingly endless journey, Fife found things to be happy about. How did he do it? Leena admired him. Even though she was the older of the two, she looked to him like an older brother. But every once in a while she struggled to see what he saw.

"Why are you so happy right now, Fife?" Leena grumbled. "How do you feel happy right now? How do you keep feeling so happy even when there's nothing to be happy about?" She didn't wait for him to answer. "There is nothing to be happy about right now!" She sat up, annoyed. Her stomach growled and turned over at the thought of stale sweetcakes.

Fife looked at Leena and smiled. "I feel happy, Leena, b'cause I'm thinkin' happy thoughts." He shrugged his shoulders like it was no big deal. "It doesn't really matter what's goin' on around me. I get to choose how I wanna feel. I get to decide if I'm happy. And if that means I gotta talk to sticks to help me feel better, then I guess I'll be talkin' to sticks, because I wanna feel happy and it's up to me. I'm not leavin' it up to the dirt and the rocks to decide if I'm gonna be happy or not."

Leena stayed silent, thinking through his words. Thoughts. She got to choose her thoughts, and her thoughts determined how she felt. How could she have happy thoughts all the time though?

"And I ain't sayin you need to think happy thoughts all the time," Fife said, as if he had read her mind. "Sometimes I wanna feel sad, so I feel sad. But when I feel sad, it's b'cause I *choose* to feel that way. It's ok to be sad, or mad, or annoyed…but please don't be annoyed with me." He winked "When somethin' sad happens, it's good to feel sad. Then when you be ready, you can work through your thoughts and change how you feel. But you always get t'decide."

Leena walked over to Fife and sat down by him, leaning her head on his shoulder.

"We're gettin' close, Leena. Close to th'sea. I can feel it. Do ya smell that salty air?"

"Salty air?" Leena asked. "Oh, is that what I smell? I didn't know what salty air would smell like, I guess." And she tried to laugh but wasn't quite ready yet.

They rested at the top of the hill a bit longer then used their breath to breathe the land around them back to life. Leena admitted that she didn't see much point in bringing back the fine, thin, dirt, but gave herself the thought, if they did it now, they would never have to come back here again. And that did make her feel better.

For three more days they walked through the forgotten land. The days were cold and the nights were freezing. Fife made a fire every night that crackled and sparked all through the dark hours. It comforted Leena to have the sound of the fire and Fife close by. Before she fell asleep, she opened her box of amethyst stones and took one out, holding it up to the fire light and then held it tightly in her fist. Leena went to sleep that night huddled under her blanket with the scarves her Mum made wrapped around her tightly, holding onto her gemstone that reminded her of her meadow and her doll with the purple dress tucked under her arm. Her dreams filled her mind with memories of her childhood. She dreamed about Mum and Aaron and the kittens.

"Mum, where's Betty? I can't find her anywhere," Leena called out to Mum as she looked behind the woodpile in their cat Betty's usual hiding spot.

"Check behind the woodpile," Mum called back from the kitchen window.

"I did, she's not there." Leena continued to search around the garden beds and in the pumpkin patch. "Where is that cat? Doesn't she know her babies are coming out soon and she needs to be in a safe place?"

Aaron came running barefoot on his wobbly baby legs towards Leena in the garden.

"KeeKee! Lala! KeeKee!" He shouted with excitement bursting out of his baby face, his big blue eyes shining in the sun.

"You found a kitty, Aaron? Show me!"

Together they ran toward the front porch, and Aaron pointed at the narrow crawl space under it. Leena bent low to peer underneath. Sure enough, Betty lay comfortably under the porch, just out of reach, with five newborn kittens snuggled tightly around her.

"She did it! She did it!" Leena yelled out.

Aaron danced a happy little dance, arms up high and marched in a circle, then crawled down on the ground and tried to get under the porch grabbing toward Betty trying to pet the kittens.

"No Aaron, you can't bother Betty. She's a mother now and has lots of responsibilities. We have to give her time. Good boy to find the baby kitties!" They both ran inside the cottage and told Mum all about it.

Leena woke up warm, bundled in her scarves, imagining herself snuggling kittens. The feeling of Aaron and Mum being so close in her memory made her forget the stale muffins, her dry throat, and the endless black dirt. More than ever she wanted to be in the meadow with them, looking for Betty, finding the kittens, being six-years-old.

"I dreamed about when I was a little girl, last night," she told Fife as they were toasting some stale bread over the fire for breakfast.

"Oh *really*? Tell me 'bout it." Fife looked interested.

"Well, we used to have a fat cat named Betty. Probably fat

because of the kittens inside her, but also very lazy and didn't do much of anything. She never caught mice or played with yarn or anything like a cat should. She just laid around." Fife chuckled, thinking about Betty. "But the day she had her babies is what I dreamt about. I couldn't find her anywhere, and my little brother, Aaron found her under the porch with her new kittens."

Leena took a bite of bread.

"Did you ever have a pet, Fife?"

"Nah, we had wild animals comin' and goin'. Like rabbits and lizards and stuff, but nothin' we ever kept in the house or made names for."

"Oh, that's no good. You need a pet, Fife."

"I agree, but jus' remember what happened last time I found a animal." Fife raised his eyebrows. "That baby fawn comin' outta the bush…them Destroyers came back, feelin' the new life. We can't have'em comin' back destroyin' everythin' we brought back. Not yet. Gotta get the others first before we deal with 'em."

Leena nodded in agreement.

"We'll be even stronger when we find the other Life Breathers. I got stronger in my breathing power when I met you, and when we work together, the life-breathing power seems more focused and works faster. I'm not nearly as exhausted now after bringing something back to life as when I worked alone." Leena sighed. "When we find the others, we will bring the animals back, but we'll need to be ready for a fight. I have no idea how we will do that."

Fife listened, deep in thought. His long arms resting on his long legs and his face serious. But then, as if a bright light appeared in front of him, he stood up and said, "We better be goin'. I can feel this is goin' to be a great day. Maybe today is th'day we find the sea," he said, raising his eyebrows up and down and up and down with a silly grin.

"You could be right." Leena laughed and shook her head. "Maybe today is the day."

They gathered up their supplies and filled their water jugs in a scrawny nearby creek.

As the afternoon rolled in, finally the scenery began to change.

The black trees had skinny trunks with huge, frayed, leaves sprouting out the top. There were black tufts of tall grasses all over the hillside. Black pebbles scattered throughout the grainy black dirt. The air did smell different. Was that the salty sea air Fife had talked about? They walked in silence up a hill covered in long, black grass and scrubby bushes. About half-way up the hill, Fife stopped.

"Do ya hear it?" he asked, breaking the silence.

Leena stopped walking and listened. In the distance she did hear something. It sounded like a dull roar. It sounded like mumbled movement. "What is that?" she asked, looking equally curious and afraid. Fife ran up the hill motioning for Leena to follow.

"Come on!" he called. The sound rhythmically moved in and out, soothing then smashing, calm then crashing again and again in a pattern. Leena ran up the hill to the bluff following Fife, her heart speeding faster than she could run.

From the top of the hill she looked down below her. A massive body of water spread across the land. Her breath caught in her throat when she tried to breathe in. Leena gasped. "We found it! The sea! We found it!" Leena felt the same joy as when she and Aaron found the kittens under the porch, but amplified. Joy mixed with relief. Turning to Fife, she wrapped her arms around his waist. Fife enveloped her in his long arms, and they hugged each other tightly.

The sea covered as much space as the sky itself, just like the riddle said. They watched in awe, wanting to sing, laugh, and cry all at the same time. But feeling the serenity of the waves, they just stared in silence.

"Is it real?" Leena whispered.

"Aww, yeah. It is," Fife answered.

The black sands stretched for miles and miles below them. The water, brilliantly blue, remained the only sign of life. No Jillian.

"I'm not sure what to do first!" Leena said. Her mind raced with excitement. "Should we breathe life back into the trees, grasses, and bushes, or should we search for Jillian? Should we meditate in gratitude or build a fire?" Thoughts and questions rushed around her giddy mind. But she continued to ramble in excitement. "Maybe we should find a food source, or maybe…it's almost night time, so maybe we should sleep and start early in the morning. Maybe we should…"

"Slow down, slow down…there be plenty of time to do all that. Righ' now we're gonna sit and watch th' sea and breathe in th' salty air," Fife said.

Leena closed her eyes and did just that. The salty air filled her nostrils. The sea. She could hardly believe it. They'd found the sea.

Relief washed over her, like the waves she watched down below washed over the sand. Leena had not realized until that moment how desperately her mind and body needed rest. The journey to the sea took nearly all her mental and physical energy. Thank goodness for Fife. Leena's heart swelled as she thought of him. Is this what love is? Did she love Fife? She didn't know. She knew that he held a special place inside her heart. She knew he could make her feel better when she felt terrible, and she knew that every fiber of his soul was filled with goodness.

"Everythin'll be alright. We're gonna find Jillian. But now we breathe… and rest," Fife said, interrupting Leena's thoughts about love. Fife inhaled a fresh breath of sea air.

Leena set her thoughts aside, without coming to any sort of conclusion.

They set up camp on the black sand of the seashore. The sea looked exactly like Leena remembered the beauty of the sea in her dream.

"My goodness, I don't think I could ever get tired of watching the waves. It is a bit windy here, though," she said, the curls of her hair flapping around her face.

"Yeah, this be a beau'iful spot." Fife set down the wood. Together they gathered rocks and arranged them in a circle to house the fire.

"Jillian could be anywhere." Leena sighed. "The sea is bigger than I thought it would be. Where should we start looking?"

Fife stood up, cupped his hand across his forehead to shade his eyes from the setting sun, scanning the shoreline up and down. The tide rolled in and pushed back, again and again.

"If we start bringin' stuff back to life, she'll be comin' to us. You'll see. We won't have to do much searchin'."

That night, Leena and Fife sat by the fire, looking at the stars.

"I hope we can convince Jillian to come with us. What if she doesn't want to leave the sea?" Leena said. "I wouldn't want to leave."

"There's nothin' t'worry about Leena. Look, it's a lucky moon tonight." Fife pointed to the sky at the slim sliver moon.

"A lucky moon?" Leena asked.

"Yeah, th'skinny moon, a crescent. See, it be smilin' down on us, lettin' us know it's all gonna be alrigh'."

Leena smiled up at the thin, crescent moon smiling down at her. In the cool night air, the thought of a lucky moon comforted every part of her soul.

"Everything will be alright."

11

Lemongrass

*"You cannot stop the tide from coming in. When the waves rise ominously, don't
tense up or run away, relax into the rhythm of the water.
Embrace the wave."*

The next morning Leena and Fife woke up before the sun and
found a lovely spot in the sand looking out towards the water to
breathe in the new day. Leena sat in her usual criss-cross style but
now with bare feet, the soft black sand on her toes. A warm
seabreeze floated through the air, unlike the cold air on the journey.
Fife found a log to sit on comfortably and he buried his bare feet in
the sand too. They straightened their backs to a tall posture and
took in a refreshing breath of salty sea air through their noses. And
then exhaled slowly and completely through their noses. The air
filled with a balancing blend of a rich, balmy, clean scent. Leena
already felt at home here. The sound of the waves created a flawless
backdrop, allowing them to focus all their thoughts on the life that
surrounded them.

For a few minutes they sat and appreciated the view. The sun still hid behind the horizon, but the orange and pink sky glowed with signs of morning. Thin clouds streaked the sky in gray and lavender. Before long, the sun made its first appearance of the day, peeking up behind the hills that rested behind Leena and Fife. When the sun rose, its light changed everything. A slow, miraculous process.

"*This* is magic," Fife said quietly.

The sun rose, little by little, until a complete and perfect circle lifted above the horizon. When the colors of the sky were washed out by the brightness of the sun, a new day had dawned.

Close your eyes and take a deep breath in… and out through your nose. Imagine you are standing on the seashore. You breathe in the clean air, and you smile. The energy of your breath is giving motion to the waves in the sea. Continue breathing. Feel your breath as it moves through your body like a wave in the sea. As you fill your lungs, see the wave as it powerfully rises to a peak. Exhale as it crashes to the ocean floor and then rolls calmly onto the shore right up to where you are standing. The cool water rushes up to your toes and covers your feet before it runs back, like a game of chase. Your breath is filling the water with life. In your mind, look around for the seagrass along the banks and up on the bluff above the sea. Breathe in slowly and the clusters of tall grass will sway and wave in the breeze. Your breath is calling to the grasses, you are alive. You are alive.

Leena paused her meditation because she smelled a scent so fragrant she could not stop herself from opening her eyes. She turned to look behind her just as the black grasses shed their charcoal skin. From the roots up, the grass turned a lovely green. The citrus-like scent reminded her of the orange taffy, but grassy and sweet. The smell of the grass brought a memory of Dad, bringing a slightly sour yet delightful yellow candy home from market.

"Wha' is that smell?" Fife said as he, too, opened his eyes. He looked around and saw the tufts of seagrass transforming.

"Isn't it amazing!" Leena said, exhilarated. The contrast of the black sand and the bright green grass, took her breath away.

"Do ya think we could eat that grass? I'm hungry." Fife looked around longingly and rubbed his stomach.

"It smells good enough to eat. I'm not sure. Let's look in the water and see what other things might be growing," Leena answered. "But first" —she pulled out her book of riddles and smoothed her hands over the brown leather— "let's start this new day by the sea with a riddle. We're going to need some guidance on where to go next in our journey after we find Jillian."

Flipping through the book, she landed on a page that felt good in her hands. She had not seen this page before. The words seemed to glow ever so slightly. It vibrated a little between her fingers. She read, *"Bright as diamonds, loud as thunder. Always falling, never still. Running forever without moving location, no lungs, no throat, but a roaring yell. What am I?"*

Fife looked puzzled.

"What d'ya s'pose that means?"

"I don't know. Something with water maybe. We know the sea roars, but running without moving anywhere…" Leena glanced around looking for ideas of what it might be referring to. She shook her head after a minute or so. Nothing. Disappointed Leena closed the book and put it back in her pack.

"Well, that will give us something to think about. Maybe Jillian will have some insight," Leena said hopefully.

"Gotta find her first. Roaring yell huh? Dunno if I want anythin' to do with that." Fife chuckled under his breath.

The two of them got up and walked to the edge of the sea. Comfortably, they walked into water up to Leena's waist. As Fife was so much taller than Leena, the water only came up a bit over his knees. Something slippery tangled between their toes, sending a shiver up Leena's back, giving her goosebumps on her arms. Reaching down, she pulled out a handful. It looked like a soaking-wet weed from her garden.

"I say we try and cook this up and see if it tastes any good. We're out of bread from the village, and we're going to need another food source," Leena suggested.

"I'll go in a lil' further and get s'more of that seaweed and see what else be in there." With Fife being a foot taller than Leena he could go further into the sea and it barely covered his belly button.

With no warning the waves rolled in higher. Fife was strong and tall but not as strong and tall as the waves. He walked out further and further and would not be able to outrun the big waves that were coming.

"Fife! The wave! Relax your body and let the wave guide you back in!" Leena called, cupping her hand around her mouth, hoping her voice would carry over the sound of the waves.

"What? Leena! Can't hear ya—" A wave crashed over the top of Fife's head and dragged him under the water.

"Fife!" Leena shouted, but Fife did not come back up. Terror flooded through Leena as she thought of Fife, caught under the water. *Use your breath Fife. Hold it tight and come back to me. Relax your body. You will float, but you have to relax. Don't breathe in.* Could he swim? She had never asked him. Her eyes anxiously darted back and forth, scanning the water for any sign of him. Running to the water's edge she continued calling his name, even though she knew he couldn't hear her. Her body wanted to jump in after him, but she knew she would not be strong enough to pull him to shore.

Leena yelled, watched and waited, with no sign of Fife. Fife was drowning. She could feel it. A piece of driftwood lay nearby. Pushing the wood into the sea, she laid her arms over the top of it, holding the wood tightly and floating with the waves.

The waves carried her up and down as she searched for any sign of Fife. Her heart was breaking. All of her hopes were dying. *Don't leave me. Come back.* A large wave carried the driftwood up and then pushed her hard back onto the shore. She swallowed a mouthful of salt water and coughed as she flopped onto the sand, the salt water stinging her eyes.

Her purple dress clung to her body as she struggled to her feet. Pacing quickly back and forth she scanned the water, yelling Fife's name.

Out further in the water the sun shone down on a blond head of hair. But not Fife's blond head. Leena squinted and cupped her hands around her eyes shielding the sunlight. Two blond heads emerged out of the sea.

Leena ran into the water calling for them, waving her arms. "Over here! Fife!" But he did not lift his head. The girl who held on to Fife looked at Leena and continued to pull him through the waves. The blond girl rode the wave all the way until they reached the shore, and they tumbled onto the sand. Leena ran to them scrambling, onto her knees beside Fife.

Fife's eyes were closed. The girl knelt beside him, holding his face in her hands. Propping his neck back slightly, she blew three breaths into his mouth. She sat back and opened the collar of his shirt, pushing on to his bare chest with her palms, and then again put her lips over his mouth and breathed three times more.

On the outside, Leena may have looked fairly calm. She stared in disbelief at the scene. They had found Jillian, but at the expense of losing Fife. Inside, her body screamed selfishly. *NO! Not Fife! I need him!*

At this desperate time she answered the question she had wrestled with earlier. And the answer was yes. She loved Fife. She did not know to what extent because she loved him as a friend. A dear, dear friend. A friend so dear to her that the thought of being without him caused her to feel as though she might gag and choke.

The blonde-headed girl said nothing. She continued to alternate between breathing into Fife's mouth and pushing on his chest.

The tears that Leena fought back were finding their way to the surface, and there was nothing she could do about it. Disbelief and sadness crowded her thoughts. This cannot be happening. Why hadn't she thought to ask him if he could swim? The terrible aching thought returned to her that she could have prevented this. Leena closed her eyes and covered her face with her hands. Minutes passed and finally she heard another sound other than the continuous crashing of waves. Leena's eyes flew open.

Fife's chest rose, and he let out a sputter of coughs. He turned to the side and water spilled out of his mouth. More coughing.

When his blue eyes opened, they looked blue like the sea, and the eyes that stared back at him were just as blue.

"Jillian?" Fife asked in a rough raspy voice. The blonde girl flinched in surprise at the sound of her own name but did not answer. Slowly she nodded her head. Fife looked at Leena and smiled.

"She found us." He rubbed his eyes and sat up slowly, ruffling his hands through his wet hair and coughing some more.

"Fife, you're alive! I thought you…." Leena's eyes filled up with tears again but she forced them back. "I thought I'd lost you and…"

"I'm here, Leena. It be alright. Jillian, she…saved me. She was under the water like a fish and I seen her but then I couldn't breathe and she…she pulled me outta the water and gave me breath back."

Jillian's wavy hair, wet and long, flowed all the way down her back. Her skin, browned by the sun, contrasted with the white dress she wore. A white string of beads hung snuggly around her neck and lit up as the reflection of the sun bounced off of it. Jillian glanced around, looking lost, but still didn't say a word. Her eyes looked curious but not surprised.

She looked up, noticing the life in the grass, green and fragrant.

Jillian wrote in the sand with her finger. "-it's-back-" She smiled. "-I-dreamed-about-you-" And she looked at Leena. "-I've-been-waiting-" Her round cheeks had an adorable dimple on one side. Leena and Fife watched curiously as Jillian wrote words in the sand.

"I dreamed about you, too, Jillian. We have so much to tell you. And so much to do. Can you speak? Or do you choose not to speak?" Leena asked and then immediately regretted it. Jillian dropped her gaze, looking embarrassed. Her face lost color, and she appeared to be very uncomfortable.

Standing abruptly she ran towards the water. She had a small frame, even smaller than Leena, but she looked strong. Putting her hands together straight out in front of her, Jillian dove into the sea and disappeared from view.

"She be a mermaid! And she is amazin'!" Fife continued to stare where she had jumped in. "I forgot to thank her for savin' me life," he said regretfully, looking lost as if he may never see her again.

A few minutes later Jillian came out of the water and swam to the shore, holding a long box in her hand. Jillian ran to them and handed the box to Leena. Leena looked at it curiously.

"Do you want me to open it?" Leena asked.

Jillian nodded.

Fife interrupted, "Thank ye Jillian. For savin' me. For pullin' me outta the water and breathin' your breath into me mouth like ya did…yeah…you saved me. Thanks for doin' that. You were really amazin' swimmin' like that out there in the sea and pickin' me up and pullin' me to shore. I dunno how you did it b'cause I be twice as long as you…" Fife rambled on until Leena stopped him. Jillian's eyes were wide, and she shifted her feet awkwardly, but smiled at him.

"Fife. Get a hold of yourself," Leena said, giggling. "She knows you're grateful. Now let's look in this box."

"Awe yeah, right, the box." Fife cleared his throat and moved his gaze from Jillian's eyes to the long box in Leena's hands.

Leena unhooked a little latch on the edge of the box and lifted the lid, revealing a rolled up piece of thick paper, completely dry, with writing on it. Picking up the scroll, she unrolled it and began to read aloud.

"My name is Jillian. I was born by the seashore to my mother and father whose names were Jon and Lillian. My little brother's name is Jonathon. I called him Jonny. Around ten years ago we were playing on the seashore building castles in the sand. I was seven and Jonny was three. It was a normal day. The sun was shining and Mother and Father had just gathered the last of the wood from the trees and were going to start building our new home.

As we played, the clouds turned from white to black almost instantly, and blackness tumbled through the sky. Jonny cried and hugged my legs. I picked him up, and I ran towards my mother but the black clouds got to her first. She completely disappeared into the cloud. The sand turned an ebony black, and everything the clouds touched also turned to black. I wanted to run and hide in the water, but I couldn't leave Jonny. My father ran to us and yelled for us to get in the water but I was so afraid I couldn't move. Then the black cloud swept up my father and he disappeared, too.

The cloud came for me. I ran to the water with Jonny in my arms, not knowing what to do, and then I heard a sound, a loud bumping sound. It pounded in my ears and my heart felt like it was going to stop beating. Then I saw them coming. An army of creatures coming out of the black cloud. Tall and dark with no faces. They held long black sticks in their hands. They beat the sticks on the sand.

My knees collapsed. I dropped Jonny onto the ground, and then I don't know what happened. I woke up hours, maybe days later, and Jonny was gone. Every-thing around me was black.

Inside my body continued to shake and rattle, like the beating of the sticks on the sand. It wouldn't stop. My anxious thoughts were disjointed and my voice, gone. My only escape was the water. The sea was all I had left. So I let the waves take me away, and I held my breath. I only come out of the water every few days to breathe in fresh air. My home is out there, in the sea. My body cannot live on the land without shaking inside. The water is the only place where my heart is quiet and my mind is clear. I don't know why I lived and my family died. All I know is, I have a gift. It's a gift I was given at birth. I am a Life Breather and I can hold my breath for days at a time.

Leena stared down at the paper, wishing there was more. Exhaling a long, steady breath, she lifted her gaze.

"I am a Life Breather, too. I'm so sorry about what happened to you. I lost my mum and dad and baby brother on the day of destruction," Leena said wistfully. "I'm so sorry about what you have been through and what you go through everyday missing them. We understand." Leena took Jillian's hand. "We're so relieved we found you."

"Yeah, yeah we know wha' it feels like to be alone. Ain't no good for nobody," Fife added with a smile. Jillian looked uncomfortable, like she wanted to leave but didn't want to be rude. Her eyes shifted from side to side, and she held her stomach. She started shaking her head slightly, squeezing her eyes shut.

"Are ye alright?" Fife asked. His eyes focused on Jillian.

Jillian shook her head. Leena could see by the way she held her stomach that she felt queasy. Jillian bent her head low as if she struggled to think clearly.

"-can't-stay-" she wrote in the sand. Her hands trembled. "-sorry-" And she lost the color in her face and looked like she might fall over, but instead she ran back to the water and dove in.

Leena sat down on the seashore.

"I don't know how to help her," Leena confessed.

"Sure ya do. She's like you. Different, but the same. She be needin' time and focus. She be needin' some peace. Peace in her mind. Peace in her heart and in her body. She still bein' tortured 'bout them Destroyers." Fife sat down beside her, resting his long arms on his knees. He was right. Leena did know how to help her.

They didn't see Jillain for the remainder of the day. They spent their time bringing the tall, skinny trees back to life and cooking up the seaweed. It actually didn't taste bad at all. Fife being so hungry, asked for a second helping.

The two of them sat by the fire, discussing what they knew about Jillian's story.

"But how come th'Destroyers didn't extinguish her? If they got her brother and she bein' right there. Why didn't they get her, too?" Fife asked.

"Maybe she held her breath, like I did," suggested Leena. "Or maybe…something else. Did you see that necklace she wore? I wonder what kind of stones those are. Did you see them?"

"I did. They were shinin'… like her eyes." Fife looked out at the sea dreamily. "They sparkled like I ain't never seen anythin' sparkle before."

"The stones or her eyes?" Leena laughed and threw a handful of sand at his legs. "I think you like her!" she teased. Leena wasn't sure how she felt about what she just said. Was it okay if Fife looked at Jillian in a different way than he looked at her? Of course it was. Her love for Fife wouldn't change. And she genuinely liked Jillian. Beautiful and sweet, Leena could find nothing *not* to like. But still, something rumbled inside Leena. A weird sensation she'd never felt before moved in her stomach. Prickly and also squirmy. She didn't like it, so she stuffed it away.

"Well I mean, she did save me life and she's real sweet and kind," Fife said in a matter of fact way.

"*And* beautiful," Leena added.

"And beau'iful," Fife repeated in the same dreamy voice.

The next day, Leena and Fife slept until the sun reached the middle of the sky. Listening to the waves rise, crash and roll in and out, soothed their dreams and kept them asleep far past morning.

They stretched out their sleepy legs. Fife yawned lazily.

"Fife, can you hold your breath?" Leena asked a bit randomly.

"Ummmm… I dunno. I guess I could. For how long?" Fife asked.

"Well, I thought maybe we could visit Jillian in her home today. In her home…under the water. I learned how to hold my breath as a child, and I can hold it for probably about an hour. You, my dear friend Fife, are a Life Breather, which means you can hold your breath, too, but it might take some practice."

Fife started practicing immediately. He sucked in a huge breath of air, his cheeks like a puffed mushroom, and his eyes bulged. Within twenty seconds his face turned red, and he looked rather alarmed.

"Let it out, Fife!" Leena said, smacking him on the back, laughing.

"Phewwwwwwwwwww!" Fife let all his breath out in one gust *so* quickly that the force of his breath blew all the way to the sea, lifting a wave up out of nowhere and smashing it down hard.

"Did I just do that?" he asked, raising a lone eyebrow.

"I…I…am not sure…maybe? Weird. Try it again."

He held in another breath for about ten seconds and let it out. "Phewwwwwwwwwww!" Again, a blast of wind blew straight at the wave, lifting it higher, and then crashing it down.

"Hmmm. Well, I'm not sure when that will come in handy, but it's good to know you have some powerful breath." Leena was impressed. "But it looks like only I'll be visiting Jillian in the water today. Sorry, Fife. But I'll try to get her to come onto the land for a bit."

Fife's shoulders sank in disappointment.

"We've got to work with her to help her feel more at peace when she's out here. Otherwise, we'll never be able to get her to come with us on our journey…and we need her," Leena said.

"Yep, we do." Fife quickly agreed, and even with his sunken shoulders, the same dreamy look came over his face along with a smile.

12

I am Peace

"Sometimes it is easier to run than to stand perfectly still, but sometimes standing still is exactly what your soul needs."

Leena left her sweater on the seashore and walked barefoot out to the edge of the water, the warm breeze caressing her from head to toe. One slow step at a time she walked into the sea, feeling the rhythm of the waves and moving with them. When the water covered her shoulders, she waved to Fife, took in a big breath, and dunked her head below the water's surface.

The turquoise light made it easy to see, and the seaweed thinned out the further out she swam. Eventually, she reached a black rock-like barrier, full of all sorts of caverns. It looked like a small village. Inside Jillian sat at a table, eating the same black weeds Leena and Fife had discovered. Looking up from her food, she saw Leena and smiled, waving for her to come closer.

Leena waved back and swam over to sit by her.

"I'm so glad you came down to see me." Jillian's voice came clearly

into Leena's mind but her lips had not moved. *"Where's Fife? Did he come, too?"*

Leena, despite her surprise at the clarity of communication through their minds, answered back easily: *"He wanted to, but he can't hold his breath long enough yet. Oh my goodness, it's amazing down here! It's so beautiful. What is this place? How is it made?"*

"It's called a coral reef. It used to be alive, full of color and sea life but now it's just a big rock with holes and shelves. This is where I live. It's peaceful down here...but lonely." Jillian looked sad.

"I understand loneliness. I lived alone for ten years, too, until I found Fife in the forest. Have you ever been to the forest?" Leena asked.

"I've heard of it, but I've never been there. Was everything, everywhere destroyed?"

Leena looked down and nodded her head. *"Fife and I are on a journey to find other Life Breathers to bring life back to the world and...and... maybe even..."* She paused, deciding not to complete her thought. *"We will need you to come with us. We need your help."*

Jillian looked hopeful. *"I want to. I really do. I've been dreaming about you for months now. I've been waiting and watching for you to come. But the problem is I don't know how to feel peace out on the land. And I can't speak. I try, but I feel so nervous and anxious inside. My heart beats fast and my insides are constantly moving. There is no stillness. I feel dizzy, like I'm going to burst all the time. The memories of the day of destruction come running back to me everytime I go on the shore. All I see is my mother and father and Jonny being taken by the blackness, and I retreat back to the water where I feel safe. I have to find peace but... I don't know how."*

Compassion filled Leena. She looked at Jillian with new eyes, like she really could see inside her and feel what she felt.

"Fife and I are here to help you, Jillian. We came for you. Come with me. I'll show you what we've learned," Leena pleaded. *"And we will stay with you. You will never be alone again. We can even bring your coral reef back to life. I'll show you how."*

They spent nearly an hour together and Leena could feel herself running out of breath. Leena pointed upward, and Jillian nodded and waved goodbye.

Leena swam straight up and broke through the water, releasing her breath and taking in a new one. The water danced around her. Now she understood why Jillian lived peacefully in the water. It felt like being cradled and rocked to sleep with a lullaby.

The heat of the afternoon sun was beating down on the black sand by the time Jillian came out of the water to find them. Her hair, woven into a braid, hung loose and wet down her back, like a princess from a far away land. Her white dress dried quickly in the sun, and she wore her shining white beads around her neck.

"What kind of beads are those?" Leena asked, looking at her necklace closely.

"-Pearls-from-seashells-" Jillian used her finger to write into the sand as she had done before.

"Seashells?" Fife asked. "What's a seashell?"

Jillian dug in the sand and pulled out a black dish-shaped object. Leena and Fife had never seen anything like it before.

"Whoa!" Fife said curiously. Jillian handed the shell to Fife, their fingertips brushed against each other. Their eyes met. Fife hesitated a moment then smiled. He looked down, suddenly bashful. He turned the shell around in his hands looking at all the sides.

"-Pearl-forms-inside-takes-years-to-grow-special-sacred."

As the waves rolled in behind them, Leena looked out at the water. "Have you always worn that pearl necklace? I mean, since you were little?"

"-Yes-" Jillian answered in the sand.

"Were you wearing it on the day the Destroyers came?"

Jillian looked thoughtful, reaching back in her memory. Then without warning, she clutched her stomach and closed her eyes tightly. Leena could see Jillian's mind spinning, her face pale and slightly sweaty. With a shaky finger Jillian attempted to write in the sand, but she blinked her eyes and shook her head slightly. She tried to stand, looking like she might run.

"No, Jillian, wait! Stay!" Leena pleaded. Jillian looked at her with worry in her eyes and shook her head no, but her knees collapsed to the ground.

Fife bent down and took her hand.

"We'll help ya." His eyes connected with hers, and he continued to hold her hand until she stood. Jillian squeezed her eyes shut. From the look on Jillian's face, Leena imagined a storm growing inside her. Jillian opened her eyes again and looked at the sea longingly, as if the pulse of the waves would calm her heart.

"Come up here and sit down on this log. Fife and I will guide you through your breathing, and I promise it will help calm you inside."

Jillian looked terrified at the suggestion that she stay. But instead of running, she followed them over to the log, pain on her face.

With shaking legs and blurred eyes, she kept hold of Fife's hand as he led her toward the log. He sat her down and put an arm around her, unable to tell if it helped her because she pulled away from him. But as soon as he went to move, she grabbed onto his shirt, her eyes asking him to stay close. Leena sensed the conflict inside Jillian, wanting to run into the sea as she had always done, but forcing her tortured body to stay on the land.

Sitting crossed-legged, Leena sat in the sand. Fife, more comfortable on the log with his long legs, stayed by Jillian. He sat with good posture and relaxed his hands, this time he chose to rest his palms down on his knees, grounding him to the earth.

"Jillian, we are going to help you use your breath in a new way." Leena spoke softly and carefully. "It will begin to heal your body. Just like we have healed the seagrass and the trees here with our breath, you can be healed, too. It might take some time, and it won't be easy for you. Are you ready?"

Jillian nodded hesitantly.

Leena continued. "Find a comfortable position with a straight back. Gently close your eyes. Listen to the waves of the sea, and let the waves sink deep into your soul."

Jillian let out a quiet sob and covered her face. Jillian's thoughts entered Leena's mind. *I can't do it. I can't do it.* Her mind raced. *I have to get out of here. I can't breathe.* With a wave of nausea she stood up and attempted to run.

"Jillian, wait! Don't go!" Fife begged.

But Jillian did not give any indication that she heard him, her eyes glossy and blank, like she could not see. In one motion she stood up and fell to the ground. Without hesitation, Fife scooped Jillian up. Her small, limp body rested easily in his strong arms. He carried her to their campsite, surrounded by the seagrass. Resting her head on the pile of soft knitted scarves from Leena's mum, he laid her down and breathed a fire to life within seconds.

Jillian opened her eyes.

"Tell us what you need. We are here for you. You are strong. I know this is hard, but I also know you can do this." As Leena spoke with heartfelt compassion, all remnants of jealousy melted away and empathy took its place.

A few minutes went by in silence. Jillian sat up weakly and looked at Leena. In a thin voice, Jillian quietly struggled to speak. "Waaater."

Fife lifted his head, eyes wide with astonishment. Jillian gave a fragile smile.

"You're not strong enough to go to th'water right now," Fife answered, controlling his voice so he didn't seem completely shocked that she spoke. She shook her head and pointed to the jug of water. "Aww yeah, ye be needin' some water to drink!"

He fetched the water that Leena had gotten out of their bag and brought it over to Jillian. Gently Fife lifted the edge of the jug to her lips. Color returned to her face, and she tried to speak again but only a soft breathy sound came out.

"Easy, Jillian. Give yourself time. There's no rush," Leena said.

Jillian lay back down and stared up at the sky.

"Lemongrass," she said.

Jonny ran barefoot along the shoreline, chasing the white birds. As soon as the squabbling birds landed on the ground, he raced up and scattered them. The birds flew high up into the sky, squawking in a noisy disagreement.

His laughter filled the air, mixing in nicely with the scent of lemongrass that floated on the sea breeze. Jillian watched Jonny chase the birds as she sat with her mother among the tufts of lemongrass. Pulling the grass up by the roots, they cut off the bulb at the base and set it aside to use for cooking. Jillian's hands worked quickly weaving the long grass strands together to make a basket. Baskets to sell at the market.

Stacks of lemongrass baskets surrounded Jillian and her mother. Her father came over to where they were weaving and borrowed a basket. Jonny came back a few minutes later with the basket on his head like a hat. The little family sat in the sand together, happy, laughing, and weaving baskets, surrounded by the scent of lemongrass.

They all saw it. Jillian's family. The dimple on Jillian's cheek appeared with her smile. Seeing Jillian smile made Fife smile.

"Jillian, I think on the day of destruction, I think…" Leena scratched in the sand as she spoke. "It may have been your necklace that protected your life and kept you alive. I have purple gemstones that were protected from the Destroyers called amethyst, and Fife was under the ground in the forest tunnels on the day of destruction." She paused and looked over at Fife, who intently focused on Jillian. "He was surrounded by amazonite stones down there, and the stones protected him. I think the pearls protected you."

Jillian glanced at Leena and then back at Fife. She looked thoughtful. "That makes sense."

"I have an idea," Leena said. "What would you think about doing our meditation in a different way today? What if we all lay on the sand? Like Jillian is right now."

"I like it," Fife agreed, and Leena and Fife both laid down in a comfortable position, the soft scarves tucked under their heads like Jillian. The three of them spread out from each other with straight backs, resting their hands comfortably to the sides of their bodies.

"Jillian, close your eyes and listen. The earth will guide you," Leena said calmly.

Inhale through the nose…and exhale through the nose completely. Inhale… Exhale…Breathing is the way to connect your body to your spirit. Inhale…Exhale…Your mind, body, and spirit are becoming one. Feel the soft breeze, and let go of any tension in your body. Let your mind relax with the rhythm of the waves. Inhale peace and exhale worry.

Soften the muscles in your stomach. Soften the muscles in your hands. Be still. Let your heart be still. Let your mind be still. Peace is filling your body, and your spirit is still. Inhale…Peace is within me. Exhale…Peace is within me. Peace is within me. Peace is within me. Breathe in a slow breath…Breathe out a long, soft breath. Feel the breath as it moves through every part of your body.

Peace is here, in my heart. Peace is here, in my mind. Peace is here in my body.

I am peace.

They rested in silence, then the sand rippled smoothly under their backs like a wave. Jillian opened her eyes and rolled over onto her stomach.

"The sand," she whispered in her thin voice as she stroked the sand with her fingers.

Fife gasped as he sat up, and echoed in a quiet voice, "Th' sand."

The black sand changed color as it rolled through the seashore. Golden sand covered the entire shore now, breathing with color and energy, and the green of the grasses and trees gave the sea a breath of fresh air.

"How?" Jillian asked, her voice still soft, sitting up to face Leena and Fife.

"This is all possible because you were able to be still." Leena scooted over toward Jillian. "Your heart, mind and body became one with your gift of breath, and together, we brought it back." Leena hugged Jillian followed by Fife who wrapped his long arms around both of them.

MEDITATION MOMENT:

    Breathe in slowly through the nose.

    Hold your breath for five counts.

    One. Two. Three. Four. Five.

    Slowly breathe out through the nose.

    Now hold. One. Two. Three. Four. Five.

    Relax your breath.

    Breathe in the lemongrass scent and visualize the green grass waving in the breeze.

    Say in your mind, *I am peace*.

13

Pearls

"A mistake: error, fault, inaccuracy, omission, slip, blunder, miscalculation, flaw. That is how we learn. Your mistakes will teach you things you cannot learn in any other way.
Learn from your mistakes. Wisdom through experience."

"What's th' water doin'?" Fife's eyes slid straight passed Leena and Jillian whose backs faced the water. The girls turned around. The water had receded unusually far. Almost so far that it disappeared. A low hiss crept through the air, followed by a low rumbling.

"Oh no." Fife gulped. They watched in confusion as the water rushed back towards the natural shoreline with such speed and force that it looked like it might swallow them. "I'm thinkin' that wave be too big."

The sound got louder and louder. Leena's stomach plummeted to the sand and burrowed a hole so deep she feared she may never find it again.

"No time to explain. Get to higher ground." Jillian's voice trembled.

Fife grabbed the packs, and they ran towards the path that led to the bluff overlooking the sea. The water behind them raged with movement. A roar crescendoed through the water. Leena never could have imagined that sound in her worst nightmares. The water rose higher than the trees in the forest and Leena knew when it crashed down, it would take everything in its path with it. Adrenaline pulsed through her body, pushing her struggling feet uphill through the thick sand.

Jillian led the way, sprinting up the path. Leena followed and Fife, hauling the packs, ran behind Leena. She knew he wanted to make sure the girls got up safely before him, but she feared for him most of all. If the wave caught them, she and Jillian could hold their breath. Fife would surely drown under the weight of the water. The thought of Fife being swept away made Leena's insides fray like the edge of a ripped blanket. She pushed the thought out of her mind. She would not let that happen. Without Fife she would never be able to continue and not continuing was not an option.

The water thrashed wildly behind them as they reached the bluff and scrambled over the edge, panting and out of breath just as the water grabbed at their heels. Sweat dripped down their faces and their backs were drenched with sea water. Jillian's unnaturally pale face tensed at the sight of her home under siege, and she covered her face with her hands.

They stood side by side and watched the madness unfold below.

"What—" Leena said, attempting to catch her breath. She brushed her wet hair from sticking to the sides of her face. "What is happening in the water?"

Jillian swallowed hard, looking like she might cry as she struggled to answer. "When the ground shifts beneath the sea"— Jillian squeezed her eyes shut and a tear slid down her round cheek— "it causes a tidal wave. It happened twice when I was a little girl." Jillian opened her eyes. "I think the vibration of the sand rolling, caused a trembling in the water and…and…"

The look on Fife's face resembled what Leena would think someone would look like when they faced imminent death. Disbelief. Dazed. Doomed.

"The waves will not rise higher than the bluff. We are safe," Jillian reassured them, her face returning to its natural color. Fife let out a sigh and suddenly looked so relaxed Leena thought he might fall over.

And then the unthinkable, the unimaginable happened. As the tidal waves raged below them, nearly reaching the bluff, Leena saw in the distance a black cloud gathering speed, getting larger as it rolled towards them.

The memory of the black cloud flooded her mind. Ravenous. Full of revenge and with more rage than the waves below.

"They are coming," Leena said under her breath. She steadied herself and looked straight into the cloud. Time slowed down. Or perhaps her mind quickened. She couldn't tell which it was. Fife still looked at Jillian and had not noticed the cloud.

Could Jillian survive this mentally? Leena reached into her pocket and wrapped her fingers around the purple amethyst. Dad's voice entered her thoughts:

Hold onto the amethyst and feel the calm. It is full of light and will make your thoughts clear when everything around you feels muddled. Inner harmony will always be your friend if you can harness the calm of the amethyst. It will be your guiding light. You are my amethyst, Leena.

Leena's fears pushed against her, and she pushed back. "I am a Life Breather," she whispered. With the howling of the waves, Fife and Jillian did not hear her, Fife still looking relieved and somewhat lost in Jillian's eyes.

"Fife, do you have your amazonite in your pocket?" Leena asked in a straight, controlled voice.

Fife fidgeted, unbuttoning his pocket. "Yeah yeah I got it here… why?" He looked up. "Oh." His calm expression fled. "That be lookin' like trouble."

"Where can we hide?" Jillian said frantically. "We can't hide in the water! There's nowhere! There's nowhere to hide!" She spoke louder with each word.

If the water was available, Leena would have chosen that option, too. The easy option. Hide.

"We're not going to hide," Leena said.

"What do ya mean we ain't gonna hide?" Fife said, squinting his eyes. "What a we do?"

"We're going to face it," Leena answered.

Fife curled the corner of his lips into a smile.

"It's coming. Whatever happens. Keep breathing," Leena instructed.

The three Life Breathers did not run. Standing firm they stared into the black cloud as it rolled savagely towards them. Fife stood in between the girls and reached out his hands to his sides, taking Leena's and Jillian's hands in his. Leena had no idea what was coming or how they would survive this, but they had no other choice.

Thick, black, suffocating, clouds billowed towards them until it hovered directly in front of their faces. The cloud tugged at Leena's breath as it approached. She held on to her breath, not responding to the pull. The cloud smoothly encircled the three like a blanket of silk, and the black smoke completely surrounded them.

It took a few seconds for Leena's eyes to adjust to the darkness. Nothing moved. No sounds. Waves and wind were still. Leena's mind stayed firm, and she continued to breathe, but something unsettling approached, though she could not see it. Leena's body went numb. Time passed. She no longer felt anything. No sense of urgency. No bravery or fear.

Lulled to sleep. That's how Leena felt. Her eyes wanted so desperately to close. Her head floated in the air as if encased in a bubble. Her mind drifting and detached from her body. She glanced over at Fife who glided along beside her in a trance. Jillian's eyes were sharp and fearful but she, too, glided smoothly through the blackness.

If only Leena had a bed. She looked at the ground—it appeared soft and welcoming. The cloud gently coaxed the air right out of her. Leena realized she was not breathing, but she was also not holding her breath.

Just for a moment. I'll just sit and rest for a moment. Placing her hand on the ground she guided her weightless body to the earth. The stone in her hand rolled out of her grasp and onto the sand beside her glowing a soft purple. Leena's eyes fixed on the illumination of the stone. Light rose out of it until it encircled Leena with a purple glow.

Clarity. Inner harmony. Guiding light.

Keep breathing.

"I am a Life Breather," she said quietly. "You cannot have my breath." Leena rose to her feet. "I am a Life Breather. You cannot have my breath," she said louder.

Jillian drew in an anxious breath through her mouth. Fife shifted. Leena's eyes narrowed. A twisty bit of black smoke twirled like a finger in front of her and reached into the pack that Fife had slung over his shoulder. Fife did not seem to notice. His glossy eyes stared out in front of him at the blackness. The smokey fingers pulled out the small bundle of sticks wrapped in moss that Fife loved so much. His family. Still he did not move. Everything in the cloud seemed to be in slow motion. And little by little Leena could feel the air being sucked out of them. *Keep breathing.*

"Fife!" Leena shouted although it came out of her mouth raspy and not as loud as she had intended. His head snapped to the side to look at her as though he'd been woken from a dream. Confused, he looked around. The wispy black smoke dangled his beloved bundle of sticks just out of reach in front of him.

"No." His voice cracked like he hadn't spoken in years. He held out his hand, trying to reach the bundle, but all his movements were slowed like, honey dripping off a wooden spoon.

And then before their eyes the stick family, snuggly wrapped together in green moss, turned a charcoal black, disintegrated to ashes and fell to the ground.

Fife's eyes darted back and forth in disbelief. "Nooooo!" he screamed with every ounce of passion in his body. "No, no, no!" He fell to his knees and picked up the black ash from the ground, holding it to his chest. His erratic breathing caused him to gag, and he collapsed. Kneeling beside him, Leena focused every breath on survival. Jillian coughed again and again.

Fife's body jerked and trembled uncontrollably.

"You must breathe, Fife," Leena whispered into his ear. "You must! You are a Life Breather."

Then she noticed his fist still clenched around his amazonite stone. Prying his fingers open a burst of pale-blue light released into the cloud. The light gathered around Fife's body and lifted him to standing. He breathed in through his nose and the blue light streamed into his nostrils and back out again with his exhale. His eyes stayed closed as he breathed, but his face contorted in pain. The pain of a little boy who had lost his family. Again.

Jillian grabbed her throat. Leena turned her attention from Fife to Jillian.

"Breathe through your nose, Jillian. Not your mouth," Leena pleaded. "You must breathe through your nose. Focus. Control. You can do this."

As Jillian calmed her breath, her pearl necklace lit up around her neck. Her face softened and her coughing halted. As the Life Breathers glowed, the black cloud thinned. Through the thinning black smoke Leena could see objects moving in the far end of the cloud. She could not make out anything for certain, but they appeared to be people and they appeared to be moving towards them. Shock swept through her, and the desire to run pulsed in her body. Did she want to run towards them or away from them? She had no idea if she needed to save them or fear them.

Before she could act on any impulse, her body buckled beneath her. She could no longer feel her legs.

A massive gust of wind took hold of the three and flipped them easily into the air, spinning them like leaves in a tornado. Leena shut her eyes tightly. Her stomach lurched as she whirled through the cloud. After spinning furiously for what felt like several minutes the cloud spit them out, throwing the three of them onto the sand, and the black cloud rolled away and disappeared.

Then Fife lost it. Leena had never seen him lose control. He crumpled into a ball, and tears raced forward from his eyes like a tidal wave. Pounding his fists on the ground, he grabbed hold of the sand and threw fistfuls of it as if he still searched for his bundle of sticks that were now ashes lost at sea.

Leena and Jillian watched him. All they could do was watch as he wept in pain. Jillian's eyes looked startled and helpless. Leena could not help but wonder if because Fife had never seen the black cloud or the Destroyers all those years ago, that the tragedy of losing his family of sticks somehow brought all that his family suffered on the day of destruction to his reality. Fife's tears ran deep. Leena let him cry. She let him process the clean pain he needed to deal with the injustice that he never understood until this moment. How could he have? He was so young.

He lost them again today. Leena's inside wept with him. Compassion for her friend grew, and all she wanted to do was hold him.

As Fife's sobbing slowed, Jillian sat beside him and touched his arm softly. Fife looked at her, his eyes red and his hair wild.

"I dunno wha t'do." Fife wiped his eyes with the sleeve of his shirt. "I feel so lost now."

Nobody spoke. They sat in silence as the minutes passed. Finally Leena broke the stillness.

"We stay together, that's what we do." Her voice was strong and unwavering. "We fight. We find the others, and we stay together."

Jillian nodded in agreement. Jillian's hands still trembled slightly as her fingers glided along Fife's arm.

The sea had calmed below. The three made their way back down over the cliff edge, even though there was no longer a path and no sign remained of their campsite. Sticks and logs lay scattered along the shore. They had survived, but not without scars. Scars that would eventually be strengths.

Leena, Fife, and Jillian walked to the edge of the water.

"I need to go home," Jillian said. She turned away from them and put her head down not wanting to make eye contact.

"It's okay, Jillian. Everythings okay. Get some rest." Jillian met Leena's eyes and gave a slight nod. Leena continued. "We've been through a lot today. And we survived. The cloud will return, but now we know what to expect. We are stronger than we were an hour ago. Stronger because we know we can survive."

Jillian walked into the rippling foam of the water and dove in.

She stayed under the water till late into the following day, nearly sundown. As she approached, Fife looked up from the campfire that he'd just started.

"Hello there!" he called, and he looked delighted to see her.

Leena smiled in relief that Jillian had returned. In the back of Leena's mind she worried that Jillian would change her mind and decide not to come with them. But Jillian was here. She came. And that brought relief.

For the next couple of days they spent their time together digging for oysters and clams.

Jillian held out a white pearl in her hand to show Fife.

"This pearl used to be as tiny as a grain of sand," Jillian said.

"Wow, really?" Fife took the little pearl out of Jillian's palm and held it up to the sun. "How? I mean, I believe ya, but how's it done?"

"This pearl started out as a tiny irritant, like a bit of sand or a random piece of something floating around in the water, that made its way into the insides of the oyster shell," Jillian explained. "As it stayed there, one layer at a time formed around the irritant to protect the oyster, until finally after many years, it created a pearl."

"Well, I'm pretty sure that be the coolest thing I ev'r heard," Fife said, clearly impressed.

"My father used to tell me I was like a pearl," Jillian said, looking out to the sea. "He said a little at a time, with each new experience in life, I would be shaped and grow stronger, just like a pearl. Learning wisdom through experience."

"That is beautiful," Leena said. "You are strong like the pearls. And wise."

"I agree." Fife handed the pearl back to Jillian. "Strong, wise, and beau'iful, like a pearl."

Jillian turned away from Fife and smiled in the other direction, hiding the pink in her cheeks. Fife smiled, too, but didn't hide it.

"I've worn these pearls since I was a baby. They were a gift from my grandmother."

Jillian touched the string of beads around her neck. "My grandmother is the one who passed on her gift of breathing to me." Jillian's voice was light and soft, like a song.

"Tell us," Fife coaxed. "Tell us more 'bout your Gran'mother.

Jillian looked at Fife shyly and then she did something unexpected. She began to sing.

Like stars that appear, one by one, reverently in the night.
Like pearls that grow in a shell of hope, with rays of sunlight.
Like a miracle, of a rainbow, finding joy on your darkest day.
Like a breath of life, like a breath of love, you were giv'n on your day of birth.

Leena had never heard a more wondrous sound, like a magical bird soothing her into a daydream. Jillian's singing reminded her of Mum's lullabies. Fife's eyes were closed, and the corners of his lips raised in a soft smile as he listened to Jillian.

"My Grandmother would sing that song to me," Jillian said. Her hair blew across her face, and she brushed it back over her shoulders. "And she would tell me about her gift of breath…and she told me I had it, too. She told me we were Life Breathers. But I never understood what that meant. I don't think I actually believed her." Jillian let out a soft laugh. "We practiced on the seashore, holding our breath for only minutes first, then for hours. She's the one who taught me to hold my breath underwater."

"What else, Jillian? What else did she teach you?" Leena asked, desperate for more answers.

"I do remember a story grandmother used to tell me. I thought it to be make believe, but after the Destroyers came, I knew."

"Knew wha'?" Fife asked, his eyes intently looking at Jillian. He leaned slightly forward waiting for more.

"I knew that all the things she told me were not just a tale about good and evil, about light and darkness, but it was real. It was the story of how I came to be. Our existence. The Life Breathers here on this planet."

The three of them sat on the sand surrounded by oysters and pearls. Leena closed her eyes.

"And then the Destroyers trapped thousands of Life Breathers inside the

cloud itself, and though the Life Breathers fought back, one by one they became weaker and weaker."

Jillian clasped her small hands over her open mouth and gasped. Grandmother continued in her intense best storytelling voice.

"A hundred of the most powerful Life Breathers escaped the cloud and decided it best to leave the realm immediately. The Destroyers had taken control over the home that they loved. The Destroyers had betrayed them and were no longer trustworthy companions, but enemies. The Life Breathers knew they needed to leave or they would become extinct."

Jillian lowered her hands from her mouth. "Where did they go?" she asked in a high voice.

"They traveled through the atmosphere until they discovered a planet with life. Earth."

"They are here? On our planet Earth?" Jillian asked, sitting up straight and smiling. Grandmother paused. Her long gray hair braided neatly to the side hung over her shoulder. She looked into Jillian's eyes. The seriousness in her face seemed to capture Jillian's full attention.

"Jillian, I am a Life Breather." Jillian stared hard at her Grandmother. Not knowing if she was still making up a pretend tale. "And so are you."

Jillian said nothing for a long time.

"Is this a real story?" Jillian asked. Her small round face looked hesitantly up at Grandmother.

"Do you want to know what happened next? Hmmm?"

"Yes," Jillian answered.

"The Life Breathers came to Earth, and since they looked like the other humans, they lived among them. Hiding their powers as needed so no one would be frightened by them. They began a new life. They blended in with the humans and became one race. Of course that means that through the course of time, new Life Breathers were born with special abilities and powers. And that is how you and I came to be."

"Grandmother, but what happened to the Destroyers?"

"They were angry. They were furious. They were determined to steal all the breath from the Earth and destroy the Life Breathers once and for all." Her voice wavered a bit.

"Grandmother if you are a Life Breather, then what do the Destroyers look like?"

"Well my child, I have never seen them. Nor would I ever wish to. But you, there may come a day when you have to face them. And you must be ready. So let's get started."

Leena, Fife, and Jillian opened their eyes. They had all seen Jillian's grandmother. They stared in amazement.

"Now that!" Fife exclaimed. "That!" He let out a nervous laugh.

Jillian's eyes looked glossy, like ice blue marbles, the ice melting into tears. She looked like her mind floated somewhere far away. Her body tensed up as she grabbed her stomach, looking down at the sand. Taking a deep breath in and out through her nose her body relaxed and she continued.

"My first memory of my Grandmother is her showing me a long, white budded flower in a cluster on a branch. It had not bloomed yet. She sat very still and breathed in and out. Slowly the bud began to open." Jillian smiled at the thought of the flower. "It was the first time I had ever seen her do anything like that. It opened up to a white flower, with a yellow middle and five petals. It smelled sweet, like honey." Jillian took a breath in as if she was remembering the scent of her grandmother's flowers. "She would put a flower in my hair tucked behind my ear every morning after that." Jillian touched her hair gently by her left ear remembering where the flower used to be. "I asked her if I'd ever be able to do that, and she laughed and said she would teach me when I was older…we ran out of time. There was so much more she needed to teach me. There wasn't time. About a year after she died, the Destroyers came. I was not prepared to face them. I hadn't even really believed my Grandmother's story."

Night came. The sunset, mixed with purples and reds— the colors melted into each other and lit the sky. The three Life Breathers watched without speaking. When the colors faded behind the water and the stars started to appear, Jillian spoke.

"I think I'm ready," she said in a more confident tone than she had before. "I want to sleep on the sand tonight…around the fire… with you." She let out a noticeable breath.

"You'd be most welcome t'join us," Fife said quietly, glancing at Leena with slow widening eyes.

Relief mixed with excitement filled Leena's heart. Finally with Jillian getting closer to being ready they would be able to continue. But they had no idea where to start searching for the next Life Breather. The riddle in the book that drew Leena's attention still made no sense. She repeated the words out loud.

"Bright as diamonds, loud as thunder. Always falling, never still. Running forever without moving location, no lungs, no throat, but a roaring yell. What am I?"

"No idea," Fife said. "It be makin' no sense t'me."

"What is that?" Jillian asked.

"Riddles." Leena pulled the book, *Riddles of Time Secrets of Stones*, out of her pack.

"Ohhhh." Jillian looked at it with interest. "May I see it?" Leena handed her the leather book, and Jillian's fingers carefully brushed through its pages. The same page that called to Leena fell open without effort.

By the light of the fire, Jillian traced her fingers along the riddle.

"Well if I had to guess, I'd say this is about some sort of water."

"Hey that be what Leena's thinkin', too." Fife looked impressed. "But what kinda water runs nowhere and is yellin'?"

Jillian sat quietly thinking for a moment before she spoke. "Well there's always a waterfall."

"I dunno wha' that is. Leena, you?"

Leena shook her head.

"It's a stream of water that falls over a cliff edge into a pool of water below," Jillian explained. "A waterfall can be quite forceful, quite loud, and it does sparkle like diamonds, all that water falling in the sunshine."

"Where do you find waterfalls?" Leena asked. "Have you seen one?"

"My Mother has. She showed me pictures she drew of the waterfalls in the canyon when she traveled there when she was younger—before she met my Father. She used to adventure all over the place until she found the sea and stayed here."

"I've never heard of the canyon. Maybe that's where we're headed next," Leena said.

With the sound of the crackling fire, mixed with the soothing rush of the waves coming in and out with the tide, they all slept peacefully.

Fife sneaked off early before the sun rose.

"Where are you going?" Leena whispered so she wouldn't wake Jillian, who was still sound asleep.

"I'll be comin' back real soon. Don't worry 'bout me," Fife said with a wink as he crawled out of his blanket and put his light blue scarf around his neck, protecting him from the cool morning breeze.

Leena narrowed her eyes and shook her head, but then snuggled back down into her scarf pillow and quickly fell back asleep, slipping into a dream.

Her hair. The color of fire. The hills that surrounded her, orange and alive. The canyon, breathing and full of life. The girl knelt on the cliff of the sandstone canyon, her feet tucked under her body. Her hands in front of her chest with her palms together pointing upward. Her back, straight, and her chin tucked slightly in, eyes closed, breathing in and out steadily. Wearing a plain gray dress and her hair short and straight. Heat pressed down around her, hot and dry. Below the cliffs were strange green trees, thick, spiked, and rounded at the top. Pointed needles covered the entire skin of the tree.

The girl continued to meditate. From behind a bush, a small red fox emerged. The fox came to the girl, and the girl opened her eyes, touching the fox's head then under its chin, inspecting it. She patted the fox and scooted it with both her hands out of the way, telling it to go.

The heat continued to press down around her without a breeze. The girl stood on the cliff edge in a warrior stance ready to fight.

Abruptly, in the distance could be heard a faint beating on the earth. Drums. A small army, coming closer and closer to the girl. Her eyes narrowed intensely, her expression fierce. Fear, nowhere near her. The sky stayed a bright blue. No clouds. But up over the ridge of the canyon came a dozen black, tall, ominous figures with black bone sticks in their grasp, pounding and beating in unison, getting closer and closer.

The girl turned her body in their direction and faced them. She closed her eyes, but only long enough to inhale a momentous breath. Opening her eyes, and with a fierce blow, she exhaled. Her breath, powerfully shot out towards the

Destroyers. The tornado-like wind grabbed hold of the sticks they held, shattering them into pieces and forcing them to lose the rhythm of their beating. Once she had gotten their attention, she ran toward a cave opening, and the Destroyers followed, slowly and still in perfect rhythm, but silently, with no beating sticks.

From inside the cave the girl shouted.

"I am a Life Breather! I will destroy you if you come in here!" She was clearly warning them but also calling to them. The Destroyers could not resist her breath. They came to the cave opening. They needed her breath. They desired it, wanting it more than anything.

As they entered the cave she continued to yell and taunt them. "I am Mandy! I am a Life Breather! You have no power here!"

The Destroyers followed her deeper into the cave until no light remained from the outside. They moved forward, closer to her. She could feel their malice. The darkness emanating from the Destroyers could be felt even through the darkness of the cave. After moments of silent staring she yelled, "You will not touch me! You will not steal my breath! It is mine! You cannot take it!"

In each hand she held a smooth, silvery-black stone. A light glowed inside of each. Holding the stones up in the air, a beam of light shot out of each rock. The light wrapped around the Destroyers like a rope, surrounding the black figures. The cave lit up, the Destroyers strangled in the center of the cave, the light suffocating them. Gasping helplessly, moaning in a rash tone, they fell to the floor of the cave, choked by the light. They collapsed and shrank until nothing remained but a pile of black ash.

Mandy stood in front of them and closed her eyes, lowering her head. Exhausted, Mandy collapsed to the ground, taking in huge breaths of air. Sweat dripped from her face and she lay there in a heap until her strength returned.

Emerging from the cave opening, the red fox pup met her at the entrance. Bending down she cupped her hands around its furry face and whispered, "You were worth it." And she smiled a tired smile. The fox leapt onto her lap and licked her face. Still sweaty and exhausted, she sat down and cuddled the animal for the rest of the afternoon.

Leena opened her eyes. The sun barely peeked out over the bluff.

She looked over at Jillian, who lay awake. Jillian's eyes were wide open and the expression on her face told Leena they had the same dream.

"You saw Mandy," Leena affirmed.

"Yes. We need to go to her," Jillian answered eagerly. "I'm ready. I know you have both been waiting on me, and I'm ready now." Her eyes were alive and sparkling. "I don't want to leave the sea"— Jillian paused and swallowed— "but I want to help, and I understand that all of us have sacrificed in order to bring life back into this world. I want to do my part. I want to give up what I love for something that is so much bigger than me." Jillian stood up, and her golden-blonde hair, which matched the sand, caught the light of the sun. She looked powerful. "I'm ready."

This is what Leena had been waiting for. They had solved the riddle and in return they were given a dream about where to go next. The waterfall in the canyon. Jillian was ready. Everything worked together for their good. It was time.

Just then, Fife came running on the path that led downward from the bluff. Short of breath he said, "Look! Look at what I found!" From behind his back he pulled out a branch that had a cluster of white flowers on the end of it. "You've no idea how long it be takin' me this mornin' to find it. But I found 'em way up and over that hill. Back further behind the lemongrass, a whole bunch a these trees in neat little rows. So I did a bit of breathin' and made 'em come alive." He looked at Jillian anxiously, still breathing hard to catch his breath.

Jillian stood in front of him now, staring in amazement at the white flowers on the branch. Her grandmother's flowers. Jillian's hair still glowed with the light of the sun hitting it, blowing a little in the breeze. Fife gently broke off one of the flowers and placed the branch on the sand. He tucked her hair back and delicately put the small stem behind her left ear, his hand brushing her cheek. The flower nestled snugly, clearly meant to be there.

"Plumeria," Jillian said smiling.

"Plu–who?" Fife asked.

"The flower. It's called plumeria." Jillian laughed softly.

"Ah right, yeah, that's what it looks like it'd be called." Fife chuckled.

"This is exactly what I needed," Jillian said, her face shining.

Standing on her tiptoes, she took hold of his light-blue scarf and gently tugged him down closer to her and kissed his cheek. He pulled her in for a hug. "It's from your gran'mother…and from me," he whispered into her ear. They stood hugging for a moment, then he loosened his hold.

Fife put his hand over the spot she kissed and leaned back, letting out a sigh. Then he plopped down onto the sand. "That right there? That be worth gettin' up early in the mornin' for."

14

Heat

"When the sun first rises up over the edge of the earth, that is the moment when you breathe it in."

Fife was thrilled to hear about the dream—Mandy, the fox, fighting the Destroyers, powerful breath—all of it.

"This Mandy girl seems like she could be my sister, bringin' back animals and fightin' and all." Fife looked impressed. "Jillian, you feelin' ready?"

"I'm ready." Jillian smiled, and her dimples showed. Fife melted just looking at her.

They spread some of the pearls they had gathered out along the sand to protect the life they had brought back. The rest of the pearls were brought in a small pouch along with a few shells from her grandmother's collection and a small tuft of the lemongrass for its calming scent.

They had been drying seaweed to bring with them on their journey, along with a few lemongrass bulbs for cooking over the fire to add some flavor.

"Well, that'll be the last of it," said Fife, looking around at the packs all full of supplies. "Guessin' it's time to say g'bye to the sea." He looked at Jillian and gave her a reassuring look with a slight nod of his head. Jillian exhaled a long sigh.

"How do we know what direction to go to find the canyon?" Jillian asked, looking around.

"We don't yet," Leena answered. "We'll ask the earth for guidance. If we ask, ready to receive, we'll get an answer."

Each of them had their preferred positions to meditate. Leena sat cross-legged with a straight back, the back of her hands resting on her knees, palms open, facing the sky. Fife sat on a log, with a tall back, his hands palms down gently on his thighs, helping him feel grounded to the earth. Jillian chose to lay flat on her back, her legs stretched out, inline with her hips and her feet relaxed, toes out and her spine long, so her body could fully relax, pressed into the sand. She rested her hands on her stomach softly.

Feel your breath, moving in and out of your body. Slow. Steady. Smooth. Feel the stillness within your body as you breathe in and out. Listen to the waves rolling in as you inhale, and as the waves roll out to the sea, exhale. In…and out…Waves and breath. Feel your body rooted in the ground like the lemongrass. You are grounded to the earth beneath you. Your roots are strong and firm. You are connected to the earth. Feel the strength of the earth. It will protect you. It will keep you strong. You can see your path clearly. You are at peace with your path. Follow the peaceful warmth of the air. The warm breeze will guide you. Follow the warm air. Place your hands over your heart and begin.

Leena placed her hands over her heart. A stillness rested inside her. Gratitude filled her heart for the earth, for the guidance it gives, and for the lemongrass scent that permeated the air.

Gradually, Leena opened her eyes. She waited patiently for Fife and Jillian to finish. Once they were all ready, they looked at each other and nodded agreeing it was time.

With their packs over their shoulders, they began their ascent up the path to the bluff that overlooked the sea. Leena noticed Jillian crying quietly as she walked, glancing back longingly at her home below. Leena understood. Leaving the meadow was the hardest decision she had ever made. Her heart broke for Jillian.

Even though Leena knew they were on the right path and all would work together for the greater good, leaving a beloved home was hard.

Fife whistled a tune as he walked, sounding like a sparrow. A few minutes later, Jillian joined in, humming along with him. Her soft, clear humming soothed them all. Jillian hummed as an intentional distraction so she would not give attention to the queasy, unsettled feelings swirling around her body. Humming seemed to calm her and she smiled as she walked. When they reached the bluff, they stood looking out over the vast landscape of water and sand one last time.

"Alrigh'." Fife sighed. "Which way?" He looked from side to side, weighing the options, trying to guess which would be best.

"Well," Leena said, facing the breeze to her left. "We are supposed to follow the warm air." It felt cool on her face and a shiver went down her back. Turning to face the right, she felt a breeze float past her cheeks, sending a warm sensation all the way down to her toes.

"Did you feel that?" Leena asked with excitement.

"Wha'? I didn't feel nothin'." Fife looked betrayed.

"Turn your body this way. Do you feel that warm air?" Leena waited for Jillian and Fife to face the same direction and feel the warm air.

"I feel it," Jillian said in her light voice. She smiled. "It's calling to us."

"Aww yeah, I be feelin' it now!" Fife closed his eyes and the warm breeze fell upon him.

They walked along the edge of the bluff for a few miles, still keeping a close eye on the sea and watching the waves dance below. In unison, they turned their bodies and veered slightly to the left after a while, leaving the path along the bluff, following the warm breeze. The further they traveled in a new direction, the blacker everything around them became. They had breathed life back into everything along the sea and the cliffs above the sea, but nothing further out. The black sand got rockier and harder under their feet. The black shrubs and small scorched trees looked gloomy and depressing through the flat dry land. Leena missed the beauty of the sea already.

Walking through the nothingness gave Leena plenty of time to think. She thought about Fife, and she thought about love. Thoughts of her parents came to her mind. Thoughts of how Dad would look at her Mum, his eyes shining in admiration, just like Fife when he looked at Jillian. The thing was, she really liked Jillian. Really, really like her. Kind and soft and smart and she could clearly see that Fife saw all those wonderful things in her, too. As Leena thought about the two of them she knew that they were good for each other and it didn't mean she had to love him any less or that he loved her less. It was just a different kind of love. She longed for a love like Mum and Dad shared. That is what she really wanted. Leena sighed heavily without noticing. Fife turned and looked at her. He smiled.

"Everythin' okay?" he asked, looking concerned. Her insides softened for both of them. No more sweeping aside feelings, no more swirling confusion or uncomfortable jealousy she just let it go and loved them.

"Yeah, everything's fine." Leena said and she meant it. Everything was fine. It felt good to love Fife and equally love Jillian. It felt good to love as a friend loves and not need or want anything more.

As they got further away from the sea, Jillian's skin turned a shade lighter. Fife noticed her pale face. Her hands trembled. Fife came up from behind her and scooped her hand into his.

"You alrigh'?" he asked. She looked up at him, and her hands continued to shake. "Here, let's have you lie down for a bit. Takin' a few breaths in and gettin' your insides feelin' right." He gently helped her down into a comfortable position.

"I'm sorry. I'm so sorry. I…I…my heart is…so fast…my mind… it's messy. What am I doing? Why did I leave?" She clasped her hands over her stomach and closed her eyes. "I can't do this."

Leena bent down beside her and brushed her wavy hair off the sides of her cheeks, which were now damp with sweat. "Yes you can. We are here with you, Jillian. Relax into the feelings. Don't push against the panic. Don't resist it. Don't fight against it. Embrace it.

Let your body embrace and accept the feeling. Only then will you be able to move on."

Jillian clasped her hands together and closed her eyes, a sheen of sweat on her brow. "My hands…my feet…they're tingling like I'm being pricked with needles. My heart is racing."

"It will pass," Leena said. "Breathe. In through your nose. Out through your nose. Good." Leena softly caressed Jillian's forehead. "Fife, get the water jug and bring it here."

Fife jumped up and rummaged around Leena's pack for the water. He helped Jillian sit up enough to get a drink.

"I feel like" —Jillian struggled to speak— "I'm dying. I feel like… I'm breaking apart inside… I want to be in the water. I can't stay…I can't stay on the land." Her voice was weak and shallow. "I'm sorry…I have to go back."

"Close your eyes, Jillian," Leena said softly. Jillian laid her head back, and Fife held on to her shaking hands that were holding her stomach.

"Take a breath in through your nose. It's time to take your mind somewhere else. We are going to focus on three new things." Leena glanced around for inspiration. "I want you to name three things you can see. Find three things that are not black."

Jillian obediently peeked her eyes open.

"The sky…it's blue." Her voice squeaked—high pitched almost like she was asking a question. "Ummm…" Her words fumbled as she searched for another color. "The lemongrass." Stalks of lemongrass hung out of her satchel. "Green." Turning her head, she looked at Fife. His pale-blue eyes looked calmly back at her.

"Fife's eyes." Fife and Jillian stared at each other. "Your eyes look like the sea."

"Good Jillian," Leena said. "Now close your eyes, and think about three sounds you can hear right now. What do you hear?"

Jillian closed her eyes.

"I hear…" Jillian stammered. "I hear the breeze blowing through the skinny trees. I hear…the muffled waves rolling far away. I hear…I hear…Fife…breathing."

Leena glanced at Fife, and he raised his eyebrows and smiled with a slight shrug of his shoulders.

"Good. Good. Focus on those things. If your mind wanders, quickly forgive yourself and bring it back to those sounds," Leena instructed. "Now, I want you to move three things on your body. First, your ankle. Rotate it around in a circle." Jillian lifted one foot off the ground and rotated it in a circular motion.

"Now, move your little finger on your left hand." Jillian followed Leena's instructions. "That's it, Jillian. You're doing great. Move your finger up and down. Move your head from side to side slowly. Continue to breathe in and out."

Jillian's breath began to regulate, and color returned to her face. Her tense body loosened and her hands stopped trembling.

"There you go. We are here for you, Jillian. You are strong, and the peace is inside you. It is there. You are peace."

Jillian sat up slowly, apologizing again and again for delaying them.

Fife delicately lifted her up and onto a big rock close by. He looked into her face as he set her down, and her eyes looked as blue and dynamic as the waves of the sea, too.

"Ya know, *your* eyes are like th'sea. The sea is still inside ya. It'll always be there. It's part of ya. Just like th'forest is part of me. And the meadow is in Leena. You're not leavin' the sea." He paused and waited a moment. "The sea is comin' with you."

Jillian stared at him like he had just revealed the most mysterious secret of all.

"Thank you, Fife." Jillian looked deeply into his eyes. "I needed to hear that." She took in a breath of the warm air and let it out in a long sigh. "I think I'm hungry."

"She be hungry!" Fife announced and clapped his hands together once as he stood up. "You're in luck b'cause imma make somethin' very special today for our first meal on our journey." Fife said with a cheeky grin. "Wanna know what it is?"

He waited, but neither of the girls answered him. They just looked at each other and shook their heads, knowing that dried seaweed and lemongrass root was all they had.

"I am gonna roast this seaweed over the fire. You ain't never tasted anythin' like this before."

"Fife, you can't start a fire right now. Not in this heat! Don't you feel the heat wave we're walking into?" Leena said, teasing him.

"Mmmmhmmmm. Maybe you're right. One of these cold nights though, I'll be makin' a fire and roastin' the seaweed. That salty crisp delicious food from the sea. So good."

"It's really not that good." Jillian said laughing.

"We can pretend though, right?" Fife raised a single eyebrow. The girls shook their heads again and laughed. They found some shade and unpacked the food.

After a bite to eat and a bit of a rest they continued to walk in the direction of the warm air.

"The air...it's gettin' warmer, ya think?" Fife asked, though Leena suspected he already knew the answer.

They talked very little for the next while. Every hour, they took a break and breathed life back into the world that surrounded them, leaving behind a world of green shrubs and tan rocks. Ahead of them were black rolling hills of smooth hot sand. The thick-trunked trees, now stalky and prickly, looked like the trees in the dream they had about Mandy, except in the dream, color covered the land. Here everything lay black and breathless.

As soon as the sun went down, cold air covered the desert. Fife made a fire and they bundled together in their scarves. Leena's pink cheeks burned a bit from facing the sun all day. Her fair skin never got this much direct sun in the meadow, not even on the hottest days.

Jillian's feet ached. Her red ankles stung with blisters, rejecting the shoes that she was not used to wearing and longing to be barefoot in the soft sand.

"I don't know how I'm going to walk tomorrow." Jillian took off her shoes and exposed the blisters on the heels of her feet.

"Oooow...that be needin' some medicine and a bandage. Only...we don't have medicine and a bandage..." Fife frowned thoughtfully. He looked around. Leena noticed he did not give up easily when sorting through a problem. It was one of the things she loved about him. "Don't worry. I'll think a somethin'."

Fife left the girls sitting by the fire and went searching for anything that might help the burns and the blisters. He came back over an hour later, empty handed.

"There ain't nothin' out here. I can't find a single long leaf for a bandage or anythin'." He sat down disappointed. "All there is, is prickly plants with big ol' thorns pokin' out'em. I must be missin' somethin'. The earth is always providin' a way, but…" Fife didn't finish. He sat there exhausted and looking like he might fall asleep sitting up.

Leena patted his shoulder. "It's alright. Thanks for trying. We'll think of something in the morning."

They each took a few long drinks of water. Getting comfortable on the hard ground proved to be difficult. They each shifted their bodies tossing and turning for a few minutes.

When they finally settled, stillness filled the air. It felt unnatural for the world to be so silent. The sea had given them a backdrop of noise to sleep to everynight, and now, nothing. Looking at the stars, Jillian broke the silence.

"I wish I was warm in my water, with the waves rocking me to sleep. I feel nothing here. It's empty."

She closed her eyes.

Fife spoke slowly in a gentle voice. "Imagine a wave rollin' in and out with the tide. Can ya see it? Use your breath to bring th'wave back and forth. Hear the wave rollin' and crashin'." Fife deliberately paused, giving her time. He licked his lips and continued. "Smell th'sea air. The lemongrass and the salt. Breathe it in. Feel the sand between your toes and the water all around ya. See yourself in the sea."

This visualization seemed to soothe her mind, because Jillian slipped into sleep as Fife spoke. As if he could sense her breathing deeply in sleep, he glanced at Leena and they gave each other a reassuring nod. Grateful and exhausted, Fife and Leena drifted off to sleep.

Leena woke up first, just before the sun came over the rocky hills, the clouds, mixed with oranges and reds, streaked across the desert sky. She sat up and looked around. Who would live here in a place like this? She could not wrap her mind around it. Why anyone would choose this? Memories of the quiet beauty of the meadow came into her thoughts. How she missed the rolling grass hills. The stream. Her daisies. She longed for a field filled with wish flowers and the sheep she had as a child. Everything about the meadow gave her comfort. Nothing about the desert gave her any comfort. Hot and prickly. Dry and flat.

Leena wanted to bring life back to the plants around her to see what they would have to work with. With Fife and Jillian still sleeping peacefully, Leena quietly left the campsite and found a place to meditate.

Straightening her back, she rested her hands and closed her eyes, breathing in and out three times. In her mind, she envisioned the desert alive, the sand a warm tan. All the strange, brilliant plants that she did not recognize, she saw them breathing and strong, green and alive. Waiting quietly in the stillness of the morning, she felt a cactus take a breath close by.

Just as she opened her eyes, the ground beneath her rumbled ever so mildly and the black earth vanished, revealing a glorious red sand under her feet. Leena thought she could only love the green grass and the rainbow of colors in the flowers from the meadow, but this! Her heart soared as she looked around at the many shades of orange, brown, red, gold, and green. This looked different than anything she had ever seen, and as different and as strange as it was, she loved it! The desert held a strange beauty. A beauty she was not prepared to see.

Curious, she got up and walked around inspecting the plants at every angle. Some were taller than her and some were short and stubby. Was it a tree or a bush? Some had oval-shaped red fruit and some pinkish orange flowers. The green pads of the plants were spiked.

Leena walked back to the campsite in search of a sharp-edged shell that she could use like a knife to scrape off the pointed spines. The plants must hold nutrients that could be useful to them.

As Leena dug through her bag, Fife sat up, and looked at her. His hair scrunched up on one side of his head like usual after sleep, his face pink from yesterday's sun.

"What are ya lookin' for?" he asked in a groggy voice. Then, seeing the life around him, he gasped. "What did ya do?" he asked in amazement.

"Thought I'd get a head start. I'm looking for something sharp I can cut those plants up with. I want to see what's inside them," Leena whispered, so she wouldn't wake up Jillian.

"Ahh, right. I'll help ya." He stood up, shaking his legs out a bit.

"I'll come, too," said Jillian. Leena looked at her surprised, not expecting her to be awake.

"No, no Jilly. You need to be restin' those feet. Gotta be keepin' you healthy. We'll fetch the plants," Fife said.

"Did you just call her Jilly?" Leena asked, stifling a laugh.

"Yeah, yeah I guess I did. It's a nickname right?" Fife said, looking at Jillian. "I mean, I thought it was cute when I said it…now I'm wonderin'…is it cute?"

"You can call me Jilly," she said with a sleepy smile.

"Well, there ya go, then. I got meself a friend named Jilly," Fife said with a big sleepy grin, too.

Leena and Fife walked out into the desert and out of earshot of Jillian so she could keep resting.

"You like her…don't you, Fife?" Leena said as they walked, nudging him a bit.

"I do. Somethin' about her makes me heart flutter with excitement n' feel at home in th' same beat. I feel all wiggly when I'm 'round her and all I wanna do is stare at her and listen to her voice," Fife answered, looking dreamy.

Leena listened as Fife chatted on and on about Jillian and all the reasons why he found her so special. Leena's smile never faded as she listened patiently.

They worked with the sharp edges of the shells to cut a variety of the thick prickly plants.

"I'm happy for you. You look at Jillian the way my dad looked at my mum. All that love. Right there. Ready to give anything." Leena sorted through the different plants they had cut up. The spikes were difficult to remove.

"I feel happy, too," Fife said. "Ooooouch!" Fife grabbed his hand. A spike had caught him off guard and stuck him right in the palm.

"Ooo, let me see it." Leena took his hand and carefully removed the spike.

"These be the worst bundle of prickly pear pots I ever seen!" Fife said with an irritated laugh.

His hand continued to sting even with the spike removed, but Fife worked through the pain and helped cut up the pads of the remaining plants. They gathered some of the red fruit-like balls also. Leena found a stemless shrub that had dense thick leaves that were greenish and fleshy that fanned out from the middle of the plant. The edges had small, jagged tips.

"Let's get a few of these, too," Leena said pointing to it.

As Fife worked on cutting off the thick leaves from the base, an oozing clear gel slowly drained out the side.

"What be this?" Fife wondered, touching the clear gel. The gel immediately cooled his skin with a tingling sensation. Without thinking, he rubbed it on his wounded palm and the pain eased instantly.

"Whoa! I think we need this stuff!" Fife looked excited as he rubbed it on his sunburned face. "Aww yeah, this is the good stuff. This is what Jillian be needin' for her feet and you for your skin burns. Try it!" He handed the thick pad to Leena.

Leena rubbed the gel onto her pink, sun kissed face and also felt the cool of the magic gel.

"This is wonderful! This will help us!" Leena exclaimed, giving Fife a quick squeeze on the arm. He gathered a few more of the thick gel leaves and they quickly journeyed back to the campsite to show Jillian.

"Look what we found, Jilly!" Fife ran to her and showed her the gel plant. He scraped some of the leaves insides to get a good amount of gel on his fingertips then asked, "May I?" as he motioned towards her feet. Jillian's face lit up.

"You found the wonder plant!" Her dimples showed with her

smile. "My grandmother used to bring that to us when our skin would get burned in the hottest times of the year. I never knew where she found it, but that's it! She called it aloe and it works like magic. Yes, yes let's put it on my heels." Jillian reached for the gel and applied some to one heel as Fife rubbed it on her other heel.

"Thank you, Fife," she said and gave him a quick hug. After they cooked up a few plants, they packed the extra food into their bags, and they were ready to go. Feeling refreshed, they left before the heat got intense and started walking again, but as they walked into mid-day it became unbearably hot. The sun burrowed into their bodies. They wrapped their scarves around their faces for protection from the sun's rays and from the wind blowing the sand up into their eyes. Just as they were on the edge of misery, in the distance, the canyon came into view.

15

The Canyon

"Think of a time you were rewarded for doing something you were asked to do,
but didn't want to do, but you did it anyway?
Was it worth it?"

Leena sensed the earth guiding them, keeping them alive. To their fortune, a supply of the desert plants gave them the nutrients needed to prevent dehydration, but that did not fully compensate for the fatigue and despair they endured. Their dry, chapped lips cried out for moisture in the form of a cool drink of water, but little water remained in their jugs.

The dry earth cracked beneath them like their lips, but in front of them, the canyon beamed with life. They knew they were getting closer to Mandy because everything had color here. The high rocks stretched nearly to the sky, streaked in an impressive reddish orange.

A slight incline made every step a struggle. Even Fife, who never showed a sign of desperation, moaned softly. Stumbling over a few loose rocks he nearly collapsed but caught himself. He bent over, his hands resting on his thighs.

"We maybe need to be rethinkin'" —Fife coughed a little to clear his dry throat— "about goin' to the top a this thing. I mean, this be the canyon right? So maybe we should wait here for this girl, Mandy." Fife looked depleted, as they all did—dried sweat on their pink faces, and their legs and arms dusty with the red dirt.

"What I wouldn't do for a waterfall right now," Leena said to herself in a low voice, wiping her brow with her arm.

"Ahh, man." Fife closed his eyes. "I could go for that right 'bout now."

Leena had never seen Fife so drained. The heat had gotten to all of them, and their weakened minds ached as badly as their feet.

Fife could find goodness anywhere, but even Fife had his limits.

"I'm serious, I actually think we need to find the waterfall," Leena said. "It has to be close. Let's go up a bit toward the inside of the canyon and find some shade. I think we could all use a rest."

They entered the canyon opening and walked until they spotted a cavern with some shade covering. They took the hot scarves off their heads and rested their backs against the cavern walls, each taking turns sipping the last drops of water from the jugs.

In her exhaustion, Leena took a deep breath in through her nose and thanked the earth for helping them. She continued to breathe in and out slowly, silently asking for guidance, longing for focus.

Keep walking. Keep walking. Keep moving.

"We need to keep going," Leena said, obediently.

Fife peeked one eye open. "Are ye serious? We just sat down. I can barely open me eyes."

"We need to keep walking," Leena said again in the same tone.

The last thing she wanted to do was keep walking. She wanted to sit and rest in the shade. She wanted to drink water, meditate, and think clearly. What she really wanted was to be in her meadow stream. Lazily floating on her back, looking up at the birds and clouds. The smallest sliver of a thought wondered how she could be crazy enough to have left. Nothing seemed clear. Nothing seemed real. How many days had they walked in the heat? How long would the earth push them beyond their natural limits? Would the Destroyers come when they were weakened by the heat? Their minds were weak now. If the Destroyers came right now, how would they survive? A pang of panic rattled her inside.

"We have to go!" Her voice shot out in the canyon and echoed off the walls. Jillian and Fife looked at Leena surprised by her tone. "We…we have to go," she said softer. "Now."

The three of them stood up, their bodies feeling as heavy as the boulders they had been sitting on. They continued into the canyon further, in silence, following the natural path that twisted and turned around the painted red rocks.

"Did ye hear that?" Fife asked and stopped walking. The girls stopped and listened. And then they heard it, too. Someone or something called out, a cry in the distance. They heard it again and simultaneously a shadow flew overhead. Leena's heart nearly lept from her chest.

"Fife, look!" Jillian exclaimed, pointing to the sky. Leena and Fife looked up at what Jillian pointed to, and they saw something they did not expect. A large brown and orange bird with a cinnamon-red tail soared high above them, calling out with a raspy scream. The hawk's cry lasted two or three seconds and then descended in pitch.

"It's a hawk!" Leena and Fife said in unison. Leena knew Mandy had restored animals to the canyon, but she was unprepared for the thrill of actually hearing and seeing one. "We're close!"

Their pace quickened. It felt cooler the deeper into the canyon they traveled, a welcome relief. In the distance they heard water rushing. Fife grabbed onto Leena's shoulder and asked in a serious voice, "Could it be? Could it *really* be? Or am I imaginin' it b'cause that could be what's happenin'. I am a bit parched and could be startin' to hear things or see things that might not be real."

"It's real! I can hear it, too!" Jillian said, wiping the sweat from her face. "Let's find that water!"

Jillian and Fife, despite their sore feet, ran in the direction of the water as if it called their names and ordered them to come. Before long they all stood at the water's edge. Ahead of them flowed a mighty stream of water falling from a high rock into a large, crystal clear pool.

"A waterfall," Leena whispered in awe.

"I'm goin' in," Fife said, as if he had just made a very serious decision.

"Me too!" cried Jillian with a wide smile, dimples showing on both sides of her cheeks like she'd never been so happy in her life. Jillian jumped in first without hesitation.

"Bright as diamonds," Leena said out loud, admiring the sparkling waterfall. It truly looked like diamonds in the sunlight.

Leena took her shoes off and carefully walked into the water, one step at a time. She wanted to feel every drop of water touch every tiny part of her skin, soaking in all the sensations to its fullest. As she stood in the water, ankle deep, she closed her eyes and breathed in gratitude for this magical place, filled with so many emotions. For days and days they had traveled and wished and searched for relief and now it lay here in front of them. The earth must be thanked.

There is life all around me. There is life in me. I feel hope. I feel peace. I feel grateful. I feel life. I feel life. I feel life.

She repeated this mantra in her mind, breathing deeply in and out.

"It's about time." An unfamiliar voice shot out and echoed through the canyon. "Do you have *any* idea how long I've been waiting for you three to get here?" The stranger's voice interrupted the good feeling that surrounded the waterfall.

Fife and Jillian stopped splashing and turned around, looking terrified, as if they'd been caught stealing. But Leena kept her eyes closed for a moment and smiled. When she opened her eyes, she turned and looked in the direction of the voice.

"Mandy. I love what you've done here. It's really beautiful." she said as comfortably, as if seeing an old friend for the first time in years.

Mandy stood at the other end of the pool. She put her hands on her hips. She wore a short gray dress that matched her steel-gray eyes and her red hair matched the color of the hills that surrounded them. She was thinner and taller than Leena. The intensity of her presence matched the intensity of her hair, the color of fire, cut short and straight just below her ears.

"I've been waiting here for you for years. I had to get things going in case you never decided to show up," Mandy said in an accusatory tone. "A few times I thought I'd need to leave and come find *you*. Do you not know that the Destroyers are getting stronger by the day and are roaming the earth more easily than ever before? Because they are. They are coming sooner than you might think." She paused. "I knew I needed to stay…and wait. So I waited."

"We have so many questions," Leena stepped out of the water and walked toward her. "There are things you've learned and done that we want to learn."

Fife cleared his throat and attempted to speak. "I…I…be Fife. This be Jilly…I mean this is Jillian." He cleared his throat again, clearly off his game, and then started to ramble as he made his way out of the water. "I meself am from th'forest. I be livin' there alone since the day it all be destroyed until the day Leena found me." Fife spoke fast. "I think I'm fifteen, maybe sixteen now, not sure…Leena be from the meadow, she's seventeen. And she taught me how to breathe life back into stuff around us and we've been making everything alive again. I mean except animals…well actually, I brought one animal back. A deer. It just sorta happened without me meanin' to. Then we traveled until we found the sea where Jillian lived. Jillian be seventeen…seventeen, right?"

He looked back at Jillian, and she nodded. "She can breathe underwater and live underwater for days at a time. It's a mystery how she done it b'cause I can only hold me breath for five or maybe ten seconds." The three girls stared at him waiting for him to take a breath, but he continued to chatter. Jillian giggled. Fife continued. "We been travelin' for days, maybe a week, I can't really remember because it just seems like we been walkin' forever. It's real hot here where ya live and when we saw th'water—" Then he stopped and took a breath before he interrupted himself with a new thought. "And we saw a big bird! And we ain't seen animals of any kind since we left our baby deer in the forest!" Then he stopped talking, his long wet hair dripping onto his face. "Yeah, that's 'bout it." He brushed his long bangs out of his eyes.

"Thank you, Fife, for the introductions," Leena said smiling.

The corners of Mandy's lips twitched, and Leena knew she was trying hard not to smile, but Fife made that very difficult.

Jillian came out of the water. Her white dress glowing, making her look royal and mysterious. "It's lovely to meet you, Mandy," Jillian said in her soft voice. "We are so grateful to have found you, and we are ready to do whatever it takes to bring the world alive again. We're ready to work together and teach each other what we know."

"Are you? Are you sure?" Mandy looked at all three of them, her eyes narrowed. Leena had the distinct feeling that Mandy questioned their strength. "Well if you're ready, then let's get to work."

Leena did not like her bossy tone—in fact it irritated her. The two of them were complete opposites. Leena wondered how they would work together for a common purpose? How would any of them work with her? Leena rolled her eyes without realizing it.

As they followed Mandy up the path that led to her home, Fife whispered in Leena's ear, "She scares me."

Mandy looked back at him and raised an eyebrow. He raised one eyebrow back and bit the inside of his cheek nervously. "I'm thinkin' she don't like me at all."

"I don't know that she likes any of us," Leena said nervously. "But don't worry, everyone likes you Fife—you have nothing to worry about." Leena reassured him, but she didn't feel any better.

Apprehensively, Leena asked Mandy a question. "How long have you known you're a Life Breather?"

"My whole life," Mandy responded curtly.

"And how long has that been?" Leena pushed for more information.

Mandy did not answer.

"I mean, how old are you?" Leena asked.

Still, Mandy did not respond. Fife and Leena exchanged looks. Leena shrugged. If she had to guess, Mandy seemed older than all of them, but not by much. There would be time to ask her more questions, but for now Leena guessed it best to walk in silence.

They followed Mandy through the winding trail up the canyon for almost an hour. The climb got steeper and more rugged. Loose rocks and dry earth made it slippery and difficult to catch their footing securely. Fife held his hand out to help Jillian over a small edge along a slope. Jillian took his hand, grateful, and they held hands the rest of the way to Mandy's home. Mandy led them to an area heavily shaded by a cliff ledge high above them. A wide cave entrance opened up to a large tidy cave home, complete with a table and chairs made from rock, and soft sleeping areas made from plants and a billowy cotton material.

"Whoa! You did all this?" Fife gasped, looking impressed.

"This is my home," Mandy said "Sit down." She motioned to the red rock chairs. They obeyed.

"I'd like to introduce you to the animals."

A thrill chased up Leena's spine. *The animals.*

16

Animals

"You get to decide how you want to look at any story. Just remember, everyone else gets to decide that, too."

Mandy whistled in a variety of tones, highs, lows, loud, soft, and one by one, different species came out of the inner parts of the cavern. First the red fox appeared, loyally trotting to Mandy's side. The fox sat upright by Mandy's feet. Then, rabbits, squirrels, lizards, birds of all kinds, bats, ringtail cats, opossums, raccoons, and snakes made their way towards them. With each new animal, Leena giggled and had to refrain from running to them, scooping them up and nuzzling her face into their bodies. Oh, how she had missed the animals. Her eyes longingly watched all the furry bodies scurry in.

From outside the canyon came some larger birds, along with larger animals, like big horned sheep and coyotes. Some looked big enough to be wolves.

Though Leena wanted to run to them, Leena, Fife, and Jillian sat astonished and still, eyes wide. Leena's heart beat quickly. The animals gathered around their feet looking up at them, as if the animals knew that Leena, Fife, and Jillian were Life Breathers, here to protect them. Leena trusted the animals instantly. Wild or tame it didn't matter. A respect bonded them all. Life on earth depended upon this open respect. With each addition, Leena's faith in their journey strengthened. They could do anything. Anything was possible.

Jillian sat down on the ground floor and put her hand out to a light-brown bunny. It freely hopped over and into her lap, snuggling in comfortably. Fife's lips broadened into a wide grin, but his excitement quickly turned as a mountain lion strolled past him. He raised his arms as the large cat brushed by his leg.

"Yiyyyyieeeeesh," he said under his breath and gulped in a breath of air, beads of sweat forming on his forehead.

"This is unbelievable," Jillian said breathlessly. "I've never even seen animals that looked like this before."

"We still have many species to bring back, but it's getting harder for me to fight off the Destroyers alone. Each time they come back stronger than before." Mandy's tone was commanding.

"Tell us about the Destroyers," Leena urged as she bent low to touch a squirrel's bushy tail. The squirrel looked into her face with his black glassy eyes. Leena continued to speak. "When Fife brought back a deer in the forest, a few Destroyers came almost immediately. We were not expecting it so we ran and hid. But in the dream, Jillian and I saw you fight them and destroy them. How do you do it?"

"Time and practice. The first time they appeared after I brought back the red tailed hawk, I almost…" Mandy did not finish her sentence. The three stared at her waiting. "I didn't know they'd be coming and I fought for my life. And now, I do what I have to do. I do it because I have a duty to the earth, as we all do." Mandy looked strong like a warrior on the outside, but Leena sensed a fragileness and loneliness hiding deep inside her. Leena could see it in her eyes. Maybe the two of them were not so different.

Mandy turned around and looked out into the canyon from the cavern opening. "I find a way to do it, however I can, because of all that we've lost. All that we lost on that day so long ago." Anger tainted Mandy's voice. Then her voice softened for the first time and she said, "I'm grateful you came." She turned back around facing them. "I'm going to gather food for dinner and tonight we'll eat and rest, because tomorrow" —she paused and gave a strange satisfied smile— "tomorrow we will fight."

Leena, Fife, and Jillian looked up at her simultaneously.

"Did she jus' say *fight?*" Fife asked, looking back and forth at each of them. "Because if she did, I'm in. I'm ready."

Mandy left to gather food, and the red fox followed her out of the cavern. Some of the larger animals left the cave also.

Fife breathed a sigh of relief when the mountain lion sauntered back out.

"Oh boy. That's a big one." He chuckled nervously.

Jillian patted Fife on the back. "You did well, Fife." She smiled at him. His eyes fluttered and he dropped his head back looking like he might melt.

Leena spent the next half hour snuggling and talking to the animals. Nothing shy about these animals. Ringtail cats and rabbits could not get enough of all the attention. She didn't realize just how much she missed animals until they surrounded her. Thoughts of the sheep in the meadow billowed into her mind. Oh how she loved those sheep, especially the lambs. Leena closed her eyes and buried her face into the soft fur of a rabbit, breathing in its scent. For a moment, her six year old self lit up inside her, and Leena longed for her childhood more than ever.

Mandy wasn't gone long and brought back a sack full of food. With each item she brought out of her bag she told them what it was called.

"This is called banana yucca. We're going to roast up the fruit. It's not edible unless it's cooked, but when it's cooked, it's delicious." Next, she pulled out a plant with white berries. "This one is called currant berries. She handed a branch covered in bundles of white berries to each of them. "Here, try it."

"Thank you, Mandy." Jillian graciously accepted the branch.

Fife put a few berries in his mouth and started munching right away.

"Ooooo, these be havin' a bit of a kick to 'em. Sooo good." Fife ate his whole bundle of berries.

After their first meal in the canyon, Fife and Jillian quickly fell asleep on the cotton billowy mats on the floor, exhausted from the heat and the long journey. Leena and Mandy stayed awake talking about what would need to be done in the canyon, before they could move on.

"Will you tell me…about your family?" Leena asked hesitantly.

Mandy's face looked frozen, and she didn't speak.

"I'm sorry. I shouldn't—" Leena looked down, fidgeting with a stick from the currant berry branch. "I lost my family, too. Sadness stayed inside me for years before I remembered my gift of breathing. I understand loneliness and—"

"I'm not lonely," Mandy interrupted. And she looked directly at Leena when she said it.

Leena stayed calm and continued. "Well, I was. Sad and lonely and I didn't want to be alive anymore. I couldn't understand why my family had been extinguished and I stayed alive. I couldn't find any happiness…until I remembered."

There was a pause. Then Mandy looked her straight in the eyes and asked, "Remembered *what?*" putting an extra emphasis on the word 'what' as if she didn't understand.

Leena took a deep breath. "I remembered that purple is my favorite color, and that my little brother used to chase chickens." An ache in Leena's throat gathered, begging her to set the tears free from her eyes, but she refused. She steadied her wavering voice and continued. "I remembered that I love the smell of lavender flowers, and that the last day I saw my mum, she made me apple tartlets for my birthday breakfast." Leena studied Mandy's face as she spoke. Mandy's face stayed still as stone. "And I remembered I am a Life Breather. That I have a gift, and the earth needs me."

Leena wasn't sure exactly why she had opened up this much to an almost stranger. A stranger who clearly didn't want to be friends at all. Leena wanted Mandy to know that she hurt, too. It wasn't just Mandy that hurt inside and buried negative feelings. They were all hurting. Still after all these years, they still mourned the loss of their families, of their childhood. Each of them feared the Destroyers and the black cloud, and each of them needed the others to defeat them. None of them could do it alone.

The air hung heavy in the stillness, with no breeze. They both let the moment sink in and gave silence some time. Mandy's face did not move. Her features were smooth and thin. Her face, lovely and sharp. Her eyes, full of rage.

"I'll tell you what I remember," Mandy said, breaking the quiet moment. "I remember that I couldn't save my sisters." Her voice was flat, dark, and cold. "I remember that they were screaming for me, and I couldn't get to them fast enough. The blackness took all three of them without hesitation." Anger flashed in her eyes. She clenched her fist."I wasn't strong enough. I should have been, and I wasn't. That's what I remember. But I'm strong enough now," she said through gritted teeth. "I will destroy them all. And I will get my sisters back."

"Back?" Leena said looking up. "Do *you* believe they can come back?"

"Of course we can get them back. That's why we're together. That's what all this is for." Her voice sounded tight.

Leena had been afraid to hope too much before. She was even afraid to think the thought. But now she could see clearly. People *were* trapped in the black cloud. She *had* seen people on the day the black cloud came to the sea. Her mind opened. It was possible that her family could be brought back—she could see Aaron again. Plant flowers with Mum. Bake biscuits. Arm wrestle with Dad. All of it. Was she allowed to hope for this unhopeable thing? But it was too late. Hope already swirled inside her. Her mind lost the ability to come back to reality for a moment. Memories of the meadow and her family were so close.

"I want that more than anything else. Thank you for sharing your hope with me. I've been afraid to hope that somewhere my family was still out there, needing me, waiting for me to bring them...back. There have been times when I felt my family, close and needing me, but I was too afraid to give the feeling life, because I didn't think…it was possible…but now…everything seems possible."

"I don't think of it as hope," Mandy said a hardness in her tone. "It is our duty to avenge those we love. It is our duty because of our gift."

They were both silent.

The silence eventually led them to their beds without saying goodnight. Leena lay awake for hours while the others slept. They existed. All these years denying herself hope when all along she could have chosen to believe they still survived. Mandy was right. And how grateful she was for that.

Thoughts of the black cloud twisted her thoughts. She could not help but feel a darkness hovering just outside. She closed her eyes, trying to block out the feeling of being watched.

Her thoughts turned towards fear. Her hand slipped into her pocket and she felt the familiar shape of the jagged amethyst stone. Reaching over to her pack, she dug until she found her doll in the purple dress. For the first time since she breathed life into the tree, Leena cried willingly, without restraint, holding her doll tightly to her chest. Tears upon tears poured from her brown eyes like the waterfall over the cliff edge as she silently grieved her family.

When she was a child, tears meant she had lost control of her emotions, that she was not strong enough to keep them inside and in line. Tears meant she was weak and lacked courage. Nobody told her this or taught her this. Believing this to be true had formed from a thought too young to even recall. It was the story she told herself for no reason at all. She wondered now, as she watched Mandy so full of anger and spite, if crying might help Mandy. That possibly tears being allowed to come unrestrained, could actually be a sign of strength and not weakness. What if tears were a key to healing. What if strength and courage were linked to tears.

There are all types of courage. Quiet courage like Jillian, optimistic courage like Fife, physical courage like Mandy. Leena wondered what kind of courage she possessed. She thought she had courage, even when doubting herself. Leena felt brave at times, but then at times so unsure and hopeless. She could not decide what kind of courage she had or if she possessed courage at all.

Holding her doll in one hand and a softly glowing amethyst in the other, Leena waited patiently, giving her tears permission to come. And then finally, sleep welcomed her.

Leena dreamed of her family that night.

Mum's black hair fell down her back, blending in with her black dress. Her face looked like charcoal had been smeared all over it. The smile Leena knew so well remained lifeless. Her features were blank and covered tightly with a black web. She had no visible mouth. Wandering in darkness, Mum walked in a trance. Marching slowly, compliantly following something that Leena could not see.

Aaron's small body looked different, no longer chubby, with his skinny legs following slowly behind Mum. He did not breathe. Dad followed close behind Aaron. Dad looked tired and old. Leena hardly recognized him. He looked as though his mind had struggled mightily before he gave in to the darkness. Others, similarly dressed with black webbed faces, wandered in the darkness. No one breathed.

Leena looked around. A dark fog surrounded her, like an enormous cloud. The vast space inside the cloud held thousands of wandering people, not breathing, just existing mindlessly. Leena ran to them and shouted at her family to breathe, begging them to wake up. Suddenly, she grabbed her throat. Leena's lungs could not hold air. An unseen hand wrapped around her neck, squeezing tightly. Her nose and mouth were clogged. She could not breathe in. Terrified, she looked around for someone to help her. Looking down at her feet she saw that her toes had turned black and the charcoal color crept up her legs. Wanting, needing a breath that she could not find, her mind desperately raced as her life slipped into darkness. Leena felt life being strangled out of her and then a last gasp of hope, a simple thought came in her despair.

I am a Life Breather.

With all the focus she had inside her, she forced herself to imagine something else. There is life all around me, there is life in me, I am hope, I am peace. Her mind continued to recall her mantra. There is life all around me. I am not alone.

As she recalled her breath, her mind went into action. A breath of fresh air swooped into her lungs. Color came back in her toes and the color spread out around her onto the other people passing by. Aaron's bare feet turned a pink shade that stretched up his skinny baby legs and finally reached his face. He turned and looked at his sister. Then he reached out to her and said clearly, "Help me breathe."

Leena's eyes flew open, and she lay trembling at what she'd seen, gasping for air.

In the darkness, Leena noticed Jillian's eyes open, too, looking deeply troubled.

"Are you alright?" Leena whispered.

Even in the shadows with only the light of the moon shining through the cave opening, Leena could see the cold sweat on Jillian's pale face. Jillian struggled to speak. "Do you feel the darkness? It's close. I feel it sometimes like it's watching us." Jillian squeezed her eyes shut. "I can't breathe. My stomach—" She rolled onto her side in pain. Jillian had one hand on her stomach and one hand holding her head. "Everything is spinning, my mind, my heart, everything inside…my head hurts so badly."

"I'm here. It's okay. I promise it will pass and you will be alright. Relax into it. Don't tense up against it. Welcome the feeling and sit with it. I promise you will be alright. I promise," Leena soothed, comforting Jillian and simultaneously glancing out the cave entrance. With the dream still fresh in her mind, the black cloud lingered in her thoughts. She could only see the light of the moon outside the cave, but her mind shuddered with the evil that still felt so near. Jillian must have sensed the dream.

"Take a slow breath in through your nose, then let it out through your nose. Slow and easy. Breathe in and out." Leena's voice stayed low and calm. "Imagine you are safe in your water. You are safe here with me. Say in your mind, there is peace in me. There is peace all around me. I am peace. I am peace. I am peace."

Jillian's body gradually calmed, and her hands stopped shaking. It had passed. Just like Leena promised. Leena held on to Jillian's hand.

"You are like a sister to me," Jillian whispered.

"Same." Leena smiled softly and closed her eyes.

17

Hematite

*"A butterfly is a beautiful creature. It was not always beautiful though, it used to be a squishy, wiggly, slow, creature called a caterpillar.
The struggle to form its wings is what creates the butterfly's beauty."*

In the morning, the birds were the first to awaken, singing as the sun filtered into the cave. Mandy's words from the night before rang in Leena's ears. *Tomorrow, we will fight.* Adrenaline pulsed through Leena's body, waking up her senses.

"So today's th'day," Fife said, his voice tinged with excitement and a little apprehension. "We face the Destroyers and see what we be dealin' with." Fife looked like a man for the first time. Leena had always seen him as a boy, but he seemed older somehow, ready to defend those he loved and fight.

Fife looked at Jillian and concern flashed in his eyes.. Dried tears streaked a small amount of dust across her cheek.

"Are ye alrigh', Jilly?" he asked. "Let's get ya somethin' to eat."

Mandy appeared in the cave entrance with her arms full of

banana yucca and white berries, a few animals following close behind her, including the red fox.

"I brought breakfast. We'll need our strength today. We have a lot to do."

Fife gently wiped the dirt smudge off of Jillian's cheek then helped Mandy with the food. They cut and cooked up the fruits. It tasted even better than the night before. Mandy appeared to be warming up to Fife and his chatter. She even smiled when he cut the plants into star, moon, and sun shapes.

As they ate, Leena said, "I think we should start the morning together breathing, to focus our minds. Let's find a good spot after we eat and do some breathing together." Leena glanced up at Mandy. "Mandy, do you have a favorite spot in your canyon that you like?"

"There are some things I need to show you before we do that. But yes, we will do our breathing. And yes, I have a spot." Mandy did not look up, leaving Leena confused and wondering if somehow Mandy felt threatened by her. It was not Leena's intention to take any sort of leadership over the group, but she sensed that Mandy wanted that position.

After breakfast they followed Mandy to an upper cave a short hike away with views of the dry earth below. They were getting closer to the top of the ridge. When they reached the upper cave, Mandy went in first. The small entrance only allowed one to go through at a time, unlike the wide opening of Mandy's home. Leena followed, then Jillian, and finally Fife. It got darker as they continued to walk down a long corridor. Mandy picked up a stick, leaning against a cave wall, and after a few deep breaths a fire lit up the tip of the torch, illuminating the entire cave. Along the walls of the cave glittered silvery black stones. Drawings covered the cave walls like murals.

"Whoa. This!" Fife said, looking keenly around the walls.

"Don't touch the walls," Mandy warned him. Fife put his outstretched hand back in his pocket, like a child.

They examined the pictures on the walls depicting generations of families. Each family that had lived in the canyons for thousands of years back were represented, set up like triangles, with a man and a woman on the top and under them, their children, followed by their grandchildren.

Mandy pointed to her family, a straight line with no parents. They recognized her image easily because of her short, red flaming hair. Standing in her family line were three other girls. Mandy, at the head of the line, looked taller, drawn in a white dress, the others in brown tones with shades of black hair.

"These are my sisters. This is Carissa." She pointed to the drawing next to hers. Carissa, slightly shorter than Mandy, looked completely different than her. Carissa's long hair was straight and black. "And this is Bethany, and this is Bree. They're twins." The twins were colored reddish brown with tightly curled black hair. Leena wondered why they looked so different from Mandy, but she did not ask.

The three of them watched and listened. "My sisters and I are all very close in age. Do you see this up here?" Mandy pointed to a place none of them had looked at yet on the far side—the markings showed it was thousands of years back. A mass of swirling black strokes. Dark figures inside the clouds.

The three of them walked over and looked at the wall closely.

"What does this mean?" Leena asked in astonishment, her brows furrowed.

"It means that this has happened before," Mandy said. "The black cloud, the Destroyers, it's all happened before, thousands of years ago. These figures here" —she pointed to figures drawn in white— "these are Life Breathers from the past. They battled the same thing we are facing now." Mandy glanced at each of them as if measuring their expressions. "Their world was destroyed and they had to rebuild it. But the black cloud continues to come back into the drawings every five hundred years or so." She pointed along the corridor at multiple black drawings. "Destroying all life and taking all the breath of the land. The Life Breathers never figured out how to get rid of them for good." She paused, then said, "That is *our* job."

Fife raised his eyebrows and nodded his head in agreement.

"We're gonna figure out a way." He crossed his arms and continued nodding as he thought. Leena loved that he looked for solutions to problems without giving up, even when the task seemed hugely overwhelming.

"It's like the stories my grandmother told me. It's all here on the walls like a picture book," Jillian said wistfully. "But I don't remember her telling stories about them coming to earth before."

Leena thought through her Mum's stories and tried to recall any stories about the Destroyers coming and the Life Breathers rebuilding the earth in the past. She couldn't recall, though it made sense.

But what could they do differently? What did they have that the other Life Breathers did not? Doubt in her own strength crept in slowly through the slightly open doorway in her mind. She shook her head. Pushed the doubt out and closed the mental door.

The four of them searched across the walls of the cave, looking at all the life that had existed over time. It really was miraculous. All the generations of humans and Life Breathers that had lived in the canyon since the beginning of time. All of the drawings of the humans were in various color tones and the Life Breathers started coming into the drawings about two thousand years ago. The Life Breathers were represented in all skin tones and always drawn in white clothing.

After some quiet time, Leena asked the question that no one else was brave enough to ask Mandy. "Why don't you have your parents drawn on your cave picture?"

"I've never had parents," she said simply. "My sisters and I were orphans. Parentless. Eventually, we were raised by a woman here, Naomi." She pointed to a figure in a white gown a few generations before her own figure on the cave wall. "Naomi was very old. She, too, was a Life Breather. I don't remember anything before she found us, but she told me she saw me breathing on desert flowers and they bloomed instantly. She recognized the gift in me and made the decision to teach me everything she knew about life breathing. When she found us, she treated us like we were her own daughters. She did not have a family of her own still alive. Naomi is the only mother I've ever known. She died when I was nine, three years before the day of destruction. I took care of my sisters after that. But I couldn't save them from the black cloud."

Nobody knew what to say, and there was a long silence.

"Tell us about these stones," Leena said, pointing to the silvery black rocks glittering along the walls.

"This is hematite." Mandy pulled out a few stones from her pocket.

"Hema-who?" Fife raised his eyebrows. The stones in the walls were jagged but the ones in her hand were smooth.

Mandy ignored Fife and continued. "These rocks I've shaped and tumbled so they're polished. Hematite is the stone used to paint these drawings. No matter what color the hematite is, it always streaks red. That's why it's called the bloodstone or the warrior stone. Other things are mixed into the drawing to create the other shades of color on the drawings. Things like charcoal, animal fat, and even spit. But to make the white, the hematite has to be heated and formed into a powder and then mixed with minerals from the desert plants." She handed each of them a polished rock. "It's very strong on the outside, but it's delicate and more fragile on the inside, which is why it's good for cave wall drawings."

Fife turned the smooth stones around in his palms.

"Hematite," Fife whispered. The stone relaxed him. Jillian rubbed her thumb across the stone again and again.

Leena examined the hematite closely.

"We each have a gemstone from our home. A precious rock that represents our part of the earth." Leena paused thoughtfully. There must be a higher purpose to the stones. Each of them had one. But why? "Mine is a purple gemstone called amethyst, and Fife's is light-blue called amazonite. Jillian's is a pearl. Each of the stones were protected on the day of destruction."

Mandy looked at her curiously.

"Let's go to the highest point of the canyon, and we'll ask the earth what we should do next." Mandy suggested.

One by one they exited the cave. They climbed up and around the winding path. Nothing about the path looked dangerous, but they were very high up. A few times Jillian looked nervously at her feet and took a few steadying breaths. Fife touched her shoulder every once in a while to reassure her.

When they reached the highest plateau, Mandy motioned them to come over.

"Come and sit. Get comfortable and relax." Mandy had a couple of the billowy cotton mats like the beds in her cave, but smaller.

Mandy knelt down, her knees on a mat, sitting on top of her heels that were tucked beneath her, and she put her palms together in front of her chest, fingers pointing up. Leena sat crossed-legged and rested the back of her hands on her knees, so her palms faced the sky. Fife found a flat rock close by and sat with his back straight aligning his head, neck and back and rested his hands palms down, grounding him to the earth. Jillian layed down with her head resting on a cotton mat and her hands relaxed over her heart.

Close your eyes. Feel your breath inside you, flowing naturally through every part of your body. Breathe in smoothly to bring your mind home to your body, uniting your body to your spirit. Feel them become one through your breath. Breathe in deeply through your nose, then exhale through your nose. Let go of any anxious thoughts. The only place for you to be right now is here. In stillness. As you breathe in, say in your mind, I am one with the earth. As you breathe out, soften your body, let go of fear. Let go of the unknown. Focus your mind on the world around you. I am one with the earth. See in your mind and feel in your heart what the earth needs. What does the earth need me to do?

The four of them continued breathing in silence. Only the sound of breath could be heard. The soothing sound of rhythmic breathing. A clear picture formed in Leena's mind, something impressive. Millions of orange and black winged butterflies flying through the desert in a massive kaleidoscope of beauty. The swarm gathered in a large desert oak tree. The tree went from green and brown to covered in orange and black fluttering wings. Every inch of the branches and trunk on the huge tree were now holding these small, majestic creatures. As Leena continued to watch the vision in her mind, the sun warmed the butterflies wings and then she heard the rarest sound, the most magical sound she had ever heard, like a softly cascading waterfall. Not the roaring of the big waterfall in the riddle, but a light delicate waterfall. The sound of the butterflies, one by one, descended from the tree. It was visually and emotionally stunning, a great fluttering of wings sweeping through air.

"Do ye hear that?" Fife asked, keeping his eyes closed. "It be a quiet waterfall or somethin'?" He kept his eyes shut.

"The butterflies are coming," Leena answered breathlessly, her heart beating quickly in her chest. She felt as though her whole body might lift off of the ground in flight, like she might become a butterfly. The swarm flew closer and Leena could feel the breath of millions of butterflies flying through the air.

Mandy opened her eyes and stood up, then Jillian, then Fife, and then Leena. Simultaneously they looked in the direction of the magical sound of millions of delicate wings flapping. Leena's breath caught in her throat when she saw them.

The butterflies swooped in and around them, swirling and flitting on their shoulders as they said hello and continued to fly through the canyon. Jillian raised her arms and twirled as the orange butterflies flew around her body. Leena's stomach felt like it flipped inside out as if the butterflies were inside her, flying and breathing. The rush of beauty and wind lasted a few minutes as the butterflies all came back to life and passed through the canyon.

After the butterflies passed through them, the four looked at each other. Jillian had tears welling up in her eyes. "I've never seen an animal like that before," she said in her light airy voice.

"I haven't seen butterflies come through here since I was a child," Mandy said, looking reminiscent. Then a quick change in tone she said, "We have about one minute before they come. Get ready." At Mandy's words, a chill rushed up Leena's spine.

The emotions from elation to apprehension switched quickly. Fife stood by Jillian's side and laced his fingers with hers. She looked up at him, and he squeezed her hand. "It'll be alrigh'." He promised her with a quick nod of his head. Jillian swallowed hard.

They were coming.

18

More Butterflies

"Never forget, hope is close by whenever you need it.
It's only a thought away, staring you in the face, waiting to be seen."

Within minutes, they heard the distant beating on the earth and could see a dozen thin, bony black figures coming towards them, long sticks in their hands, in unison pounding them on the earth. The horribly familiar pounding of the sticks vibrated inside Leena's body. Her heart tightened with fear, and for a moment, her mind slipped back to ten years ago, and she was tucked quietly between two bales of hay, small, innocent and afraid. Thump thump boom! The darkness of the Destroyers brought a hushed evil that crept towards the four with each dark step.

The fear wrapped around Leena's chest and spiraled through her insides as the Destroyers got closer. Her heart beat furiously with terror. Sweat dripped down her back. Her stomach in knots. Where was her courage? Find it! Find it! She begged herself silently. Her fists tightened.

Jillian dropped Fife's hand and put her hands over her stomach, the color fading from her face. "Not now!" she whispered. Taking a heavy breath in through her nose she held it for five seconds, then released the breath and held again for five. Inhale five seconds. Hold five seconds. Exhale five seconds. Hold five seconds. Reaching up she touched her pearl necklace. The pearls glowed in response.

The sun emerged through the clouds in the sky. Jillian's white dress glowed brilliantly. Her long blonde hair blew in the wind and looked like gold as it caught the sunlight. Fife looked over at her in complete awe, his mouth and eyes wide. The earth gave her the stability she needed. Her quiet courage rising to the challenge.

Mandy held tightly onto the hematite stones. "Come and try," she said through clenched teeth. The Destroyers continued marching, sticks slamming the ground in angry thuds. Mandy's eyes, focused with intensity. Courage poured from every muscle in her body.

Fife's eyes stayed fixed on Jillian a few more moments and then turned to the Destroyers that were getting closer. Leena couldn't be sure but he seemed to smile vaguely as they marched closer. He looked...almost excited.

Leena relaxed her clenched fists. *I am a Life Breather. I am a Life Breather.*

As the Destroyers approached in steady rhythm up over the ridge to the plateau, Mandy inhaled a breath. Taking her lead, Fife did the same, and they both held their breath. Seconds later, Mandy and Fife's minds seemed to synchronize, and they released their powerful breaths at the same time. Combining like a tornado, a whirlwind blew fiercely straight at the Destroyers, thrashing the tall, black figures, causing their sticks to fly out of their grasp and smash to pieces on the side of the canyon. The Destroyers whipped around in the gust of wind and were tossed harshly to the ground. The sinister beings rose up and continued marching toward them again, steadily.

Looking at them more closely, Leena could see that they were hairless and faceless. Tight black webbing stretched over their thin faces. They draped themselves in translucent netting that covered their hunched bodies. The Destroyers reached out their arms, sending pangs of suffocation shooting through the four Life Breathers, like small pulses of lost air. Leena's body shuddered and twitched in response. *No.* She reinforced in her mind. *No.*

Leena readied herself and continued her steady breathing, fighting through the pangs of suffocation by using her breath, but as they got closer, she could feel the darkness approaching, and it became more torturous to breathe.

But through the pain, they persevered. They kept going. They would not give up.

I am a Life Breather. I am a Life Breather. "We are Life Breathers!" Leena yelled out. "You will not touch us!" Courage erupted through her as she yelled out to the approaching Destroyers and in that moment, she no longer feared them.

At the same time, all four of them rushed towards the looming black creatures, and Mandy held out the hematite stones, pointing the stones at the Destroyers. The pearls from Jillian's necklace glowed, and out of each pearl shot white streams of light that caught hold of the hematite and together made an immense crashing sound. The streams of light combined together and formed a single beam that looked like a braided rope. The Destroyers howled and gasped for breath, but the beams of light held them tight.

One of the Destroyers freed an arm from the light and reached out towards Fife. Fife fell to the red earth, clutching his throat, wheezing for air. Leena quickly dropped to his side and took his face in her hands.

"Fife! Fife! Take a breath! Breathe in!"

Fife continued to gasp for air. Leena could feel his throat burning inside him and his throat turned a charcoal black. Leena placed her hands on his neck. His eyes were desperate, his mouth open, begging for breath. Wish flowers came to Leena's mind. Every part of her mind channeled on giving him breath. Leena breathed a focused stream of air directly into his open mouth, with so much specific direction that each air particle landed exactly where it needed to inside his body.

"I will not lose you! You will breathe! You are a Life Breather,

Fife!" Leena yelled at him. Hearing Leena, Jillian whipped around and the pearls no longer faced the Destroyers, breaking the strands of light that tied them together.

"No Jillian!" Leena called to her. "You must stay focused!" Jillian's desperate eyes matched Fife's. Reluctantly she forced herself to turn back to the Destroyers who fought to free themselves of the remaining bands of light.

Jillian's pearls once again connected to the light of the hematite stones, binding the black terrors and strangling them tighter and tighter.

Leena's breath streamed into Fife's mouth and down his throat. His blackened neck returned to flesh color and life returned to his body. He sputtered a raw thank you, forcing himself to stand. The four Life Breathers stood in front of the hideous black figures. Their bony black bodies thrashed violently on the ground as they could not get breath to sustain themselves being strangled by the light of the stones. Until finally, after one last strangled scream, they fell to their ruin. The Destroyers shriveled to a pile of black ash at the Life Breather's feet.

Exhausted, terrified, exhilarated, and relieved all at the same time, the four fell to the ground, sweat pouring down their faces, their energy completely consumed.

"That was the most amazin' thing" —Fife paused to catch his breath— "we've ever done. We can do anythin'." His laugh mixed with triumphant tears. "Course I 'bout died." He rubbed his throat that still ached. He hugged Jillian and Leena, pulling them both close. They sat hugging and laughing through tears, taking in everything they just experienced.

"We did it," Mandy said quietly as she closed her eyes and put her head on her knees.

That night around a fire lit inside Mandy's cave, Leena opened the book of riddles.

"What is that?" Mandy asked, holding out her hand.

"Riddles of Time Secrets of Stone." Leena handed it to her. "The riddles in it have been guiding us to our next destination. Only we don't know where we're going next."

"Well, we better figure that out. We'll need to leave the canyon first thing in the morning." Mandy said flatly. As Mandy held the leather book, she carefully glided through its pages. "There are hundreds of riddles in here. How do you know which one you're supposed to answer?" Mandy asked curiously without looking up. Before anyone had the chance to respond, she stopped on a page about halfway through. "Oh. I see." Mandy read aloud the riddle the book guided her to:

"Where a goat can live higher than a bird. Where you can climb, but not on branches. Where roots remain but do not grow. Where tiny white stars fall from the sky. You will find him. Where am I?" Mandy looked up. "Any ideas here?"

"All them clues 'bout roots and branches, I'm hopin' we're headed to another forest." Fife chuckled.

"It says *not* branches. Roots that *don't* grow." Mandy looked exasperated.

"Don't be spikey," Fife said back at her. "I'm only hopin'. I can hope, can't I?"

Mandy did not respond to him but appeared deep in thought.

"Well—" Leena started…

"Them white tiny stars could be snowflakes." Then, realizing he'd cut Leena off, he apologized quickly. "Oop sorry, Leena, you were sayin'?"

"No it's fine, I was just thinking about the roots, what other things have roots besides trees and plants?" As she asked that her, Dad flashed through her mind. Her Dad. What connection did he have to this riddle? Why had she thought of him? Mountain goats. Dad was always talking about those goats that walk on the sides of the mountains. "Snowflakes, yes Fife. I think you're right." Then slowly, thoughtfully, carefully she said, "I think we're supposed to go to the mountains."

"You will find *him*." Jillian repeated part of the riddle. "That would make sense. Mountain goats are as high up as birds, you can climb a mountain, the roots of a mountain lay under the ground, and snow."

"Roots? Under th'mountain?" Fife raised both eyebrows. "I had no idea. I never seen a mountain or seen a mountain's roots. I got s'much t'learn."

Their chatter around the riddle and the mountain faded into stories they remembered from childhood.

Leena told them about the time her dad set up a picnic in the meadow for Leena and Mum just before Aaron was born. They made a table out of a flat rock and had little, flat rock chairs. Leena remembered it being the finest meal, bread and jam with bundles of grapes. And that reminded her of the last lunch they spent with Dad in their little home before he left for market.

Jillian told them about her grandmother's collection of seashells and showed them the few shells she had brought with her, passing them around.

"We used to spend hours searching and digging on the seashore to find the most beautiful shells with the best shine on the insides."

It was Fife's turn to share. He let out a big sad sigh. "I be wishin' I still had me sticks." Mandy looked at him sideways. "Then ye could all meet me family." He looked down in his empty hands like he half expected his precious bundle to still be there.

"What am I missing here?" Mandy asked.

Jillian reached into her pocket and pulled out seven small currant berry sticks wrapped in a desert oak leaf.

"I know it can never replace your family...but..." Jillian looked shy and unsure. Everything stood still. Time, talk, breath, thoughts. All still.

Fife stared at the bundle in Jillian's hand.

"Ye did this for me?" Fife's voice barely escaped his mouth. He looked at Jillian with so much unbridled passion Leena thought he might kiss her on the mouth right in front of them all. But he didn't. He just gazed at her. Holding the sticks out to him, she still looked hesitant.

"I can't believe ye did this?" Fife tenderly took the bundle of currant berry twigs wrapped in a leaf into his hands and closed his fist around them. He cleared his throat and spoke.

"Introductions." He cleared his throat again for dramatic effect. The girls smiled, even Mandy.

"I'd love for ya t'meet me family. Here's my mama." He carefully unwrapped the sticks and held up a tall slender stick. Then he held out the other six sticks that varied in size. "This here is me brother Cliff and here is Jack, Paul, and Ron. These two lil' sticks are me sisters, Lil and Rose." He smiled broadly as he held up each one.

"I love them, Fife. They are part of you," Jillian said as she looped her arm through his and leaned her head on him, pressing her cheek into the skin of his bare arm.

Fife smiled, and even in the darkness his face turned noticeably pink.

"Thank ya, Jillian. I mean it. This means th' world t'me."

Leena told them about her dream inside the black cloud and seeing her family trapped within it. She described their webbed faces and blank expressions and how they moved slowly without breathing. Fife, Jillian, and Mandy all listened attentively, their eyes fixed on Leena as she spoke. Their faces lit up as she told them about her baby brother and color returning to his small body.

"Our hope is that once we find the last Life Breather, we will be able to restore *all* life to the world." Leena looked at Fife. "*All Life*. We will meet your family, Fife. We will do everything we can to save them."

"Sometimes I feel my sisters are so close." Mandy had not shared feelings about her family before. The others looked up in surprise. "I know they are still out there…somewhere…waiting. When the time is right, we'll bring them back. I need my sisters…" She wiped her eyes before a tear could fall, her gaze darting to Leena before she continued. Her gray eyes were filled with anger. "It was my fault. I couldn't save them. I'll never forgive myself until I can bring them back." She covered her face with her arms and buried them into her knees, letting out a sob. Her body trembled as she cried. "I miss them so much. I'm so tired of being alone."

It was the first time any of them had seen Mandy show tender emotion. The significance of this moment was not lost on Leena. This meant Mandy trusted her new friends. This meant Mandy was finally starting to heal.

"We will find them, Mandy. Together," Jillian said as she put her arm around her. "And you're not alone anymore."

Leena reached into her bag and pulled out the gray scarf they had brought from the village market. "This is for you. From my mum." The scarf matched Mandy's eyes and her dress. Draping it around Mandy's neck, Leena said, "It looks good on you, and will keep you warm as we travel to the mountains tomorrow."

Mandy smiled uncomfortably, wiped her eyes again, looking embarrassed that she'd shared so much of herself. "Thank you for the scarf. I do like the color."

They fell asleep that night wrapped together in blankets and scarves around the crackling fire, like a family would. Tomorrow they would begin their journey to the mountain. Excitement and apprehension moved through Leena as she thought about the last Life Breather. The thrill of going to the mountains breathed inside her. She longed to feel the closeness to her dad by going to the place he called home.

Just after Leena had drifted off to sleep, she heard Fife and Jillian whispering to each other, and it startled her awake. Leena peeked an eye open and she saw them as they quietly tiptoed out of the cave, the evening crickets singing by the light of the moon.

A strange feeling came over Leena. Curiosity yes, but something more. An uneasy fear that tipped her senses, making her not trust the darkness unless they were all together. She hadn't trusted the darkness ever since that first night, lying awake with the eerie feeling of being watched, like something dark waited, watching and studying them as they slept.

What did Fife and Jillian think they were doing? Wandering out in the night just the two of them? It didn't seem like a very good idea to Leena. Leena rolled her eyes.

Curiosity, mingled with a protective urge, pushed her out of the cave after them and she silently followed behind them, unnoticed. Fife held Jillian's hand as they walked all the way down to the waterfall. A few raccoons followed close behind them. When they got to the waterfall they sat down side-by-side and put their toes into the water, hands still clasped together. Leena stayed far enough behind to remain unseen. She tucked herself behind a bush and became invisible.

"I uhhhh…be wantin' to tell ya somethin', Jilly." Fife spoke slowly and carefully. He turned and looked into Jillian's round face. Their knees touched, and her foot wiggled next to his under the water.

Leena looked away, now so uncomfortable she genuinely wished she had not followed them.

"What is it?" Jillian said, looking divine with her long hair cradling her face and cascading like a waterfall down her back.

"Well, I think ye are the most lovely person I ever been 'round," Fife began.

"You haven't actually been around that many people, Fife." Jillian teased.

He let out a laugh but then looked at her with serious eyes. "True, yeah, that's true." He waited a few moments and took a deep breath. "But I know love. And I am in love with you."

They both giggled like children, with their fingers still intertwined and their toes snuggling under the water. Leena fully realized she should not be spying on them. She had no intention of intruding on their love story. But what was she supposed to do? She couldn't just let them go off by themselves without anyone knowing. She rolled her eyes again and resisted sighing.

"You are of course beau'iful, but I be thinkin' you are so much more than that." He gazed at her. "You are kind, and smart, and ye mus' be a little crazy b'cause you seem to not notice that I'm tall and awkward and not at all what ye deserve. But seein' as that I may be the only boy left on the earth…do you think I might have a chance?"

There was a pause. The warm air was still. Jillian spoke.

"I am in love with you, Fife." Her voice sounded like a bell ringing in the warm night air—like a lullaby. Fife closed his eyes and smiled.

With his hand that was not holding hers, he touched her blonde hair delicately. "You are me favorite girl in the world. I love Leena like a sister, and Mandy, well Mandy still scares me a bit, but I s'pose she's like a sister, too, but you…you are not like a sister t'me. You are someone I want to hold and look at and talk with and tell all my secrets to."

"You have secrets?" she asked playfully, trying not to giggle.

"No, no, not real secrets, just you know… me inner thoughts and fears and the stuff it's hard to tell ev'rybody, I want to tell you all of it. I wanna tell you everythin'."

"I understand exactly what you mean," Jillian said softly. "I feel like the butterflies we brought back to life are inside me, everytime I'm with you."

"Yes butterflies," he said, his face so close to hers now he could feel her warm breath on his cheek. She closed her eyes and leaned closer. Closer and closer until their lips were touching. Their mouths connected in a kiss. A simple and soft kiss.

"Your lips…are the sweetest thing…I've ever had on mine," Fife said, gazing into her eyes, the shades of their blue eyes connecting them. Jillian smiled and her dimple showed. Fife touched it with his thumb. "You are adorable."

Leena drifted off to sleep behind the bush. When she awoke, still in darkness, the birds were singing, giving the signal of a new day. She could still hear Fife and Jillian talking and laughing by the waterfall.

As quietly as she could, she ran up the trail and back to the cavern. By now, dawn had arrived, and she found Mandy awake bustling around, getting things packed and organized. She seemed focused and on edge.

Mandy refused to make eye contact. Grabbing a bristle broom,

Mandy brushed the floor and swept everything into a tidy pile. She gathered the banana yucca and many bundles of white berries and collected them, forcefully stuffing them into her already full pack.

"Let me help," Leena offered. No answer.

So Leena rolled up the cotton bedrolls and placed them neatly in the corner of the cavern.

Fife and Jillian had still not returned.

"Where are those two?" Mandy demanded, erupting from her silence. "Don't they understand we have the most important thing in the history of the world to do right now? They are being selfish, you know?"

"They are in love," Leena said simply.

Mandy turned and looked at Leena for the first time. "In love?" she asked half disgusted and half amused. "How in the world do they have time to think about love right now? That's ridiculous."

Just then Fife and Jillian came giggling through the cavern opening, completely consumed in their own world, and suddenly their love became glaringly obvious.

"Oh, hey, love birds," Mandy said in a raised voice. "Did you know we are leaving today for the mountains? To find the last Life Breather that lives there? And then to fight against all the Destroyers and bring our families back into existence?" Mandy yelled. Clearly, she had reached her breaking point to whatever inner struggle she wrestled with.

Jillian looked startled and Fife looked genuinely afraid.

"Uhhhh yeah...we were just...ummmm...talkin'...out by th'waterfa—"

Leena interrupted Fife's explanation, patting his shoulder. "Fife, it's fine. Everything is fine."

"Well, I don't think it *is* fine!" Mandy said angrily, and dropping her broom, she walked out.

Fife tightened his lips and closed his eyes. He drooped into a sullen position on the floor and covered his face.

"This be awful. Th'guilt. Now she's terribly ticked off and I dunno how to make it right." Fife shook his head, distraught by how he had affected Mandy and the emotions she might be feeling about leaving her home today.

"She'll be alright, Fife. We know she tucks all her feelings deep inside, and when they explode out of her, it's usually aimed at someone or something that isn't really the cause of her pain." Leena sat down by him and put an arm around him. "But you're sweet to care. Let's get the rest of the things packed up. She'll come back when she's ready.

They filled the water jugs and packed their clothes and supplies into their bags. Jillian and Fife finished sweeping up the pile of dust and debris that Mandy had walked out on. They wiped down the rock table and chairs and washed up the cooking utensils. Mandy returned within the hour and offered a stiff apology to Fife and Jillian.

"Let's get out of here, before I change my mind," Mandy murmured.

19

Despair

"A rock. It's a simple thing. Or is it?"

The fox whined at Mandy's side begging to follow her. Kneeling down she patted his head. He snuggled his face into her side.

"I'll be back," she told him and kissed his furry red head. He whimpered as she stood up. She held her hand out motioning to stop. "I'll be back," she repeated. The fox obediently sat back. And with that, they left Mandy's cavern home, clean and tidy with beds layed out waiting for her sisters when Mandy returned.

In her bag, Mandy had a pouch full of smooth hematite stones and another sack full of a fresh and enticing smelling plant.

"Hey wha' is that smell?" Fife asked, looking at Mandy's sack.

"This is a plant that Naomi used as a medicine and healing oil."

"I'm likin' this Naomi gal. And I like that smell." Fife hoisted his pack over his shoulder and put his tan cap on his head.

Leena looked over at him. Fife reminded her of her dad just then, always putting on his cap just before he'd leave on his journey. Suddenly the reality of what they were about to do drizzled over her like a thick, heavy syrup. They were going to bring her dad back. Or at least try. So much time had passed. Her heart ached painfully as she thought about him wandering somewhere in a cloud with no air to breathe. The torture endured by so many. Gloom sidled up to her. The inevitable doubt that continued to push into Leena's mind, slipped through the ajar mental door. With the near sleepless night, she did not have the strength to close the door before the doubts slid in through the crack.

Within a short time, sadness spread through Leena's body as she walked up the path to the plateau. Thoughts about her family, and how long it had been since the day she had seen them, brought darkness along with them. She missed them intensely. She longed for them. But she realized she had spent so much of her life without them, and she wondered if she would even recognize them—or if they would recognize her—when they were reunited. *If* they were reunited. Guilt and shame escorted more sad thoughts that continued to play through her. By the time someone spoke, Leena's mind was far away.

"Leena, Leena!" Mandy said multiple times trying to get her attention. Leena looked at her, confused without smiling, and didn't answer. Mandy asked her again, "Do you want me to lead the way? I've been to the mountains before, I know the direction to go..." Mandy looked at her strangely tilting her head. "What's wrong with you?"

"I'm fine," Leena said blankly, but she wasn't feeling fine at all. She had no idea how to explain the sadness creeping over her, and she had no desire to explain it to them.

"Whatever you say," Mandy said callously. "It's about a four day walk, and the weather will change quite a bit as we move north, so say goodbye to the sun. It's about to get really cold. Have you ever seen snow, Jillian?"

"No, I haven't. I've heard of it, but I've never seen it."

Then Fife's chatter began and the telling of stories about the snow, the Founding Forest Feast that happened every winter, and the great snow beast story that his papa would tell them. His words melted together, and Leena tuned him out, not hearing any of it.

She was lost in a dark world, thinking about her family, and how sad they must be. With no desire to pull herself out of her sadness, she mourned them all over again.

The heat followed them as they made their way out of the red rock canyon hills. They camped in a flat desert spot surrounded by desert shrubs. Around the fire that night they heard animal sounds. Howling coyotes and a few frogs singing in the distance. It was different from the quiet of the forest or the soothing waves on the seashore. Mandy's cave had kept out most of the night sounds, but the call of the wild animals filled the open air now.

Leena stayed silent. The others glanced at Leena every now and then, noticing her mood change, but nobody mentioned it. She found her spot by the fire and stared at it emotionlessly. Emptiness. A hole. Disconnected from her body. Darkness. Was she even really here? Leena could no longer feel. Numbness. No more aching. No more hope. No life inside her.

Fife continued to tell stories about the forest. Jillian faced him, her wide eyes glued to his. He kissed her forehead before she went to the other side of the firepit, snuggled up in her blanket, and fell asleep. Fife stayed awake watching the fire, poking at it with a stick. When Jillian and Mandy were asleep, Fife looked at Leena, the fire reflecting in his eyes.

"What are ya thinkin' about?" he asked in a hushed voice.

Leena didn't respond. She had not felt like this since she lived in the meadow before she found her breath again, and the sadness had come on suddenly. She could not explain it.

"Leena," he whispered. "It's me. You can talk t'me."

"I'm tired that's all." She did not look at him. She did not want to explain anything to him. An irritation fidgeted in her body.

"I noticed ya didn't eat any dinner." He got up and sat next to her.

Her face felt like stone. She couldn't pinpoint the reason, but it felt looming and dreadful inside her.

"What can I do for ya? I wanna help. You've helped us all so much. I just wanna help, that's all." He looked concerned.

Leena looked at him and answered softly. "I know, Fife. I'm not sure what's happening. I feel sad and alone—"

Fife interrupted, "You're not alone..you've got us."

"I know, Fife. I know." Leena paused as she gathered her thoughts. She trusted Fife with everything in her. If she was honest with herself, she knew things would always be a little different now that Fife loved Jillian in that special way that Leena's dad loved her mum. Leena and Fife would always be friends, and would always share that time in their memories when it was just the two of them, but it would be different now. She understood but didn't like it and it only added to her sadness.

"I was thinking about my family, and I want them. And I'm confused because I miss them, but I've lived so long without them, I don't even know them anymore." Leena shook her head. "I know it doesn't make sense. Is there any hope?" She closed her eyes and covered her face with her hands. "Because I don't feel it anymore."

"We all be dealin' with troubles from our past, Leena. Give yourself grace. It'll be alrigh'. And just know I'm here for ya."

"I kinda miss you, Fife."

"What'd ya mean? I'm here."

"I know, but…"

Leena pressed her lips together. "I just wonder if I'll ever find someone to love like you love Jillian. Like my dad…loved my mum. I just miss you. I know you're here. I know you'll always be here for me, but eventually I'll need something more."

Leena could tell by Fife's expression how much he cared about her. His eyes filled with love, and he smiled at her. "Leena you're th'most lovely person I ever met. Don't you worry 'bout a thing." His words should have comforted her. But they didn't.

She pulled her scarf tightly around her, and hoped for sleep that did not want to come to her. Fife sat awake for a while watching the fire, clutching his bundle of currant berry sticks wrapped in a desert oak leaf tightly in his hand. Leena watched as he kissed the bundle goodnight, lied down, and closed his eyes.

Morning came with a pink sunrise. The sun was such a bold pink that the circular shape of it could be seen glowing in the sky like the full moon. Bright pink clouds eventually faded to a pale pink and then into a light lavender gray. A hawk soared and cried out across the morning sky. Leena lay awake staring into the sunrise, still feeling fragments of eerie dreams lingering in her mind— dreams of her dark past in the blackened meadow.

Mandy got out of bed first. She started the fire and boiled the water to cook with. Fife got up out of his warm bed to help, his hair bundled into a mess on one side of his head. Leena almost smiled when she looked at his hair, but didn't.

Jillian woke up slowly to the sound of the morning fire and lay there enjoying the desert sounds. She watched Fife as he cut and boiled and cooked the cactus plants. He caught her looking at him and he winked at her.

Leena felt the deep longing to breathe but could not find the strength. What was happening? Why did she feel so dark inside? It was like a thick veil had been placed over her mind. Like a cloud that would not leave. Her thoughts were heavy without relief.

"Would you like some food, Leena?" Jillian asked, offering her a cooked cactus pad.

Leena shook her head and whispered, "No, thank you."

Mandy watched the interaction and didn't hesitate to share her opinion.

"You need to eat, Leena. We need to be at full strength this week. The mountain alone is going to be more difficult than anything you guys have walked through yet. Eat."

Mandy didn't leave it open for discussion and tossed her a piece of yucca. Leena took it but stayed silent. Her empty stomach did not give the usual hunger cues. The thought of food made her wince. Leena looked at the yucca plant, turning it over in her hand. Mandy's eyes pressed into her.

Feeling no desire to eat, Leena bit off a small bite. The bite of yucca she had in her mouth seemed to not want to be swallowed. It held no flavor and the gummy texture made her stomach turn. She gagged, unnoticed by the others, and finally swallowed the bite down.

"I think I'll go for a walk." Leena got up and dusted the sand off her legs.

"Lemme come with…" Fife offered and stood up.

"No, I need to be alone. "

"Leena, I dunno if that's a good idea right now. We're here for ya and want to help. How can we help?"

Leena felt irritated, even though she knew Fife's concern for her was sincere.

"I won't be long. I'll be alright," she said without smiling or saying goodbye.

"What is wrong with me?" Leena whispered to herself as soon as she was out of earshot from the others. She knew better than to let the darkness and doubt filter back inside her, but at the same time she felt too weak and exhausted to break free from it.

The sun shone brightly now in the cool of the morning. She noticed that the land as far as she could see still had color. Mandy must have traveled a great distance as she brought back life to the desert. Gratitude pricked her heart for Mandy.

Leena sat down and closed her eyes, trying to summon the desire to take in a deep breath.

In her mind came the image of her goat Prickle. He chewed on the weeds, and she could see her six year old self hugging him. Her arms wrapped around his neck. Prickle grunted, looking at her in a sideways glance without moving his head, just his eyes. Those beady goat eyes. The thought of that scene made Leena smile in spite of herself.

Was she the same person as that little girl so many years ago? So much had happened. The little girl who tended her garden and blew wishes off the dandelions, now no longer innocent and oblivious to life's challenges. Everything was different now. She was different now. So much had changed. She was stronger, in some ways and weaker in others. Stronger in the power of life breathing, but weaker because she no longer trusted herself. So many things could go wrong. Would she really be able to bring her family back? The fear that she would fail overwhelmed her to the point of breaking.

And what about Fife, Jillian, and Mandy? Would they *all* survive? She could not bear it if anything happened to them. Then what? She could not go on alone again. If any of them survived, without the others, all would be lost. None of it would be worth it. They had to survive together. Knowing now what it's like to have true friendship, she never wanted to be without it.

And who was the other Life Breather? Why had the earth withheld any dreams or visions concerning this new person they would soon meet from the mountains?

The desire to breathe stirred inside her. Sitting there, she realized she wanted to feel freedom from the sadness. But how could she when the thought of being happy seemed unnatural and even wrong? Leena wrestled with the questions swirling through her thoughts. The wrestle inside her continued until she felt the words deeply—so deeply it vibrated her soul: *Just breathe.*

With the determination building in her body, her posture straightened. Leena inhaled a slow, steady, intentional breath through her nose. Then exhaled even more slowly. The words of Mum fell into place in her mind.

You, Leena, have a gift. It is a gift that has been passed down from your great great great grandmother. My baby girl, you were given the gift of breath. With practice, hard work, and time, you can learn to control your breath and with that, control the world around you. But only if you truly connect with your spirit and if your intentions are pure. You are a Life Breather. There are only a few Life Breathers left in this world. There will come a time when your gift will be needed, and you will need to find the others.

Be ready my darling.

Mum's voice articulated so clearly, it seemed as if Mum stood right in front of her, whispering the words into her ear. Leena could hear her voice, smell the sweet scent of vanilla bean on her skin, see her hazel eyes, and feel her breath. Mum was real, and she trusted Leena after all these years to free them all.

Mum's voice saved Leena in her moment of despair, and now Leena was going to save Mum.

Hope trickled back into her body. The darkness slipped off of her heart. Light filled her insides. Gracefully, she got up and faced the direction of the mountain.

"I am coming," she said. "I am coming."

By the time Leena arrived back at the campsite, Fife had cleaned up and had everything packed and ready to go. He approached Leena and took her by the shoulders softly.

"You good?" he asked quietly.

"Yeah, I'm good. Really good." Leena let out a sigh. "I'm exhausted, but I'm ready."

"Good." Fife winked. "B'cause it's time." And he put on his cap and shouldered his pack.

This time Leena smiled, thinking about her dad, putting his cap on his head, ready for an adventure. This time, Leena was grateful that Fife wore a cap that reminded her of her dad.

"Where's Mandy?" Leena asked, looking around.

"I dunno, I thought she'd be back by now. I'm thinkin' she may've gone lookin' for ya."

"That seems strange," Leena said mostly to herself. "Why would she have come looking for me? Did you see which way she went?"

"She wanted to do her meditation alone this morning," Jillian chimed in. "I saw her go up to the ridge. But she should've been back by now. She said she wouldn't be gone long."

"Was she upset?" Leena asked.

"Now you say it, maybe she did seema bit ruffled 'bout somethin'...but ya never know with Mandy right?" Fife let out a nervous laugh.

"Yeah I guess you're right." Leena looked around. "Well I guess we'll wait a bit and if she doesn't come back, we'll need to go look for her.

The three of them waited and waited. Jillian hummed softly to pass the time and Fife drew pictures in the desert sand.

"I'm going to go find her," Leena said. "Something doesn't feel right."

Fife looked up from his doodling.

"Sh'we come?" Fife asked.

The jagged rock formations jutting up through the desert looked like a place Mandy would go to breathe in a new day. A dry riverbed wove its way along the trail nearby.

"We need water. Fife you and Jillian stay here along the riverbed and breathe some life back into this stream if you can. I'll go up on those rocks to see if Mandy is there."

Fife looked unsure. "I dunno Leena. We can't have both ya lost."

"It'll be okay, Fife. I promise. Something is happening here, I can feel it. And I know I need to be the one to go."

Fife and Jillian exchanged looks.

"Alrigh' we'll stay. But you'll hollar if ye need me?"

Leena nodded and hurried along the path towards the ragged rock ridge. Leena's heart raced. Her legs moved quickly. As much as she wanted to call out for Mandy, it didn't feel right. She stayed silent along the narrow trail.

As she climbed, Leena held onto a rock with a groove on it like a handle and pulled herself over the edge of the highest ridge. She let out a groan of pain as her knee caught the edge of a jagged corner, bruising it hard. Sweaty with dirt clinging to every exposed part of her body she shuddered at the thought of her appearance. And a rise of frustration boiled inside her that she would come all this way to find a girl who didn't even like her. Leena knew Mandy had a good heart but she had never shown her a sip of kindness.

When she had climbed up safely over the edge, Leena looked at the bruise on her leg and dusted off her purple dress that turned more of a burnt orange with each passing day. Searching the ridge for any sign of Mandy she spotted beside a scraggly bush, a gray scarf. Despite her waning energy Leena quickly ran to it.

She stuffed the scarf into her pack and wildly looked around. Behind a mound of rocks close by she saw Mandy kneeling, her eyes closed and her hands, palms up, resting gently in the air out at the sides of her body. On each hand her thumb pressed the tip of her first fingers. The greenish, silvery plant with round leaves surrounded her in a circle.

Quietly, Leena came and knelt down a few feet away from her. She pulled her posture up tall and sat on her heels just like Mandy. Then she lifted her hands so they were not resting on her legs, but in the air at her sides. Imitating Mandy, Leena also pressed her thumbs to her first fingers, making it look like her thumb and first finger were an arrow pointed to the sky.

Breathing in deeply, Leena smelled a sharp woodsy-sweet smell, almost like the rosemary Mum grew in the garden, but it also held hints of honey, citrus, and mint. Breathing in the new aroma, her body completely relaxed. If Mandy noticed Leena there, she did not acknowledge it. Leena let her body, mind, and spirit become one. A deep breath in through her nose. Slow. Then releasing the breath through her nose. Slow.

As they meditated together, something happened to Leena that has never happened before. Her thoughts did not sound or behave like her own. Her mind, bossy, and contentious. She felt tough, able to battle a thousand beasts, but fragile, too, like she might break into a thousand pieces at the same time. The contrasts clashed inside Leena like dissonant chords. Love and hate mingled in the same beat of her heart. Anger and peace intertwined. The conflicting emotions felt unmanageable. She continued to breathe through the emotions. Breathing in the scent…*eucalyptus.* Now she could visualize the green plant growing freely in the desert. The fragrance swirled around her body and caused all sorts of images to appear in her mind…no it was Mandy's mind…inside Leena's.

Hide and seek. If we had not played hide and seek. That silly stupid game. Carissa begged to play. "You count! We'll hide!" Carissa had bossed. I went to the cave to hide my face and count to one hundred. Bethany and Bree, the twins at nine-years-old. Carissa ten. I was twelve and their sister, but also their mother. Naomi took us in as her own when she found us alone. I was only three at the time. I have no memories before that day that Naomi found us. The twins were just babies. Naomi told me I was like her. She could do all sorts of magical things with her breath. Return dead plants back to life within seconds, make food grow out of the hard desert earth, make water flow from dry riverbeds.

But when she died, that left me to be the mother at nine years old by myself. Cooking, cleaning, washing, protecting from wild animals, making sure they learned the ways of the canyon. All of the responsibility, mine! And I failed! The Destroyers came. I knew I was a Life Breather, and I was not strong enough to save them.

When the black cloud came, Naomi was no longer there to guide us and protect us, only I could do that. And I failed. The black cloud found my sisters in their hiding places before I could. I counted in that stupid cave, surrounded by the safety of the hematite and I left my little sisters screaming in the darkness. The guilt will never leave me. The anger I carry with me has been my only companion all these years. I cannot let it go. If I let it go, I will lose control of it. If I hold on to it, the control is mine. But in reality the anger controls me and I'm afraid of it.

The earth calls to me 'Let it go.' But I can't. I cannot feel the ease of forgiving myself. I was in charge. I am the Life Breather. I am the one with the power to stop them. My baby sisters. Gone. Life extinguished. All because of me.

"No, Mandy!" Leena opened her eyes and called out, interrupting the mental connection. "No! It was not you. You were a child. It all happened for a reason, and it is not your fault."

If only Mandy could see what Leena saw. All the potential for good and kindness that sat waiting inside of Mandy. The potential for love and healing. Leena wanted her to have it more than her soul could explain, but Mandy had to want it. It was not Leena's decision to make. Mandy had to decide if letting go of her anger and all the pain and all the fear buried so tightly inside her was worth giving up. Throwing out. Leaving behind. Turning away from.

Mandy's eyes flashed in anger. "What do you know!" Her eyes filled with raging tears that did not dare fall from her eyes. Even Mandy's tears were afraid of her.

"I know what it's like to be alone!" Leena shot back. "And helpless and unable to save the ones you love. I know what it's like to have the gift of breathing and then discard it and live in the darkness of my own mind." Leena gasped for a new breath, then hushed her tone. "I know what it's like to let it go and move on and it feels like freedom! You must let it go, Mandy. None of this is your fault. This is all exactly the way it is supposed to be. We are supposed to work together, breathe together, and heal together to restore the earth together. Not alone and in anger, but together in friendship." Leena spoke passionately, now out of breath again.

Mandy's body softened faintly. She buried her face with her hands and said, "I don't know how to let it go."

Leena waited a moment before responding.

"Let's do it together. I'll help you if you let me. Will you let me help you?" Leena waited patiently for an answer. Leena could feel Mandy's resistance. In a way, Mandy loved her own anger. It protected her from being vulnerable. The conflict inside Mandy grew. Leena could feel it radiating off of Mandy so strongly that it seemed to burn the air around them. Leena silently pleaded.

Mandy we cannot go on with this journey until you choose to let go of your shame. Please. Shame is poison. It will never leave unless you tell it to leave. You have to choose to throw it out of your mind by replacing it with a new emotion and a new thought. The time is now! The Destroyers won't hold off forever! They will come! All of them! The only way we will be strong enough is if we are all together. All five of us! That is the only way! And we can't do it without you! We have to get to the mountain! Don't you understand!? You must give this up to heal!

Leena's mind screamed through her pleading. And to her surprise Mandy looked up at Leena and nodded in understanding. Mandy's inner struggle now laid out plainly in front of both of them. If Mandy did not let go of the anger, she would not be ready to go to the mountain.

Leena knew that letting go of the shame that plagued Mandy, the anger that ruled her actions, and the fear that caused so much pain, remained one of the most difficult things to do, but one of the most critical, if Mandy was going to heal.

The resistance from Mandy still pressed hard on the air around them, but as with all of Mandy's emotions, a contrasting emotion tagged along as well. With the resistance came the desire to change. And the desire to change burned the air now with more strength than the defiance.

Mandy nodded again.

They prepared themselves by sitting comfortably with straight backs and took a few cleansing breaths in and out.

Breathe in through your nose. Breathe out through your nose. As you breathe in, think of a rock. Imagine holding the rock in your hands. That rock is fear. Hold the fear. Feel it. Feel it deeply. Sit with fear. It's okay to be afraid. Now, visualize yourself throwing the rock of fear off the edge of this ridge. Throw fear over the cliff and out of your mind. Let the fear go.

Pick up another rock. This rock is pain. Hold your pain. Feel your pain. Cry if you need to. Let it flow through your whole body. Feel every bit of your pain. Now in your mind, look at your rock that is pain. As you throw your pain into the chasm below, feel the pain being released from every part of your body. Let it go.

Pick up your last rock. Anger. Hold the anger. Feel it in your body. Let it rage. Let the anger stir inside you. Find where it is inside your body. What does it look like? Is it hard and heavy or does it billow like smoke. Don't push it away. Let the anger move through you. Wait until you're ready. Now hurl the anger rock off the edge of the cliff and down into the depth below.

Let it go. Let the anger leave your body. Release it. Each time you breathe, relax, and let it go. Let it go. Forgive yourself. Forgive yourself.

Let go of the fear, the pain, and the anger. Forgive and let go.

Leena opened her eyes. She watched Mandy's tears run anxiously from her closed eyes, finally free. Leena knew that feeling. The feeling of letting yourself cry. She let herself cry the first night in the cave, and it changed her. Allowing the feeling without resisting the feeling. But knowing *when* to let the feeling go is the important part.

Standing up, Mandy looked over the edge of the ridge.

"So much of my life has been focused on fear, pain, and anger that to let them go feels liberating and also like I've lost control." She looked at Leena for understanding. "When I threw that last rock off the edge, I felt the anger leave my body and something else replaced it."

Leena stared at Mandy in silence, listening, quietly knowing that Mandy's heart had softened, and healing had begun.

"Anger, replaced by…I'm not even sure what to call it, but an absolute calm covered me inside for the first time. Really calm." Mandy closed her eyes.

"What? What replaced it, Mandy?" Leena asked.

After a long thoughtful pause Mandy said, "I feel love." She looked at her hands and arms like she saw her body for the first time. "For myself. Compassion. For myself. I feel acceptance of my past, and I feel the desire to forgive myself. I feel washed clean and worthy of love from others." Mandy let out a surprised airy laugh then her eyes filled with tears. She blinked allowing the tear drops to gracefully fall down her cheeks.

The two girls, who were so very opposite from one another, looked at each other, neither of them knowing what more to say. Leena's compassionate heart overflowed with love for this girl. Without thinking, Leena reached out to Mandy, and they embraced.

Leena and Mandy walked down the path as Fife and Jillian were on the way up to find them. Mandy and Leena were laughing and chatting like close friends. When Leena looked up and saw the other two coming to meet them, she waved and smiled. Fife's forehead wrinkled as he opened his eyes wide in confusion and looked at Jillian.

"Are you seein' what I'm seein'?" he asked. "Mandy looks…she looks…"

Jillian finished his thought. "Happy?"

"Yeah, yeah, happy. Really happy," Fife agreed.

Mandy approached them and looked sincerely sorry. She reached out to give Fife a hug, but looked as though she only meant to embrace him lightly. Fife pulled her in for a tight squeeze.

Mandy let out a sound of being squished. "Ohhf. Alright, alright."

"We're gonna be in this t'gether for awhile. We're a family, n'family forgives and understands. And we're all healin'," Fife said, with a big grin. He put his hands on his hips and stood back in admiration looking at Mandy.

Mandy gave Jillian a hug, too, and whispered, "I'm happy for you and Fife. He's really special."

Jillian let out a soft laugh. "He is."

MEDITATION MOMENT:

Kneel with your heels tucked underneath you.

You might place a pillow between your feet and your bum if that's comfortable.

Relax your arms and place your hands out to the sides of your body.

Thumb and first finger touching pointing to the sky.

Breathe in the eucalyptus scent.

As you breathe it out, let go of one negative thought you struggle with.

Let it go.

It is no longer a part of you.

Let that thought float away in a cloud.

20

The Mountain

"You think it's hard to travel uphill in the heat? Everything in life has its opposite.
Downhill in the freezing cold has its challenges, too."

The air blew in colder around midday. Wind brushed their faces, chilling them deep inside. Fife got Jillian's white scarf out of her pack and she wrapped it around her head and neck to shield her from the biting wind. The snow had not come yet, but they could see the clouds gathering, and the snow-capped mountain range looked massive before them.

As they got closer, Leena could see that the mountains were black underneath the white snow, which meant that the Life Breather that lived there had not given the earth its breath yet. However, they could see flashes of green in groupings of trees scattered along the mountain range, which helped guide them in the right direction.

"What do you s'pose he'll be like? The other Life Breather...

have ya seen him in a dream or anythin'?" Fife asked Leena when they stopped and passed around the water jugs.

"I haven't seen him at all. It's strange. I had dreams about each of you before I met you," Leena said, shrugging her shoulders and looking around. Why had she not dreamt of him? Why was he hidden from her view? She didn't share this with the others, but it secretly gnawed at her.

"Well, we know he hasn't brought back animals." Mandy sounded a bit harsh. "Since we haven't seen a bird or insect since we left the desert. And the mountain itself is not breathing, so he must be young. And maybe not that powerful."

"Maybe he's waiting for us," Jillian suggested. "Maybe he is powerful but knows he needs us before he can make any real change."

Leena nodded thoughtfully, agreeing that giving him the benefit of the doubt was the decent thing to do. Unnecessary judgment and jumping to conclusions about someone they knew absolutely nothing about would only end in disappointment. So she kept her options open and curious.

"We should ask the earth if there's anything we need to prepare for before we head up the mountain," Leena offered.

"I agree," Jillian said.

After they each got some food and water, they prepared to meditate.

They spread out. Individually this time.

Leena found a spot surrounded by green bushes and sat criss-crossed, resting the back of her hands on her knees, her palms open to the sky in a relaxed cup shape. She breathed in slowly. Then out slowly. Steady and calm. This time, instead of meditating with words, she formed images in her mind of what she hoped for.

In her mind, she traveled up the mountain. A tiny log cabin nestled in a group of green trees. Smoke billowed out the top of the little chimney. The mountain cabin, alive and breathing. Through the tiny windows of the home, she saw the light of the fireplace glowing.

Smiling, Leena continued to see the things she hoped for most.

She visualized Aaron emerging out of the black smoke, alive and breathing, running to Leena's arms, kissing her a thousand times on her cheeks.

She saw Fife reuniting with his mama and brothers and sisters. They ran to him, recognizing him immediately. Now Fife was the oldest and the tallest in the family.

Jillian on her seashore, collecting shells with her brother, Jonny, walking by her side. In his hand he held a pink starfish. They laid down on the sand and spread out their arms and legs, both of them looking like starfish. Opening and closing their arms and legs, making star shapes in the sand, laughing in the sun by the sea.

Mandy sat on the edge of her cliff. From behind, two little girls, with dark skin and tightly curled black hair pulled to the sides in pony tails, came to her and wrapped their arms around her. Bethany and Bree. Carissa came and joined in the hug. Mandy held them as the animals gathered around.

Who is the boy in the mountain? Why couldn't she see him? Leena's mind reached for any sign of his face, his voice or his story, but she was not allowed to see him. Curiosity overwhelmed her to the point of agitation. Sighing, she let go of the nagging questions. All would be revealed soon.

Opening her eyes, Leena searched for the others. They had finished and now sat quietly talking together waiting for her.

"I'm ready," Leena said as she approached them. "Did any of you see the boy from the mountain? Or feel anything about him?"

They shook their heads. Leena felt a twinge of relief knowing that they had not gotten a sneak peek into this new Life Breather before she did. But guilt stopped her from basking in the relief too deeply. She scolded herself mentally for it.

They continued to walk, eventually reaching the snow covered base of the mountain. Every few hours, they rested and lit a fire to warm their freezing hands and feet. When the heat of the canyon had pressed down upon them, Leena would have never believed that the cold could be worse than the heat. Now she knew better. This was worse. Far worse. Mandy had been right. This was the hardest thing they had endured on their journey. All of them quietly suffered.

When the sun went down, the frigid air turned torturous. The four of them huddled together to gain warmth from each other and they kept the fire going all night. The snow surrounded them, but the earlier clouds had blown off. The open sky, spread out over the earth, was clear and full of stars.

Leena woke up several times throughout the night. Staring out into the blackness, she felt a tightness in her chest, making it hard to breathe. Breathe in. She told herself. Now breathe out. Reminding herself over and over. Leena repeated *I am safe.* She continued to remind herself that the Destroyers would not come yet. It was not time. Not unless they called for them by bringing back the animals or massive amounts of earth all at once. *I am safe.*

But her thoughts betrayed her, and she did not believe it. She could feel the shadows hovering not far off. Watching, studying them. Leena tried to recall her hope meditation, imagining Aaron running to her and seeing the mountain cabin warm and welcoming. Eyes closed she reminded herself to breathe in and out, until finally she slipped back into sleep, but her dreams were dark and mangled with images of humans trapped in nets, like fish caught at sea. They flipped and squirmed without relief. Leena wrestled with the tangled net, trying to free the trapped people, but she couldn't figure it out. She pulled a knife from her pocket, but the blunt knife could not cut the nets. Helpless and exhausted from the dream, she willed herself to wake up, her mind stressed and her body cold. So cold. She lay awake until sunrise. The clouds had gathered again.

The gray morning sky stretched as far as they could see and brought with it snow. Jillian, fascinated by the pure whiteness of the flakes, reached her hands up in the air catching as many as she could.

"It's magic!" Jillian said, holding out her hands to the sky.

"We should reach that crest up there," Mandy said, pointing, "around the middle of the day today. We're very close. So be on the lookout for any signs of life."

The snow continued to fall. As they struggled up the steep mountain path, Leena wondered if they were headed in the right direction. This was nothing how she imagined the mountain. Leena's mind felt frozen. Her thoughts muddled. Reaching into her pocket she soothed her fingers across the amethyst. The quiet glow warmed her insides just enough to take the edge off and clear her thoughts.

Out of the corner of her eye, she saw a flicker of light. Had she imagined it? She turned to look in the direction of the light. There it was again. It looked like a flickering candle.

"Look!" Leena said, pointing her numb finger up at a crest to the right. "Did you see that light?"

The others looked in the direction Leena pointed.

"I can see it!" Fife said, his cheeks pink from the cold. "If we go up this path we should be right on track to th'flickerin' light."

Mandy agreed, and they took the next trail that veered off to the right and curved around the side of the mountain. Leena felt like a mountain goat, walking along the edge of a mountainside. The beauty of the mountain she could not deny, but as far as comfort goes, it had much to be desired.

The flickering light became clearer as they approached. It came from a little log home tucked in the mountain on a small ridge. This was Leena's hope. She had seen it before in her mind. Excitement and relief filled her, and she let out a heavy sigh. They were close. This was happening. Breathing in and out slowly, she thanked the earth. Leena showed gratitude to the earth to acknowledge the help and gifts given. Without gratitude, Leena knew the earth would give less. Or maybe the earth wouldn't give less, perhaps she would not see the gifts from the earth in front of her if she did not show a grateful heart.

"That! That's a home! I think we found him!" Fife exclaimed.

Their pace quickened. Their hope guided them onward through every difficult step.

Bushes and trees, green and alive, surrounded the log home. A stone path, recently swept free from snow, started about a half a mile from the home and led them all the way to the front door. A flurry blustered in Leena's stomach, like butterflies in a snowstorm. Her excitement spun around nervously. Curiosity bubbled inside her, and Leena had no idea what to expect when the four of them came to his door. Was he old or young? Expecting them or surprised?

The snow had stopped falling and the sun shone low in the late afternoon sky. They walked up the stone path. All along the edge of the home, grew an herb with a refreshing scent. The smell of mint captured the air as they made their way to the door. Leena breathed it in, and it calmed the storm inside her.

"So, who's gonna do the knockin'?" Fife asked, his eyes dazed with excitement. He rubbed his hands together. Leena couldn't blame him. Finally, there would be another boy in the group, though Fife didn't seem to mind being surrounded by girls.

"Leena should knock," Jillian said in a soft voice.

Leena swallowed. She took a smooth breath in to clear her mind and then knocked on the small wooden door. They waited.

Seconds later, they heard soft footsteps walking along the wood floor inside. The door opened. A dark-haired boy about their age stood on the other side of the opened door. When Leena saw him, she inhaled a quick breath and her eyes opened wide and filled with tears. Around the boy's shoulders, hung a royal blue scarf.

She *had* seen him before; in the vision, while on her Dad's carriage in the marketplace. The blue scarf her dad sold to the boy and his Father lay in front of her. Without thinking, Leena reached out her hand and touched the scarf gently. Could it be? This seemed too impossible to believe.

"It's you," she said under her breath as she caressed the soft blue scarf with her fingers.

He smiled, and relief filled his eyes. Looking at the ground, he bowed to Leena and said, "My name is Lance." Then he looked up and added, "I'm so happy to finally meet you." His voice was smooth. He looked completely calm, and he welcomed them into his warm home. Fife had to duck his head slightly under the doorway as he entered. The ceilings were low, which kept the heat of the fire inside the cozy mountain cabin.

"Welcome to the mountains. I know you've all traveled a great distance," Lance said, taking a big breath in and looking at each of them as if he already knew their faces. His face remained calm, but underneath, excitement beamed in his eyes.

"I'm Fife. My home's in th'forest." Fife offered a handshake. "This be a big ol' mountain you're livin' on." Fife chuckled, and the boys shook hands, an instant respect passing between the two.

"I'm Mandy. I live in the canyon. I've been waiting a long time to make this journey." Mandy said, looking around the small home. "Thank you for being ready for us."

Lance gave a genuine smile and nodded his head.

Lance turned to Jillian.

"Hi, I'm Jillian. I am from the sea." Nervously, she smiled and looped her arm through Fife's.

Lance turned and faced Leena. "And you?"

"I'm Leena." She smiled into his warm face. "I live in the meadow."

"It's so nice to meet you, Leena." He said in a tone that reminded Leena of honey.

Around the fireplace, on the smooth wooden floor, were large soft pillows. A small wooden table rested in the corner, low to the ground with two cubed pillows on the floor at either end. It appeared to have one other room off to the side that had a small cot for sleeping. Leena wondered if all mountain homes were this tidy and cozy. The warm crackling fire and the soft pillow chairs along with the lingering smell of herbs, reminded her of home. Now she saw clearly what her Dad missed about the mountains.

"You all must be starving. I'll prepare food, and would you like some tea?" Lance asked them politely.

"Yes, please." Jillian said, and the others nodded with smiles.

"Come, sit down." He motioned to the pillows on the floor.

Lance brought them hot tea, and they sipped it slowly. It warmed every part of their cold bodies and cleared their minds.

Leena held her cup with both hands wrapped around it. "This is the mint that you grow just outside of your home, right?"

"Yes." He nodded and appeared surprised that Leena could place the scent. He looked directly into Leena's eyes. His eyes were dark brown, angular and narrow. They were beautiful, and Leena did not want to look away. "It reminds me of my father."

"I saw you. I saw you months ago in a vision." Leena paused to sip her tea. "You were a young boy at the marketplace in the village with your Father and he bought…he bought that scarf for you… from my dad."

Lance smiled and folded his arms in front of him. "That was your dad? He had the finest scarves. It was exactly what we needed. I remember the pies, too, the cherry was particularly delicious. I remember that day well. I was nine. It was just before we left the market to return home. Two weeks later…" Lance looked at the floor. "The black cloud came and destroyed everything."

When they finished their tea, Lance brought them some cake-like crackers. He called them poms. Leena had never heard of them before. The poms were delicious, soft and sweet, and the four of them ate until they were filled.

Lance went into the backroom and brought out four bedrolls and small head pillows. "Do you have blankets?" he asked as he began rolling out the beds.

"Yeah, we do," Fife answered and helped Lance with the pillows and straightening the beds.

"I think I'll let you all get some rest," Lance said, "Unless there's anything else I can get for you tonight. I'm sure you are all in need of sleep."

Fife, Jillian, and Mandy settled into their bedrolls. Fife on the far end of the room, and Mandy and Jillian close to the fire with a spot for Leena beside them.

Leena walked over to Lance by the door of the other room.

"Thank you, Lance," Leena said graciously. "I can't tell you how happy we are to finally meet you. I was worried because I'm usually intune with what's coming next. I have dreams…" She tapped her finger on her leg awkwardly and looked down as if she wasn't sure she wanted to share that yet.

Lance chimed in. "I have dreams, too." He said thoughtfully, easing the awkwardness. "I have been having dreams about you for a while now."

Leena's mouth fell open, and she raised her eyebrows. "You have? About all of us?"

His deep golden-brown skin reminded Leena of silk. So smooth. Leena noticed his hands were strong but also gentle, his nails clean and trimmed. As Leena looked at Lance, her stomach fluttered inside in a wonderful way. A way she had never felt before. Lance was a good-looking young man with an easy, genuine smile. As he spoke Leena looked at his lips. Full and soft. Leena quickly brushed the thought aside.

"No. Just you… actually," he said slowly after a pause. His polished voice was polite, and he seemed well educated.

"Oh. Well…I hope it was…helpful," she said, clearing her throat, even though she didn't need to, but not knowing how else to respond. She felt flattered and amused. She wrinkled up her nose and timidly asked, "What did you see?"

He laughed for the first time then looked thoughtful. "I saw you in your garden, with your daisies. I saw you smash the stone with the mallet that had the purple gemstones inside, and I saw you bring your meadow back to life. I saw you leave the mushrooms for Fife on his doorstep. I saw you go under water and speak with Jillian to help her. I saw you on the ridge with Mandy breathing and helping her forgive herself. I saw you sad in the desert by yourself." He looked at her intently. "I feel like I know you." Lance paused and gave a soft laugh before he continued. "Probably much better than you feel like you know me. And also…" Lance stopped himself and glanced to the side looking embarrassed. "Never mind."

"What? What were you going to say?" Leena asked.

"It's nothing. I'll tell you…sometime." He smiled and regained his composure easily.

"Well, okay then." Leena said. And she was grateful he couldn't see the butterflies flapping wildly inside her.

21

Lapis

*"Learn from the past. The past will guide you in the present and bring you
wisdom for your future.
Past, present, future, it's all connected."*

Morning emerged quietly as the mountain cabin absorbed the light of the sun rising. They had all slept deeply and comfortably. Leena opened her eyes. She saw Lance over by the stove and she could smell bread baking, a welcome and delightful smell. Memories of her childhood poured into her mind. She breathed the memories in through the smell of the bread. Mum baked bread nearly every day, and the warm, hardy scent made her feel right at home. At the low table Lance set place settings for five, with five small tea cups and five small plates.

Fife stretched out his long legs. "What can I do t'help?"

Lance handed him the teapot full of hot water and Fife poured water into each cup. The mint leaves simmered on the stovetop and filled the home with calm.

The girls came over to the table. Now, instead of two, there were five cubed cushions around it. Lance put a warm flatbread on each plate and passed around the mint leaves to add to the hot tea water.

"Did you all sleep well?" Lance asked.

"I can't remember sleeping better than that…ever," Mandy said.

"I tell ya what," Fife began, "this little mountain home be th'most comfy place I ever slept in."

"Did you sleep alright?" Leena asked. "I mean all these new people in your home after being alone for so long."

Lance hesitated with his answer. An odd silence hung in the air, causing Leena to regret she asked.

"Well, to be completely honest" —he cleared his throat— "I really don't sleep all that much. I haven't slept more than a couple hours a night since the day it all happened." He motioned for them to sit down. "Have a seat." He continued, "I struggled a lot as a young boy, being alone and not being able to process the trauma of losing my father, and I have never really recovered as far as sleep goes."

Leena had never heard of this before. "Oh, I'm so sorry."

"Don't be." He smiled gently at her. "I get a lot of reading done at night. My Father collected books about all sorts of cultures and histories. I spend most of my time reading and studying. And I have your mum to thank. The blue scarf was the one thing that brought me comfort all those years growing up alone, surrounded by black-ness. It saved me, reminding me of life."

Leena's heart overflowed. She grinned and took a bite of her flatbread.

After everyone ate, Lance gave them each a warm coat and gloves in preparation for going out on the mountain. "There are some things I need to show you, and you'll probably want to bundle up."

As he handed Leena a knit hat, his hand touched hers, and they caught eyes. She pulled the hat down over her ears to keep them warm, her curls dangling out.

They followed Lance up a well groomed trail and into a cave already lit with torches. Long icicle-like formations hung pointing down from the ceiling of the cave. Leena, Fife, Jillian, and Mandy looked around in amazement.

"Whoah! What is this thing doin'?" Fife asked, pointing to the formations hanging from the ceiling of the cave.

"Those are stalactites. It's produced by precipitation of minerals from water dripping through the cave ceiling."

"Ahhh, right. That's what I was thinkin' it was," Fife teased. Jillian laughed and shook her head.

The cave wasn't big, but it did go back deeper than Leena originally thought. Lance led them to the back of the cave where he had a rock chair and table. On the table were neat stacks of clay tablets with writing utensils beside them. To Leena, it looked absolutely intriguing. Curiosity about all of it made it impossible to keep from smiling.

"My father kept records of history from centuries back. My grandfather also, and my great grandfather." He pointed to the stacks that were on shelving that had been built into the cave wall. "This is called papyrus, and this is a writing pen made from a reed. This here, is a stylus made from ivory and is used to write on these clay tablets. Most of these are hundreds and hundreds of years old."

Carefully, they admired the records and saw that most of them were written in strange symbols in a foreign language.

"How'd ya read it?" Fife asked, looking at all the unfamiliar markings. Fife had learned to read as a small boy and continued to practice on his own, while raising himself, but he had never seen symbols like this before. None of them had.

"I learned the native language of my father as a young boy, and this ancient language here," he said pointing to the clay, "is similar, so through the years I've been able to translate most of it."

Mandy focused on the markings in the clay. "What does this symbol mean?" She pointed to an image that repeated often. The symbol had a straight vertical line. At the top of the line on each side were shapes that resembled wings or flower petals. Coming out of the top, was a brief diagonal line shooting out to the right.

"That means *Life Breather*. And this here means *Destroyer*." Lance pointed to the two different symbols.

Leena stared in awe at the symbol on the tablets. This truly was incredible. The cave drawings in the canyon and now this. Every answer to every question through time must be here in this cave.

Without warning something inside Leena's pack moved. Bumping against her back. Shocked, she shifted her body and then the strap on her pack flung open, and out flew the small leather book, *Riddles of Time, Secrets of Stone.*

The four turned their attention to Leena and the book as it floated out in front of them. Leena watched in wonder, not knowing what to expect.

"Whaaaat?" Fife gasped and held both sides of his head before he covered his mouth with his hands. Then lowering his hands, he said quietly, "It's alive." Fife's eyes were round, like his amazonite marbles.

Jillian let out a small squeal.

The book hung in the air in front of them, and the pages turned themselves. A light emanated from the old book in front of them.

"What book is this?" Lance asked in hungered curiosity.

"It's a book I brought from the meadow. It's been guiding us with riddles to where we need to go next…but I thought since we found you…it was complete."

The book opened to a page of its own choosing and glided smoothly through the air to the stone table. Gently floated down until it landed.

The five Life Breathers gathered around the book on the table.

Lance read the open page.

The day comes nigh that darkness swoons.
Life filled with air soon all consumed.
No breath, no life, but five remain who still as yet
Gather in the remnant breath
The stones to bring round circled in
One of calm and guiding light
One of harmony, heals in optimistic glow
One of peace, purity with wisdom gained through time and trial
One of protection, balance and battle, strong and fragile alike
And the last One of knowledge, truth, and compassion for all

Combine the five and circle round the light a hole formed in the ground
Out the cloud of darkness spell
A new day comes and new life breathes to begin again
Trust and live and heal them till life again brings breath to all

As Lance finished reading the riddle, the other four stood around him, clinging to every word he spoke.

"Do you know how long ago this book was written?" Lance asked. "Or where it originated?"

Leena shook her head, wishing she had an answer. "I don't know. I mean it has my grandmother Lacey's name in the front. She was a Life Breather. I'm guessing it was passed down to her at some point."

Lance went over to a shelf that held a few old books, and he selected one that looked almost identical to *Riddles of Time, Secrets of Stone*. Similar size and color.

On the cover it read: *Time and Knowledge Revealed.*

"This book has baffled me for years. The pages are blank, but my Father told me it was the key to knowledge."

Lance opened the book and lay it beside the other on the table. Both books burned with life. On the blank pages of *Time and Knowledge Revealed* gradually appeared pictures. Detailed artwork of stones and planets. Charts and maps of the universe. Each time the book of riddles turned the page to a new riddle, the book of knowledge turned to a picture illustration of the answer. Then the ever-changing book of secrets showed story after story of all the bedtime stories Leena and Jillian had heard through their early childhood of the Life Breathers and the Destroyers, the matching book at its side creating illustrations to each story.

The five of them watched and read, drinking in all the information of the past.

Lance said, "The Life Breathers that survived the last destruction, have been preparing for this for hundreds of years by passing down this riddle, this prophecy to each new generation. Preparing us. For this purpose. To rid the world of the Destroyers one final time."

Lance reached into his satchel pocket and opened his hand to show them a beautiful deep blue rock with swirls of golden flecks mixed with the blue.

"This is called lapis lazuli. It's found here in the mountains, and it has protected this mountain and me from the Destroyers many times."

Leena reached out and touched the lapis reverently. She recognized the smooth, warm rock as the gemstone her dad described from the mountain caves. Out of her pocket Leena pulled the amethyst. It glowed a brilliant purple in the darkness of the cave, its jagged crystals pointed and clear. Fife dug into his pouch and took out a round amazonite marble, glowing pale blue as the morning sky. Jillian touched her pearl necklace, and the white pearls shone brightly. Mandy held out in her hand the hematite stone, and it sparkled as it caught the light of the torch.

The stones vibrated in each of their hands. Communicating. Connecting. Suddenly light poured from the center of each stone. A blast of wind whipped through the cave and vibrated the walls around them. Leena, Fife, Jillian, Mandy, and Lance stood still, watching the lives of the stones bond as the lights reached towards each other, calling to one another. And at last each gemstone made a circular web linking them all together.

"This is what the Life Breathers of the past did not have." Lance's tone was filled with excitement as he spoke louder than he had before to be heard above the noise of the gusting wind. "These five stones have never been united before. The traits needed from each stone fused together as one. All are needed to conquer the Destroyers. Calm, harmony, purity, balance, and truth."

The light connecting the stones slowly dimmed, and the rocks rattled in their palms for a few seconds. The wind turned to a soft breeze. A calm covered the cave. A complete peace settled deep inside them. Fife broke the silence.

"Holy moly jolly firepots!" Fife grabbed his hair with both hands. "I know I say this about just about everythin', but that be truly one of the most amazin' things I ever seen! And in th'past few weeks, I been seein' a lot! So that's sayin' a ton!"

Jillian wrapped her arms around his waist and looked up at him with adoration. Filled with excitement, he kissed her on the lips, then he looked at the others. "We are gonna destroy them Destroyers!"

"Slow down, Fife," Mandy said in her usual bossy voice. "There's more to it. We need a plan and we need time to prepare."

"Mandy's right," Lance spoke up. "But your enthusiasm is fantastic."

They stayed in the cave for hours, reading through the ancient records and asking Lance questions. He knew so much about the history of the earth through every age of time, and he passionately shared his knowledge with them.

"Well, I don't have all the answers," Lance admitted, "but what we do know is that the black cloud is a force that originally is not from earth. At some point in time, long ago, the Destroyers, as we call them now, lived in another realm with the Life Breathers. They lived in peace. The Destroyers in their greed stole the breath around them and desired to continue to take and take. The Life Breathers knowing that they needed to start anew, fled to earth to survive in harmony with humans. The galaxy they originated from gradually ran out of oxygen. The Destroyers left their planet searching for air to breathe—searching for the remaining Life Breathers." Lance looked around at each of them. "Another five hundred years passed, and once again the black cloud and Destroyers returned in need of breath. And once again, the Destroyers stole the breath from the earth. And the cycle continued. Until now."

"We will break the cycle," Leena said with confidence.

"Yes." Lance looked at her with admiration. "The Destroyers return to their realm and subsist off the breath they gathered, until they run out again. They wait for the Life Breathers on earth to breathe the earth back entirely before they come again, but when an animal is brought back, they cannot control themselves, and they will come immediately to steal the air it breathes."

"We've also experienced the black cloud returning when we brought back massive amounts of land at one time. The sand of the sea. It created such a commotion in the waves, that the black cloud must have been drawn to it. But otherwise they won't come until we call them by bringing back life. Although…" Leena stopped herself, unsure if she wanted to share more.

They looked at her waiting.

"I have felt something. Something in the darkness that watches in the night. Waiting. Patiently. I feel sometimes as if I'm being studied. It's terrifying."

"I've felt it, too," Jillian added.

Leena looked at Fife, Mandy, and then Lance to see if any of them had felt it. All three shook their heads.

"Not me," Fife said. "Wonder why you two feel it and we don't."

Later that afternoon, before the sun set in the western sky, Lance offered to show them where he does his breathing routine every evening. They bundled in their scarves and jackets and headed up to a peak. The sun still hung in the sky, but also the moon hung in the opposite direction. The serenity on the mountain peak was exhilarating and the view from the peak, breathtaking.

Lance led them to a flat area called a shelf, which gave them plenty of room to spread out a few feet apart from each other. There were no comfortable places to sit or lie down. The snow covered the flat mountain shelf making the ground cold and icy.

Leena whispered to Lance close to his ear, "What pose is best?"

He smiled. "I prefer tadasana."

"I don't know what you just said." Leena giggled quietly, her breath heating the side of his face.

"It means mountain pose." Lance whispered back, looking at her.

"Show us?" She looked into his smooth face, their faces so close they were nearly touching.

He turned from Leena and spoke to all of them. "I prefer to stand while I do my breathing, if I'm outside, for obvious reasons. It's really not very comfortable to sit on a floor of ice."

"Yeah, I was wonderin' 'bout that." Fife laughed.

"You can spread out a bit if you'd like and place your feet about hip width apart. Feel all four corners of your feet grounded to the earth, fully connected." They followed his directions closely. He continued to instruct them. "Close your eyes, and notice the energy traveling up your legs. Now tuck your tailbone under and tuck in your ribs, to activate your stomach muscles. Roll the shoulders towards your ears then back down. Imagine a thread of light pulling your spine up straight, and then stand just a bit taller. Even you, Fife. Taller than you already are, my friend." They all smiled. "Now as your arms hang at your sides, turn your hands so the palms are facing forward and fingers are straight. Some muscles will stay engaged, but relax the ones you can. Relax your jaw, relax the muscle between your eyebrows. Relax your face."

When he had finished teaching them how to stand correctly in mountain pose to meditate, they began to breathe.

No one said anything, but in their minds they were focused and connected to each other.

Close your eyes. Breathe in and out three times deeply through your nose… slowly. You are calm. Breathe in. You are in harmony with the world around you. Breathe out. You are pure. Breathe in. You are balanced within yourself. Breathe out. You see truth.

Now, relax your breath, and let it easily flow through you at its regular pace. Feel your face soften and your legs firmly grounded to the earth.

Feel the life around you and let it bloom.

Welcome into your soul, new beginnings and simplicity.

Leena felt something familiar glide through the air. With her eyes still closed she sensed something happening around her. Something that made her feel like a child. Her body felt strong and composed, but also giddy. With her hands at her sides faced out, she felt a tickle on her palm, and at the same time smelled a mild earthy scent. What happened? Why was this so familiar and out of place up here on this mountain peak? Why did she feel transported back to her childhood? Curiosity overcame her, and she opened her eyes.

Her breath caught in her throat and her eyes grew big. Everyone opened their eyes when they heard Leena gasp. She clapped both hands over her mouth softly. Hundreds of daisies bloomed all over the shelf of the mountain peak and all around them weaving in between their legs, blowing gently in the breeze. The snow had melted away, and a daisy field had sprung up like springtime in the meadow. The petals of the flowers were delicately waving under their outstretched fingers. No words would come to Leena's lips, leaving her completely speechless.

After a few moments, she looked at Lance and asked in a small, high voice, "You did this?"

He closed his eyes and made a half smile with a charming shrug of his shoulders, like it was no big deal.

"It won't last long. The cold will come back and freeze them out, but…" He began to collect the daisies into a bundle. "But we can bring back as many as we can hold in our hands to my home and enjoy them there." He bowed and handed Leena a bouquet of daisies.

Instead of taking the bouquet he held out, she wrapped her arms around his neck and hugged him. Lance closed his eyes and wrapped his arms around Leena.

"Alright, alright that was amazing," Mandy said, rolling her eyes, clearly impressed by the grin on her face.

"How'd ye know how to do *that?*" Fife asked as he tucked a daisy behind Jillian's ear.

Lance hesitated and looked slightly guilty. "I've… been practicing. Nearly every day for a year."

Mandy raised a solo brow. "Well I think we can all appreciate the *why* behind that," she said with a taste of sarcasm, glancing at Lance, then Leena, then back to Lance.

"Thank you," Leena said, looking at Lance. "That was beautiful of you."

MEDITATION MOMENT:

Stand tall and straight with your feet shoulder-width apart.

Palms facing forward.

Feel your feet grounded to the earth.

You are in mountain pose.

Tadasana.

Breathe in the peppermint scent slowly.

As you breathe it out, close your eyes and relax.

22

Three Truths

"What are your three truths?"

Each night the five practiced their gift of breathing together on the mountain shelf. On the third night as they finished up and started on their way back down the path, Lance took hold of Leena's gloved hand, tugging her gently back.

"Will you stay here with me for a bit?" Lance asked quietly. "I'd like to show you something."

"Ummm yeah…sure I can stay," Leena said a bit clumsily, looking at Fife, not knowing how to explain. Fife winked at Leena and he casually encouraged Jillian and Mandy to follow him. The other girls didn't seem to notice and headed down the path with Fife.

"What is it?" Leena asked Lance.

"Well, after I had my first vision of you—" He paused. "Well actually the first vision I had of you was before the day of destruction. I dreamt about you and your brother finding some cats under a porch. I had never seen a cat before. Not ones that small anyway.

We had mountain lions here, but nothing as small as meadow cats." Leena looked confused as she thought about her cat Betty and how enormous she had seemed. "But the next time I dreamt about you I was probably thirteen or fourteen." He looked down at his feet. "I saw you in fields of purple flowering bushes. Rows and rows of the purple plant. In my dream I could smell a strong lovely scent, and in the dream I was with you."

"But how…" Leena didn't understand. Lance looked at her and waited for her to finish her question. "But how were you with me? And I don't have lavender fields in the meadow, just one lavender bush."

"It wasn't a vision, it was my own thoughts transferring into a dream. In the dream I pulled some mint leaves out of my pocket and held them out to you." Leena looked at him hesitantly, wanting to interrupt and ask ten more questions, but also wanting to stay quiet and hear the rest of his dream. "You rubbed the mint leaves and held them up to your nose and smiled at me. And then you broke off a small bunch of lavender flowers and held them out for me. I rubbed them in my fingers and then breathed in the scent. Then I…I…"

Out of his pocket he pulled a bundle of mint leaves and held them out to her. Leena looked surprised and delicately took the mint leaves out of his open palm and held them close to her nose, breathing in the refreshing scent.

"Well I wish you would've given me a heads up and I could've brought some lavender from my pack to share with you." She smiled like a child.

He took her gloved hand in his and led her off the mountain shelf and up a new path that he had never taken them on before. "There was a time when the dreams I had about you were the only thing I looked forward to about the night time. In that dream I had of us together, I could smell the lavender, and I longed for the scent after the dream had ended." He stopped walking and turned to look at Leena. "I longed to be with you."

Leena stared back at him, wishing she could've had dreams about him. Her blank mind could not think of a single thing to say.

What did this mean? Why was Lance telling her this? She knew because of the love she had seen growing up between her parents, what love looked like. But she also knew it took time to grow and develop. Attraction was not love. If it were, she would already be in love with Lance as she was clearly attracted to him. He had spent so much of his life thinking thoughts about her and seeing her in dreams, but she had only just met him.

Looking away from him, she wiped her mind of all giddiness and forced herself to behave normally. Trying to think rationally she tried to reason *why* he had dreams about her. To what purpose besides loneliness? Casually she cleared her throat and looked around.

"Why do you think you had dreams about me? You said your first dream was the baby kittens right?" Leena made the mistake of looking at Lance again. She studied his smooth, brown face in the moonlight, her hand still bundled in his. Then her eyes moved down to his neck, and with her free hand, she touched the blue scarf that protected his neck from the cold and had protected his life when he was alone for all those years.

"The scarf…" She looked back up at his face. "Your Father purchased the scarf from my dad's cart at market only weeks before the day of destruction. Betty had her kittens a couple weeks before that day. Maybe the scarf somehow connected us. At least it connected your mind to me." Connecting the dots logically felt important to Leena. After all, she didn't know anything about Lance, not really. And he seemed to know everything about her.

"That's some good figuring-out skills. I think you're onto something," he said, looking impressed and nodding his head. "Come on, I still have something to show you."

They walked in silence for a few minutes. As they rounded a little turn in the path, they came to an opening where small rocks covered the ground and in the center was a large lavender bush. The moon shone directly onto the purple plant and the scent radiated off of it. Leena looked at Lance as she bent down and touched the living shrub, breaking off a small bundle and cradling it in her hands.

"Is there anything, *anything* you cannot do? I can't believe it! How long have you been growing this lavender? It looks like it's been here awhile."

"I missed you so much that I went in search of a lavender shrub years ago. I wandered for many many days looking for one, and when I found it, I breathed it back to life and brought it up here. That way I could always feel close to you."

"Lance I…" Leena didn't even know how she was going to end her sentence, or what she planned on asking him. Her mind swirled. "I don't know what to say." She shook her head faintly. "I really don't know what to say."

Lance stood close to her, but not too close. It was just the right amount of closeness. He seemed to Leena to be the easiest person to be around, even when she had nothing to say, even if she felt clumsy or foolish. It was easy. The moment she looked into his eyes, her mind smoothed out again—no more swirling. He made everything smooth.

"So you never said how your dream ended…I mean I smell the mint, you smell the lavender…and then what?" Leena asked, eyeing him playfully.

He tucked his lips inside his mouth for a moment and said, "That's a fair question." He waited and gathered his thoughts. "In my dream we placed the lavender and mint leaves together and it made a new scent."

"Hmmmm… yeah I bet that smelled good." Leena took in a deep breath to steady herself.

Lance smiled shyly and took the gloves off his hands. Leena set down the mint and the lavender on the ground and Lance tugged her fingers loose from the warm gloves she wore. Then he carefully placed the mint back into her bare palm. She rubbed the mint leaves in her fingers to release the scent. He picked up the lavender and gently rubbed it between his fingers releasing the scent and placed it with the mint in her open hand. At the same time, they each bent down to smell the aroma of the two fragrances together. Their faces almost touching. Leena lowered her hand, but their eyes stayed close and connected to each other.

"That's a beautiful new scent. What happened in your dream next?" Leena whispered, her lips parting slightly.

"This." Lance touched her cheek with his fingers and cupped her face in his hand. She could feel his hand trembling just enough to know that he was feeling butterflies inside him, too. He kissed her cheek and then kissed her lips. Leena never wanted the kiss to end.

Lance picked up her gloves from the ground and tucked them back on her hands.

"You know," Lance said, "you literally made my dreams come true tonight."

Leena giggled and turned away. "It doesn't seem fair. You know my whole life and I don't know anything about yours."

"I'll tell you anything you want to know. I'm an open book." He said and Leena smiled. Lance continued. "I actually am kind of like a book. I've read thousands of them over the last ten years, so if it's one thing I know, it's books. I can be boring, I can give information, I can be funny, I can be sad, I can be exciting…well maybe that's a stretch. I'm not sure how exciting I can be."

Leena laughed into her gloved hands. "Well, I just hope" — Leena paused, fidgeting with her gloves— "I hope you can be patient with me. I'd love to get to know you and feel as close to you as you feel to me, but that will take some time."

"I'll wait," he said quietly. "I'll wait as long as it takes. I have waited this long, and I could wait another hundred years if you needed it. Or more."

"I don't think I'll need a hundred years." Leena looked up at him and extended her hand out to his. He took hold of it without hesitating.

They stayed there by the lavender bush enjoying the scent of mint and lavender long enough that when they returned to the cabin, the others were fast asleep.

For the next two weeks they studied and learned all they could by reading the writings on the records kept in the cave and asking the earth for guidance on the best way to move forward with a plan. Preparing for battle against the Destroyers consumed their thoughts and their conversations.

Coming up with a plan was not as easy as Leena had hoped. They each had different ideas about how it should be done. Mandy wanted to lead them all into a cave so they were trapped but Lance felt that realistically no cave would be big enough. Leena, Fife, Jillian, and Mandy did not know how numerous the Destroyers' army was. But Lance did. He had seen them on the day of destruction.

"On that day, we were finishing up working in the caves, my Father and I." Lance had never spoken about that day before, and the other four listened closely, gathered around the fireplace in his home, sitting on pillows. Lance sat leaning forward with his arms resting on his legs.

"We had collected the lapis all day and had quite a few bags full of stones. As we came out of the caves from high up on the mountain…" He hesitated and took in an audible breath,"…I could see them, down below, I could see them coming." Lance's eyes glazed over, seeing every detail in his mind. "Thousands of them marching toward the mountain, beating their sticks on the earth, perfectly synchronized." He clasped his hands together and placed them under his chin and closed his eyes. Lance looked lost in thought as he brought the disturbing memory to the front of his mind. "And the monstrous black cloud rolled in fast."

"Get into the cave," his father said quietly but firmly. "It has begun."

"No Father! I want to stay with you!" the young boy pleaded in defiance.

"You know who you are. You must be spared. I cannot survive this. The day has come. You have been trained well. In time, the others will find you and the five will save us all."

"No, Father! I'm not ready!" The boy clung to his father's legs.

"You are ready." His father's voice softened but stayed firm. "Do not forget the records and the book Time and Knowledge Revealed. It is the key to all mysteries." His father knelt down and lovingly caressed his son's cheeks. The

stomping got louder and the cloud more furious. Other mountain dwellers in the distance screamed and fled from their homes, trying to outrun the cloud and the Destroyers' army. Urgently his Father said, "You must get into the caves now, and stay there with the stones." Then looking directly into his son's eyes, he said, "You are a Life Breather, Lance. You will save us all. Now go."

Lance's small, shaking legs ran back into the cave, and he hiked in as deeply as he could. He sat down and brought his knees to his chin, clutching his royal blue scarf around his neck. Using his breath, he calmed his shaking insides as the Destroyers stormed the mountain with ease and the black cloud flooded through nearly every space. The lapis in his hands protected Lance as he waited deep in the cave.

Hours passed. He emerged from the cave entrance. A small dark haired boy of nine stood alone on the edge of a mountain peak.

Blackness surrounded him.

Lance looked drained of all his energy, and he hung his head. Leena pulled her pillow over close to him and put her arm around his shoulder. He looked relieved and calm as her soft fingers rubbed his arm.

"You were strong," she said. "To obey your Father and go into the cave." With her other hand she lifted his chin and tilted his head so he looked directly at her. "That took courage."

He nodded his head faintly. They all sat quietly for a few minutes. Then Lance broke the silence.

"They will never all fit in a cave. We have to beat them on the ground. The level ground. The flatlands," Lance said softly.

"What's th'flatlands?" Fife asked.

"The flatlands are just beyond the mountain to the west. If we traveled up and over to the other side, there is a stretch of land that is level in all directions for miles. If we could somehow get them to assemble there, we might have a chance to use the stones to paralyze them."

Mandy spoke. "Fife and I share a gift of powerful breath. When we inhale and let it go with force, it's like a typhoon."

"That's true. It's one of me secret weapons." Fife nodded. "Only, I didn't know it was actually a true gift, but I will gladly accept it. What do ye have in mind?"

Mandy continued to explain. "We'll need to disable the Destroyers from their sticks. The sticks have the power to extinguish the life that it touches, so in the past I've used my breath to disarm them by forcefully destroying their sticks so I only have to deal with them. Without their sticks, they are weak. They can still attack, like they did last time with Fife, grabbing hold of his throat from a distance, but as long as we keep them strangled with the ropes of light I think we can contain them. It worked pretty well last time, right Fife?" Mandy eyed him.

"Yeah, yeah that's right." Fife answered, rubbing his neck, remembering the attack.

"But what about the black cloud?" Leena asked. "Fife, Jillian, and I have been inside that cloud and it's massive and there's no air to breathe in there. It took all our focus just to remind ourselves who we are and what our purpose is."

Lance repeated the prophecy from *Riddles of Time Secrets of Stones* for memory.

"The day comes nigh that darkness swoons. Life filled with air soon all consumed. No breath no life but five remain who still as yet gather in the remnant breath. The stones to bring 'round circled in. One of calm and guiding light. One of harmony heals in optimistic glow. One of peace, purity with wisdom gained through time and trial. One of protection, balance and battle, strong and fragile alike. And the last One of knowledge, truth and compassion for all. Combine the five and circle 'round the light a hole formed in the ground. Out the cloud of darkness spell—A new day comes and new life breathes to begin again. Trust and live and heal them till" —Lance paused and finished slowly— "life again brings breath to all."

Jillian listened quietly, her arm looped with Fife's and sitting close together on the pillows. She spoke for the first time.

"It mentions twice the idea of circling the stone around together. I think we should pay attention to that."

"I agree. The stones play a significant part," Lance said. "That is what the Life Breathers of the past were missing. Combining calm, harmony, purity, balance, and truth into one. Yes, circling the stones together. Each stone in turn."

They continued to talk through their plan and finished the evening meditating separately in the warm home by the fire. Each of them in their preferred position. This time, Lance sat cross-legged next to Leena. The mint herbs simmered on the stove, giving off a strong, fresh, illuminating scent.

When they finished, Fife, Jillian and Mandy got into their bedrolls and drifted off to sleep. Lance breathed a small flame to life on a candle and headed to the table, grabbing a book from the shelf on his way over.

"What are you reading tonight?" Leena asked curiously, following him across the room.

"This is called 'Diamond Sutra'. It is the oldest book that we have in our collection. I've read it before, but it still fascinates me each time. I spent years studying it and translated it to our language."

"What does it say?" Leena asked, peering over his shoulder, her hair falling over his shoulder and brushing across his cheek.

"Lots of things," Lance glanced up at her and smiled.

"Like what?" Leena pushed teasingly.

He began to read in little more than a whisper. "So you should view this fleeting world—a star at dawn, a bubble in a stream, a flash of lightning in a summer cloud, a flickering lamp, a phantom, and a dream."

"That's beautiful."

"It is." Lance agreed.

Leena sat down on the pillow chair across the table from him. She rested her hands on the table and leaned toward him slightly. "Do you believe we can do this? Is this going to work? Is this our destiny and our purpose?"

Lance pondered his answer before he gave it. "There are only a few things I know as truth," Lance began. "One, the earth knows us. Two, this is our purpose, and three…" Lance tilted his chin down then glanced up at Leena without moving his head. They stared at each other. She waited patiently for his third truth. He reached over and twirled a ringlet of her brown hair in his finger. "And three, I am in love with you, Leena." His gaze did not falter. He confessed his love as a truth. Something that is. A truth that will never change.

Leena looked at him seriously. "You. Love me?" she asked, with a smile curling up on one side. "You love me." She stated again, this time not in the form of a question.

"Yes, I do. I adore you. I believe in you. I trust you. I love you." Lance took her hand that still rested on the table in front of him. "When this is all done I want to be with you. I want to go to your daisy patch in the meadow with you, and I want to meet your family. I even want to meet your goat."

"How do you know about Prickle?" she asked, laughing quietly so she wouldn't wake the others.

"A dream." He shrugged his head to one side in his charming way.

"Can I ask you something?"

"Yes of course, anything."

"In your dreams you've had about me, have you noticed anything wrong with me?" she asked in a serious tone, her throat hurting because of her need to cry but forcing it back.

"Wrong with you? No. Why would you ask that?" He looked at her gently.

"I seem to sway back and forth in my conviction. One minute I am strong and courageous, full of hope, and then the next minute I'm afraid and hiding my tears, and I allow despair in. It's all so overwhelming sometimes, I just feel there must be…must be something wrong with me. If I were stronger like Mandy, I could fight and stay strong even in quieter moments. If I were happy like Fife and always looking for the good, or if I—"

"Leena. Stop." He shook his head. "You are not weaker because of your weaknesses. Don't you see? This is what sets you apart. You feel the fear and the hopelessness and you choose to push on despite it. It is a gift, Leena. That is courage through the fear. It is resilient courage. It makes you human that you are afraid, but the important thing is you don't give up. You keep going. Every time."

And that was her answer. Lance had answered the question that had haunted her mind. *What kind of courage do I have? Do I even have courage at all?*

The answer to her own personal riddle. Having weakness is her strength. Her eyes filled with tears, and she did not stop them from coming. The throb in her throat eased as she allowed the moisture to escape her eyes without restraint.

"Thank you, Lance."

He lifted her hand and kissed it.

They sat holding hands across the table for hours, talking about the meadow and the future. She wanted nothing more than to talk with Lance until sunrise, but he would not allow it.

"You should get some sleep," he said gently.

"So should you."

"Me? Nah. I couldn't sleep right now if I tried. I'd just lay there thinking about you for hours, and I'd still be laying awake when the sun came up over the mountain."

Leena smiled at him and said, "Just so you know, I am a Life Breather, and I think it's a little remarkable that the only time I feel out of breath is when I think about you… in a good way."

She released her hand from his and quietly said goodnight.

23

Icefall

"Expect the unexpected. Plan to change your plan. Be flexible. Things will ultimately work in your favor."

The five gathered on the mountain shelf early the next morning and divided out the stones so each of them had equal amounts of amethyst, amazonite, pearls, hematite and lapis. They formulated their plan, agreeing to bring the mountain back to life first. After that, they would need to travel to the other side of the mountain and down to the flatlands. Once they reached the flatlands, they would use their combined breath to bring back all the animal life of the world at one time, in hopes that it would gather enough momentum to call in all the Destroyers and the black cloud.

Fife and Mandy had the gift of powerful breath so they would use that gift to fight the Destroyers, while Leena, Jillian, and Lance held their breath and journeyed into the cloud, position the stones in a circle as the prophecy instructed, and rely on the power of the stones to help destroy it once and for all.

After they divided out the stones, they sealed them tightly in pouches with a long strap that hung across their chest and at the side of their bodies.

"Well, I think we're ready," Leena said, looking out over the land.

Mandy added, "Let's go get a good meal. We're going to need it."

The others agreed, and they hiked back down to Lance's home.

They each packed a small, lightweight pack and agreed they would return after the battle ended to retrieve their other belongings. Quiet filled the warm home as they ate. The smell of mint permeated the air. They sipped their tea and ate the sweet poms and flatbread that Lance had baked the evening before.

No one spoke.

Leena thought about her family. Aaron. Mum. Dad. She could feel them closer now. They seemed so close. This was her purpose. She was made for this moment in time. Her heart felt calm and courageous one minute but uncertainty continuously crept in the next. Would their plan work? Was this the best way? Were they really prepared? The words of Lance from the night before echoed in her memory. *You are not weaker because of your weaknesses. Don't you see? This is what sets you apart. You feel the fear and the hopelessness, and you choose to push on despite it. It is a gift, Leena. That is courage through the fear. It is resilient courage. It makes you human that you are afraid, but the important thing is you don't give up. You keep going. Everytime.*

Resilient courage. Yes she could do this.

Leena could see the anxiety on Jillian's face. Fife rubbed her back in smooth motions, but the color in Jillian's face drained. She doubled over on her pillow, holding her stomach.

"I think I'm going to be sick." Jillian barely managed to get the words out before she rolled to the side and off the pillow completely, fainting.

"Jilly!" Fife said, alarmed. "It's alrigh'. Your'e gonna be alrigh'."

Jillian lay unconscious, and Fife laid her body down flat and elevated her feet with a pillow, brushing her hair off her face. Lance quickly wet a cloth with cool water and handed it to Fife. Fife smoothed the cloth over her forehead and stroked her cheeks with his thumb.

"You are strong, Jillian. And I will be with you th'whole time. We are gonna beat 'em. We are gonna win. I know it." Jillian slowly opened her eyes. The concerned faces of Leena, Fife, Mandy, and Lance looking down at her.

"I'm…I'm so sorry," Jillian said in a weak voice. "Maybe I'm not strong enou—"

"*That* is ridiculous," Mandy said. "Of course you are strong enough. You are a Life Breather. You survived *living as a child* on your own for ten years after your family was taken by the Destroyers. You *are* strong enough. And we need you." Mandy looked at the others and continued. "We are all strong, We are going to do this…together." Mandy, who rarely showed her emotions, spoke passionately. She looked at her hands and twisted her fingers uncharacteristically. "I want you all to know that… you are like a family to me." She looked up and met Leena's eyes. "Thank you for being brave." She took a deep breath and said, "I love you guys." The other four stared at her, looking shocked. Mandy narrowed her eyes and added, "Now let's do this."

"Yyyyesss!" Fife said, lifting his fist. "We were born for this, and we can do anythin'!" He helped Jillian to a sitting position and got her some mint tea. The color returned to her face as she breathed in a few refreshing breaths.

"I'm ready," Jillian said.

"Me, too," echoed Leena.

"Alright then, let's go," Lance said, and he grabbed his pack.

Fife put his cap on his head and they all walked out the door of the cozy mountain home and onto the cold mountain.

When they reached the top peak, they each stood in mountain pose and breathed in the crisp air. The five of them stood straight and tall, facing the open air at the edge of the mountain with the wind blowing into their faces, blowing their hair back and their palms facing the pressing wind.

Gently close your eyes. Feel the muscles in your face soften with each breath you take. Breathe in calm. Breathe out despair. Breathe in harmony. Breathe out distraction. Breathe in purity. Breathe out worry. Breathe in balance. Breathe out pain. Breathe in truth. Breathe out and feel gratitude for life. Let the gratitude fill your heart. You are strong. You are a Life Breather. Breathe life now.

The mountain took its first breath. The five opened their eyes. The mountain rippled like a wave and made a dull roar, billowing down the mountain side. Something happened just then that the five did not foresee. With the rippling wave of the mountain's first breath, a layer of snow collapsed just above them from the next peak up and the snow began to slide downhill. A mass of snow, rock, ice, and dirt rolled and tumbled down toward them. Instinctively, Lance reached for Leena's hand, clasping it and with urgency. "Get to the cave! An icefall!" They ran in the direction of the cave of records, down the snowy path as the avalanche of snow came crashing towards them. This was not part of the plan! It wasn't supposed to happen like this! Leena's mind raced and the guiding hand of Lance was the only thing that kept her steady as they ran.

Just as they reached the path to the cave a massive snowslide collided with the mountain shelf they were on. Fife tried to shield Jillian as the next wave was about to strike, but the torrent came too fast and swept her under a snow bank.

"No!" Fife yelled out. His voice pierced the wind and echoed off every rock. His long arms flung recklessly as he dug into the bank looking for any sign of Jillian. The others ran to his aid, all of them digging furiously, the snow crashing around them.

Finally, Fife saw the end of Jillian's white scarf, its tassels blending in with the snow. With tears of terror he continued to dig, his hands frozen and purple. The scarf led Fife to her body and he pulled her out, scooped her limp body into his arms and they ran into the entrance of the cave moments before a cascade of snow barricaded the opening. They were all safe in the pitch dark cave. And they were trapped.

"Jillian! Jillian! Please be okay. Please." Fife sobbed in the dark. "Please don't leave me. I don't wanna do this without ya." His tears flowed wildly. Jillian remained unmoving in his arms.

Mandy and Lance quickly breathed fire to life into the torches that surrounded the cave walls.

Jillian's face was still. Her body, motionless. Fife took her hands and warmed them in his, breathing on to them. For the second time today, Fife held Jillian who looked as though she were asleep, unresponsive. He held her and cried, clutching her small body close to his and rocking back and forth.

Leena sat quietly breathing in and out through her nose. *There is life all around me. There is life all around me.* She breathed in and out her mantra begging the earth for a miracle. They could not do this task without Jillian. All five of them were needed. Each stone, each Life Breather. Leena continued to breathe and she could feel Mandy and Lance silently breathing behind her.

"You are a Life Breather, Jillian! Breathe now!" Fife commanded her. Within seconds, her body jolted with life and she took a gasp of air into her lungs.

Fife's body relaxed, and his head rested on Jillian's head. He whispered in her ear, "Who told ya ye could fall asleep like that? In the middle of an icefall." He breathed heavily. "What would I do without ya, now that I know what my life is like with ya?"

Jillian smiled weakly, and wrapped her arms tightly around him.

Unexpectedly, they heard a terrifying, thunderous sound, beating in unison far in the distance. Lance closed his eyes and bowed his head. "They've come."

"It's too soon!" Mandy protested. "We needed more time to get off the mountain to the flatlands and now we're trapped in this cave!"

Leena's heart sank. Their plan was not going the way it was supposed to. The way they *needed* it to. What now?

Fife stood up and paced. "Why're they here already? How'd they know? We ain't even brought back animals yet." He continued pacing. "Okay, okay there be a solution to ev'ry problem. We gotta find it…what is it?…" As he paced, ideas raced out of his mouth. Most of which were not possible by any stretch of the imagination or by any power. But still Leena was grateful he continued to think.

The sound of thousands of sticks beating on the ground got louder. They marched closer.

"All this snow. We gotta get rid of it," Fife said casually like he was telling them about the food he wanted to eat for lunch. Something strange happened inside of Leena. She could see something in her mind. A shift.

"Have you ever changed the season?" Leena asked Lance, looking up at him quickly.

"The season, like from winter to summer?"

"Yes," Leena said. "I've never tried it but I remember my Mum telling me that her grandmother would do it all the time. And you, you have made daisies bloom in the winter on the mountain. It must be similar."

"That would…melt the snow…and the snow would turn to water…a flood."

"Yes, it might buy us some time," Leena offered. "Not to mention it would open the mouth of this cave."

Fife smiled. Leena glanced at him with a nod of her head in appreciation.

They could hear the Destroyers marching up the sides of the mountain. Thump thump boom! Thump thump boom! In endless repetition. The Life Breathers sat in breathing position in the cave and called on their power of breath to change the cold winter season on the mountain to a summer day.

Each of them in their minds visualized all the things of summertime, blocking out the beating and hearing only sounds of summer. The warmth of the soft air, catching frogs in a pond, the gentle hum of bumble bees, cotton blowing through the breeze, walking barefoot in the grass, gathering wildflowers, the campfire crackling, the sweet scent of roses in bloom, building sand castles by the sea, playing hide-and-seek until the late but still warm hours in the evening, roasting mushrooms over the fire, stargazing, blue, cloudless skies that extend forever.

Drip. Drip. Drip. The snow covering the cave entrance began to melt. Summer was on its way! Leena bloomed inside like a flower, a thrill filling her chest but the beating of the sticks on the earth continued.

At that moment, the sound of a rushing wave gushed outside the cave. The snow that blocked the entrance crashed down and flooded the cave with a foot of water before it rushed out the entrance and down the side of the mountain.

From inside the cave, they could see water thrashing ferociously through every path on the mountain. The beating of the sticks relentlessly continued. As the falling water slowed near the cave entrance, they ventured out just in time to see a massive wave of water rolling over the upper peak and down onto the army of thousands of Destroyers below, breaking the rhythm of the sticks and scattering them all off the edge of the mountain side.

"We need to get to the flatlands!" Lance yelled out.

The five ran up the mountain path, now lush with greenery. Summer heat filled the air. Running up and over the ridge, they made their way down the other side of the mountain, now able to see a clear view of the flatlands from above. Their pace quickened as they changed direction and ran downhill instead of up. The path on the other side of the mountain was not well defined, so they followed Lance's lead weaving in and out of brush and rocks. They could no longer hear or see the Destroyers. But Leena knew the flood would not eliminate them, it would only delay them.

The five stuffed their scarves into their packs, sweat sliding down their faces from running in the heat of summer. At such a fast pace, they reached the base of the mountain in little time. Their bodies should have been exhausted, but they felt nothing but strength. Leena gathered a strength inside her she had never known before. A strength that burned like a fire that refused to go out. She could feel the light inside her. Everything up to this point had prepared her for this. They could not fail. Not with the help of the earth and all of nature on their side.

The five of them stood together at the base of the mountain. They stood straight and tall looking out at the Destroyers who had gathered on the flatlands a half a mile in front of them, the sticks in their bony black hands. Both sides were ready for battle.

Their first step off the mountain signaled to the Destroyers to beat on the earth once again. One stick at a time, their chant began. The army of deathly black figures marched militantly towards the five.

"It's time," Lance said without a trace of fear.

24

Circle of Stones

"When you find yourself in the darkness, take a moment to breathe, focus, and
remember who you are.
Never give into the darkness.
You are a Life Breather."

The five Life Breathers stood upright, confident, and faced the enemy in front of them. The monotonous, deliberate beating of the sticks rang in their ears. A deathly sound of drum beats smothered the air. The army marched towards them, but the five felt no fear. The black cloud, nowhere in sight.

"It's time to bring the animals back," Mandy said. Their well defined plan had failed. The Destroyers were already here, but their need for the animals of the earth was even greater now. Not just to bring the Destroyers back, like they had planned originally, but for the strength in numbers.

They nodded in agreement. With three deep, smooth breaths in and out they repeated their mantra.

There is life in me. There is life all around me. There is life in me. There is life all around me. I can see the life of the earth. I feel the life of the earth's creatures, great and small. Breathe. Breathe. Breathe life. Fulfill your destiny and return to the earth.

Louder than the beating sticks, the sound of thunderous hooves and paws stampeding down the mountainside and across the flatlands ruptured the air. Birds of all kinds filled the sky with a warcry. Eagles and horses. Hawks and mountain lions. Rhinos and llamas. Giraffes, coyotes, elephants, wolves, and hundreds of other species fiercely made their way down the mountain and out onto the flatlands, gathering around the Life Breathers, facing the army of Destroyers.

The Life Breathers inhaled a great breath of gratitude and relief at the sight of the wildlife returning. A herd of bull elk stood together and pawed the ground ready to attack. Lions, panthers, cougars, tigers, cats of all sizes joined as allies. The animals were part of the earth, and they were ready to stand and fight. Leena, Fife, Jillian, Mandy, and Lance watched in wonder at the bravery in the hearts of these creatures.

The Destroyers continued to march closer, now only a couple hundred feet away. The darkness of their presence pressed upon the earth.

"Fife, are you ready to hold your breath?" Mandy asked with a sly smile.

"Yeah, but rememba, I can only hold it for… 'bout ten second." Fife winked.

"That's all we'll need."

The two of them filled their lungs with air for a count of ten and in unison exhaled, creating a cyclone of powerful wind that ripped through the air and whipped into the army of the thousands of Destroyers, knocking them down, wrenching their long bone sticks from their grasp and shattering the sticks to pieces on the dusty earth. The dark figures emerged from the ground and continued walking steadily toward them in silence, emotionless, featureless, lifeless, breathless.

The sky looked dizzy.

The summer blue swayed.

Leena recognized the early signs. Her heart flipped inside her. "The sky. It's moving. The black cloud is coming!"

Each of the five pulled their gemstone out of their pouch that hung at their waist. They would need to enter the black cloud together. Originally they thought Fife and Mandy would fight off the Destroyers while Leena, Jillian, and Lance placed the stone inside the cloud, but now it was clear. They had to be together.

Leena held her amethyst, a symbol to the earth of calm. Fife held up his amazonite, the stone of harmony. Jillian put a small pearl between her fingers and held it toward the sun. It shone brilliantly in the light. A sign of purity. Mandy grasped the hematite, symbolizing the balance within herself. And Lance held up the lapis lazuli, the stone of truth. Bright bands of light exploded out of each and connected the stones, creating blazing rays of light that focused on the thousands of Destroyers in front of them.

The black cloud rolled in the sky, gathering speed as it got closer to the ground. The rays of light wrapped around the Destroyers, the golden strings tightening around each of them, choking them as they sputtered and thrashed for breath.

The Life Breathers held the stones out with the connecting light-ropes with immense effort. It took all their energy to hold the stones as the Destroyers thrashed against the ropes that held them.

The animals stood silently at attention, waiting for the signal to attack. Mandy turned and looked at the animals. With one nod of her head they roared in recognition. Now pressing forward they charged the Destroyers, racing towards them with such rage trampling the black faceless figures under the force of the stampede. As the golden bands of light from the gemstones continued to hold them captive and squeeze the life breath out of them, the animals pounded them into the ground until they turned to no more than ash on the flatlands. The animals continued stomping the black dusty remains into the dry earth until the Destroyers no longer left any trace of existence. On Mandy's command the animals retreated to the mountains, keeping them safe from the force of the looming cloud.

The black cloud approached, hovering over the flatlands with suffocating smoke. With no time to celebrate the victory over the Destroyers, the five turned towards the black cloud and prepared themselves mentally to enter. They closed their eyes and breathed in and out through their nose, smooth and steady. Out of their pouch they took their handful of gemstones, one of each.

The black cloud swirled in front of them. A quiet rage filling it with movement. Jillian reached out for Fife's hand, and he grabbed it tightly. Leena looked at Mandy and Lance and nodded.

"Let's go," Leena said calmly, despite the commotion inside her. Their hearts pounded. Adrenaline raced through their veins. With undying courage, the five Life Breathers stepped forward into the darkness.

Immediately, the black cloud sucked the breath out of them as they were surrounded. *Stay focused. Stay present. You are a Life Breather. Breathe.* Leena's mind felt choked along with her body. *Remember who you are. You are Leena. You are a Life Breather.* She could see by the look in the others' faces that they were experiencing the same struggle. Her breath vanished momentarily. Wildly she threw her head from side to side looking for help. *Stay calm.* Something or someone unseen whispered. Without being able to think, focus, or breathe normally, it became nearly impossible to see clearly. People wandered through the cloud, gliding in the darkness. *Focus. Focus. Breathe.* Her mind silently battled with itself to give her breath away or fight to keep it.

It would be so easy to let it go. If she let go of her breath and gave the cloud what it wanted, she could stop struggling. Stop fighting. Stop existing. It would be so easy.

So many people wandering in the darkness. *Help them. Breath life into them*, the whisper urged, but suddenly Leena could no longer remember what gave her life. A darkness covered her mind and her heart felt lonely. *Who am I? What am I doing here? What is my purpose?* A new whisper began. *You are nothing. You have no purpose. You are alone.*

Leena lost the feeling in her legs and just as she was about to collapse, an arm wrapped around her waist and pulled her in close. Leena could feel his breath on her, the focused air from his mouth traveling in a steady stream directly into her mouth. Each particle of air went exactly where he told it to go in her body. She heard Lance's voice.

"You are a Life Breather, Leena. Find your family."

My family. I am a Life Breather. The darkness inside her mind melted away, like snow to summer, and light flooded through her entire body. She opened her palm to see the stones still in her hand, waiting. Looking around she saw Fife, Jillian, and Mandy kneeling down placing their stones in one circle together. They were going slowly, no doubt fighting the same mental battle that Leena was. Lance, by her side, dropped to his knees and added his stones with the others. Mandy concentrated hard on her purpose. Jillian trembled but pressed forward, taking deep breaths in and out. Fife looked confident and determined. And Lance looked at Leena, nodding his head, reassuring her.

Leena's stones were the last to be added to the circle. Placing each stone, one by one, she thought about what it represented. Calm. Leena was the amethyst, a guiding light to all. Harmony. Fife was the amazonite, spreading happiness and positivity. Purity. Jillian was the pearl, pure and peaceful, learning wisdom through experience. Balance. Mandy was the hematite. Finding balance within herself, a true warrior. Truth. Lance. Lance was the lapis. He was truth, knowledge and protection.

After they had placed the stones into the circle, the minds of the five became one. The cloud swirled, writhing in anger, and a great wind whirled around them. Together, they stood up and looked into the foot-wide circle of stones on the ground. Their hair blew wildly, but they remained calm. The five blew a steady breath into the center of the gemstone circle, breathing the circle to life. The stones glowed in response. Then with a loud gasp, as if the earth itself inhaled a breath, a hole opened up inside the circle of gemstones and a powerful suction drew in the black cloud through the opening of the earth's chasm.

The black fog sucked into the earth with such force that the five held onto each other tightly and stood back, watching in amazement. The wandering people continued to walk aimlessly as the cloud disappeared into the depths of the earth.

The blackness thinned, becoming easier and easier for the five to breathe without focused attention.

The black cloud disappeared, sliding out of control into the hole, moaning and grasping for power until it was finally, completely gone.

The hole within the circle of stones sealed itself closed.

Exhaustion collapsed onto them. Jillian fell into Fife's arms and sobbed tears of joy, but also tears of fatigue. Fife held her, and they sat together on the flat, hard ground, crying and laughing, Fife caressing her long, blonde hair. Leena grabbed Mandy in a hug and then turned to Lance.

"We destroyed it," Leena said, her voice shaking. Her breath still heaving. Lance took her trembling hand in his and touched her face gently. Relief passed over her body like a warm wave. The earth had arranged everything to work in their favor. The icefall, the flood, the Destroyers coming before they intended, all of it so they would enter the cloud united. This soothed Leena.

"We did," he said in a soft voice, "Let's go find our families. They're waiting for us."

Leena's eyes searched through the mass of people. "How will we ever find them? There are so many people."

"We save them all. Eventually...they'll find us," Lance responded, full of compassion. The masses of people gravitated slowly towards them.

"They are coming for us, to save them," Leena said, full of hope, scanning the crowds.

The five walked among the multitudes of people. One by one, the Life Breathers breathed gently onto the faces of the wanderers. As they did this, the black webbing melted away and each took in a cleansing breath. Color returned to their faces and trickled down their entire body. Faces lit up with joy and life spread across the flat-lands like butterflies on a desert oak tree. Love erupted with each hug of glorious reunion that surrounded the five.

After hours of giving breath back to the masses of people, Lance came upon a man, shorter than him, but of similar build. He knew him before he breathed gently onto his face. Lance stared at the man in front of him and the man blindly stared back. Lance touched the man's shoulder and leaned in closer to him.

"Father." A tear fell down Lance's cheek. A gentle breath came out of Lance's mouth and onto his father's face, giving life and color back to his body. A man with the same deep golden-brown skin and black hair streaked with grey, inhaled his first breath. As he exhaled, he looked at Lance and said in a fragile voice, "My boy. You saved me." They both looked down at the earth and bowed to each other in profound respect, and embraced. Leena watched the miraculous scene, letting the tears fall without wiping them.

Shortly after Lance reunited with his father, Leena saw Mandy running through the crowd after three small girls. She found her sisters. Without pause, she breathed onto their faces and without waiting for the color to return she fell to her knees, clasping them in an hug. The three young girls, Carissa, Bethany and Bree, knew Mandy's face immediately even though time had aged her and they wept, crying out her name in gratitude and disbelief.

Leena began to search more urgently for Mum, Dad, and Aaron, but she did not see them anywhere.

Jillian's voice rang out, calling to Fife, "Fife! I found them!"

Fife came running to Jillian as four young men and two little girls came running as fast as they could toward Fife, colliding together with a family hug in a mess of tears, laughter, and chatter.

"Did ya save us, Fife?" one brother asked.

"You be the tallest brother in th'forest!" another shouted.

"How'd this 'appen?" asked a third.

"How long's it been?" yelled out the last brother.

"This is Jillian! She saved you all!" Fife called out with laughter. "And she's gonna be part of our family." He kissed Jillian on the lips. Then he bent down and kissed Lil and Rose each on their noses. They giggled and reached up for him.

A woman approached, still covered with blackness, standing in front of Fife. He stared at her, recognizing her small frame and curly hair. He lovingly touched her face with the tenderness of a little boy.

"Mama?" his voice squeaked, barely audible, but with just enough breath coming from his mouth that it gently brushed against her face. The blackness dissolved and pink cheeks and long blonde curls emerged. His Mama. She looked up at him and did not say a word. Her eyes squeezed shut and she put her hand over her mouth.

"It's alrigh' Mama, it's me," Fife said, carefully pulling her toward him and hugging her. She grabbed onto him tightly and he lifted her feet off the ground.

"I'm so sorry, son. I couldn't get t'ya. I couldn't find ya soon enough," she said helplessly through sobs.

"No, no Mama. Imma be fine. Look at me! I'm jus' fine." And he laughed as they hugged. His Mama buried her face into his chest, clutching him tightly like she'd never let go.

A buzz of excitement filled the air as everyone reunited. With so many faces and people all over the flatlands now, alive and rejoicing, it got harder to see those still trapped in darkness.

From far away, Leena saw a man and a woman with a young toddling boy beside them, still in a trance. Leena ran as fast as she could across the flatlands toward them. As she got closer, she slowed down as she could see it was not Mum and Dad. Her heart dropped and she fell to the ground, covering her face with her arms. Lance ran behind her, following her to the small family. He gently breathed life into their faces. As they breathed new life they began calling "Jillian! Jillian!" Leena looked up. It was Jillian's mother and father and her little brother, Jonny, looking just like Mum, Dad, and Aaron would've.

Jillian looked over in disbelief at the sound of the familiar voices that she had not heard in ten years. She ran to her family. Jonny saw her coming and recognized her long, blonde, wavy hair and white pearl necklace. He cried out to her and ran to meet her. They met in the middle and she picked him up and swung him around as if they were playing by the sea.

Lance took Leena by the hand. "We'll find them. Don't worry. We'll find them."

Many of the people made the trek up the mountain. It would be a long journey traveling back to their homes.

Leena, Lance, Fife, Jillian, and Mandy continued searching for Leena's family. Their families followed along, continuing to hug and cry and tell stories of what had happened over the last ten years with lots of laughter.

Inside Leena, an ache grew. What if she never found them? All the hope she had put into being with her family felt further away.

"Sit with me, Leena." Lance guided her to an open area, away from everyone—away from the noise and chatter of loved ones reuniting. They sat down together in a quiet place.

"Let's breathe," Lance said calmly. "I know they're out there. There are thousands still wandering. We need to call your family to us." As Lance spoke, a tear slid down Leena's cheek. She scooted close to him and leaned her head on his shoulder.

"Thank you for believing," she sobbed. "I want to believe, but…"

"Trust the earth, Leena. They are here. Close your eyes. I will guide your thoughts."

Leena closed her eyes and listened to Lance's smooth voice.

Sit in a comfortable position. Bring your spine up straight so you feel connected to the earth beneath you. Grounding you. There is a thread of light coming from the top of your head connecting you to the sky. Breathe in through your nose. Feel your breath move through your body. Giving life to every part of you. Breathe out through your nose. Release all worry and despair. Breathe in. Breathe out. Relax every muscle in your face. Relax your jaw. Let it drop down inside your mouth. Drop your shoulders. Soften your hands. Breathe in. Breathe out.

See your dad. See him putting on his cap as he leaves with his carriage full of goods to sell at market. See the royal-blue scarf sitting on the top of the pile, waiting for its new owner. Smell the pies as they ride off in the carriage. See your mum. Her long, straight hair, looking just how she looked on the day of your seventh birthday, when she made you apple tartlets and gave you your purple scarf. See your brother, Aaron. He is searching for you, just as he searched for the kittens on the day they were born. He will find you, just as he found them. He needs you, Leena. Breathe in. Breathe out. Find him in your mind. See him. Call for him to come.

"I can see him." Leena spoke out loud. "I can see him!" She still had her eyes closed. "He is close." She opened her eyes and looked around.

Leena and Lance stood up, their eyes searching in all directions. Three dark figures walked towards them. Two taller. One small. Leena looked at Lance with big eyes, and hope illuminated her body.

Memories flooded through her, like a river. Mum and Leena baking biscuits with flour on their faces, watching shooting stars, sitting on the soft grass late at night, slow roasted 'shrooms over a campfire, Aaron flapping his arms like a duck, Mum holding a wish flower out for Leena to practice on, playing cards with Dad and digging for purple gemstones. Everything came all at once like magic. Memories are magical. The ability to remember glimpses of time as if it were yesterday. Magic.

They walked closer and closer towards each other. Leena wanted to run, but she continued to walk with patience, wanting to savor the memory she was making now. Mum looked slender and poised, even clothed in black, walking gracefully towards Leena. Dad, still wearing his cap, his lips were webbed closed and emotion-less. Aaron, still in his little overalls, now charcoal black instead of green, that he wore on that day so long ago. They were coming to her and she was going to save them and bring them home to the meadow. Indescribable joy filled Leena's soul, a joy so powerful she thought she might burst and collapse under the weight of it. Her insides trembled, but she looked as calm as a sunrise.

Standing face to face, Leena gave a soft, healing breath on Mum's cheek and kissed her. Color spread evenly through Mum's face, and her pink lips returned. She smiled as soon as she could move her mouth. Mum stared into Leena's eyes.

"You are a Life Breather," Mum whispered, and she hugged Leena as tears swelled in her eyes.

Leena kissed Dad's cheek. Dad inhaled and opened his eyes. With tears brimming, he said, "My darling, Leena." He held her face. "You have truly grown up to be a beautiful princess." He hugged her and kissed her forehead. Then he looked at his wife. His most beloved treasure and kissed her deeply. "I've missed you so."

Leena kissed Aaron's forehead. Color flooded his face and spread down his body, just like she had visualized in her meditation.

Aaron recognized Leena instantly, even though she had grown so much, the purple dress and dark curls giving her away. His wide smile went from one side of his face to the other.

"LaLa!" he shouted and reached his arms up so that she would pick him up. Leena swooped him in her arms and they squeezed each other tightly. Then he looked around with his big, blue eyes and asked, "Where are we?" They laughed and agreed it was time to go home. Home to their meadow.

The five spent the next few hours breathing life back into all who wandered in darkness before they walked back to the mountain path, Lance held Leena's hand as she told her family all about their journey. She told them about the cave of records and the mint tea with Lance, the pictures on the cave walls and the animals in the canyon with Mandy, Jillian's home under the water and searching for seashells and pearls, Fife and the deer and his beautiful rocking chair. Mum and Dad listened with complete fascination to all that Leena had experienced. The good and the bad over the last ten years of her life had all played a part in creating who Leena had become.

When they reached Lance's home, he invited them in. Lance's Father had already arrived, ready to serve all their families tea and poms. Leena's Dad was in heaven being back in a mountain home. They stayed and rested there along with Mandy and her sisters, Jillian and her family, and Fife and his family. All bundled together in the cozy little home. Laughing and talking into the night. So grateful to be together, alive and breathing.

At one point, Lance leaned over to Leena and whispered into her ear. "I want to stay with you. I don't want to be separated from you by a canyon, desert, sea, village and a forest. I'll never survive." He looked at her with searching eyes.

Leena smiled shyly but did not look up at him. After a pause, she said, "Well" —her eyes met his— "I have heard of mountain boys being quite happy in the meadow."

Lance's face beamed. "I would follow you anywhere, my meadow girl."

Epilogue

Leena sat cross legged on the bank by the stream, hands resting on her knees. Eyes closed. Breathing in and out through her nose. The stream giggled and gurgled the way it should, hopping over rocks, laughing, dancing, and breathing.

In her mind, Leena could see Mandy. Her red silky hair, now long, reaching the middle of her back, pulled into a loose braid. Mandy cupped her hand around her mouth and called, "Come for supper!" The girls bustled in along with a parade of animals. The twins, thirteen now, and Carissa, fifteen. Mandy beamed looking at them. Leena had never seen her look so happy, so satisfied, so fulfilled. Healing comes in all shapes, colors, and sizes. For Mandy, it came from deep inside herself. It came first through a love she found within herself and *then* through the love she had for others.

Leena breathed in and out and thought about Fife and Jillian.

The salty sea air swirled around them in the breeze that only the sea knows, mixing in with the lemongrass scent. They held hands walking along the shoreline. Jillian wore a long white flowing dress and a pearl ring on the finger of her left hand. A crown of white flowers rested on her head.

"Are ya packed up and ready?" Fife asked. "We'll be leavin' at first light."

"I'm ready," Jillian said in her airy voice.

"I think I love th'sea as much as I love th'forest." He put his arm around her softly as they watched the waves roll in and out.

"It was a lovely idea to have our wedding here by the sea and our honeymoon in the forest," Jillian said, smiling up at him.

Fife faced her and held on to her shoulders, gazing into her blue eyes. "I'd marry you anywhere. I'm jus' thrilled ya said yes."

Out of nowhere, Leena breathed in the scent of lavender just as a bundle of purple flowers was placed snugly into her open hand. She opened her eyes. Lance settled down beside her.

"How's the breathing this morning?" he asked.

"Wonderful. You joining?" She looked at him, her eyes alive and bright.

"I think I will. As long as you don't mind Sage joining us as well."

Leena beamed. She peered into the basket Lance brought with him and gazed at the sleeping baby girl nestled inside. Sage's wispy soft hair was impossible not to touch. Leena caressed the brow of her sleeping baby. Sage stirred. Leena tapped Sage's tiny nose and pulled her blanket closer to her chin.

"How did you sleep last night?" Leena asked Lance.

Lance nodded his head thoughtfully. "Really well. I think I'm learning to sleep through the night, finally."

Leena giggled. "You and Sage both."

Lance laughed softly, nodding his head. "Do you know what I love most about the meadow?"

"The…warm air?" Leena teased.

"Yes, yes I love the warm air," he teased back. "But do you know what I love *most*?"

"Hmmmm…the flowers?" she guessed playfully.

"Guess again. I'll give you a hint. What I love more than anything is not the grass or the stream or the big willow tree. It's not the baby lambs or the birds singing first thing in the morning. It's not even the cherries. It is someone more lovely, more magical, more gentle than any of that."

Leena looked into his brown eyes, touching his smooth and strong hands. She knew it was her. He had told her everyday for four years that he loved her more than anything.

"Is it me?" Leena asked, and she laid back onto the soft grass and looked at the cloudless sky.

"It is. And never forget it." He looked down at her, his eyes shining. "I've written it in the book of records, so actually it will be remembered for centuries to come. It's a truth."

"And you know what else is truth?" Leena asked him, raising her eyebrows. "That I love you, my mountain boy."

Lance closed his eyes and smiled. "I never get tired of hearing you say that."

Leena laid on the grass quietly for a few minutes, then sitting up she said, "You know, I thought when we found our families again that we wouldn't need to use our power of breath anymore." She paused and looked at him with serious eyes. "But we need it everyday. Our breath heals the big things, but it also heals the little things." She looked down at the grass and pulled out a few strands. "There are still times when I feel hopelessness inside for no reason at all." She laughed quietly. "I know it doesn't make sense." She looked down at the lavender in her lap and played with the blossoms in her fingers. "But if I turn to my breath and breathe through the feeling, it lifts when it's ready." Leena looked up at Lance. Completely calm. Nothing moved or ached or swirled or fidgeted inside her. Every part of her body, mind, and spirit embraced the calm.

Just then, she heard little running feet approaching behind her. Aaron came trotting down the path to the bank by the stream, and stood beside Leena and Lance, out of breath. Aaron carried a basket full of fresh-baked bread and vegetables from the garden. Being six years old now, he was missing one front tooth, and his hair was untamed.

"You want lunch?" Aaron asked, plopping down the basket. He put his bare feet in the water. "Mum made me bring it."

"Mmmmmm, looks delicious. Thank you, little man." Lance said, handing a slice of bread to Leena. Leena held the warm bread in her hand.

"This does look delicious."

Aaron noticed Sage sleeping in the basket beside Lance. He stepped out of the water and looked in. "Hey, Sagey, you awake?" He said, rocking the basket as gently as a six year old can. Sage opened her eyes and stared up at him. She wiggled a bit then closed her eyes again. "Still sleeping." Aaron sighed and trotted off.

Leena looked down at the bread in her hand. She thought about Mum and how she had made it with her own hands from the grain that Dad had planted and harvested and the eggs from the chickens and milk from the cows. The earth had been so good to Leena and her family.

"Most of the time, life in the meadow is wonderful. I learned through our journey that not everything in life is wonderful. Some-times sad things happen." She paused, looking at Lance while she formulated her words. Lance looked at her, genuinely interested in her thoughts. "And when the sad thing happens, it's good to feel sad. Feel it and breathe. Sometimes, life is frightening. And when those things happen, it's good to feel fear. Feel it and breathe."

The passion in Leena's voice made Lance smile. Leena closed her eyes and inhaled through her nose, filling her lungs with nour-ishing meadow air along with the hardy smell of fresh baked bread. This time the smell of bread took her mind back to a small moun-tain home, sitting around a fire with her four closest friends, in the midst of a destroyed world, and Lance, her newest friend, serving her bread to remind her of home. He had always been there. Even when she did not know it.

Leena paused and looked out at the meadow that lay past the stream. She breathed in the sweet scent of the lavender. "Any feeling that comes in this life, sadness, joy, distraction, focus, worry, peace, guilt, compassion, loneliness, love—feel it. Breathe it in, and really feel it." She inhaled. "Then breathe it out with gratitude."

Leena exhaled completely. "That is how breath can heal us all."

The End

Scan this code for access to free guided meditations that correlate with the five Life Breathers, Leena, Fife, Jillian, Mandy and Lance. YouTube @lifebreather5

Acknowledgments

I usually glide quickly over acknowledgements when reading a book. It's only now that I've written a book and feel the deep gratitude for so many people that I get it. I get it! I want to tell everyone about these amazing people who helped me along my book journey! Forever changing me and changing my book for the better. Big hugs and most sincere love to you all.

My fabulous beta readers: My husband Dave and my daughters Nicole and Lauren. My sisters Ylfelynn, Jandi and Tess. My parents Danielle and Dennis. Amy, my first beta reader from Upwork. My teenage friends, Annie, Grace, Isaac, Gwenn and Audrey. My friend Laura. My nieces and nephews, Wyn, Myles, Pierce and Penny. Meditation coach Jesika and her daughter Bree. THANK YOU! THANK YOU!

Kisses to my husband Dave who took the time out of his very tight schedule to read the first draft of my manuscript and give me honest feedback. He does not read fiction, ever, let alone young adult fiction, so this was such a gift to me from him. Thank you for really honestly loving my book! Thank you for ALWAYS encouraging me and believing I could do this big thing.

Hugs to my daughter Nicole, who spent so much time on my rough, rough, rough draft. Giving me detailed tips, advice, and suggestions. I could not have done this without you. And for the beautiful illustrations. Amazing. Hugs to my daughter, Lauren, who always believed in me and asked me daily how my book was coming along. She was one of the very first to finish the first draft. Thank you for being genuinely interested and curious about my book. Love you both as much as Lorelai loves Rory, as much as Anne loves

Diana, as much as Mary Lennox loves flowers, and as much as chocolate loves peanut butter.

My sons, who I know will read my book someday soon, Nathan, Derek, Kurt and my son-in-law, Jordan. You guys are the greatest blessings, and I love you with all my heart.

I started learning about meditation in 2019 and did a 40 day Christian meditation challenge in the spring of 2020. It was such a powerful experience for me. This program changed the way I pray. I see myself differently now. I understand why breath is important and how breath can heal our minds, spirits and bodies. I am forever grateful. Currently, I use a meditation app called CoCreate by Brooke Snow. Amazing stuff. Go try it!

I participated in an online meditation class hosted by Jesika Harmon and Kim Stoddard, called The Women's Mindfulness Workshop. These women are knowledgeable, creative and beautiful. Highly recommend!

To meditation coach Jesika Harmon—words are inadequate to describe how much it meant to me that you took the time to read my first draft when you didn't even know me personally. And then to meet with me online and give me feedback. And *then* for you to pass it on to your teenage daughter! Your thoughts and excitement for my book were invaluable to me. Thank you with all my heart.

Thank you, C.A. Farran author of Songs of the Wicked for being part of my journey! Thank you for being willing to read my finished book before anyone else! You are a gorgeous soul with a fabulous imagination and breathtaking writing skills.

An enormous amount of love and special thanks to Friel Black at Grey Moth Editing for taking so much time and putting so much love into editing my book. Always positive, encouraging and insightful. I'll be forever grateful. Your kindness is above and beyond. You are brilliant. You will always be a moonbeam and a kindred spirit to me. Thank you endlessly for the way you handled this creation of mine with such love.

The gratitude to my Heavenly Father and Savior Jesus Christ for helping me through this creative process is the deepest of all. I am in awe that I can call on help from heaven in my little life and receive all the ideas and motivation that I need from a heavenly power.

Thank you, readers of my book! My sincerest hope is that you find something in this book that inspires you to look deeper into your own mind and use your breath intentionally to feel peace.

About the Author

Krystal Pederson is a believer in magic, miracles and meditation. Meditation has taken on new meaning in her life over the past few years. Seeking stillness and training her thoughts has become a hobby, and she believes in the power it holds to heal.

Krystal lives in Oregon with her husband, Dave, a tall, handsome, basketball player she met on an airplane in the mid 90's. They have five adorable children that are quickly growing up and leaving the nest.

She enjoys playing the piano and taught piano lessons for fifteen years. Planting flowers and having dirt on her hands is her favorite place to be.

Find out more about Krystal at www.krystalpederson.com and on Instagram @krystal_breathes_words. She also offers free guided meditations that correspond with her book on YouTube @lifebreather5